AF32601

CHEAP

HAVENS

For Tyler, Emma, Corey, Dan, Christy, Kyle, Andrew, Zac, Vytautas, Tuva, and my twelve other roommates.

1

Already up a half-hour honing a respectable spine crease on the toiletry aisle's latest poolhall-mumble revved cataclysmic romp, bringing the sci-fi zeitgeist to its next logical beer-helmeted jackknife into the literary kiddie pool. Waspy mores scandalously buttered under a succinct-defying ubiquity of indomitable, churgling bubo-effluviants, too gratingly nipping at sapient to dare call zombies. Backwashing its own cordycepted three-chord plot by page sixty-two, with a butt-lipped double twist heart-of-gold villain reveal into a grizzled stoic pals versus barrage of soggy-yet-neurocalamatously-pustulent-gums bloodbath retrospective.

But that's too many hissy baritone yips from the kitchen this early on a Sunday to mean anything besides a bit too hungover waffle-iron operation. Alright, shapeless yet unaccountably sumptuous pajama bottoms, it's your moment. You, me, and the smoke detector all know there's no margin of error here for fiddly drawstrings and essentially ornamental buttons.

Oh hey, pardon me, and good morning, leery anthropomorphically cross-pawed pug mix I thought I'd just met in passing as somebody's fling's weekend favor. Finally got that hallway operations chief promotion? Yes, that's scalding batter you smell. Sorry dog, can't say I second getting at it through the baseboards.

Giggly goo to you too roomie, but you know there's no harm in letting that resting shit-eating grin face soften a bit. Is there some irony I'm missing in batting a thousand with iron-based cookware burns? It all must just look more fantastically absurd out from behind that deflated bouffant gone mane.

(L) Morning. On to waffles?

(R) Yeah, I wasn't sure how much latent trauma I'd have to wade through otherwise.

(L) Smart. You might be invited to petition for forgiveness pending the forthcoming chewiness to crispiness ratio.

(R) Oh, are we pontificating this morning?

(L) Mm. But I do endorse your using "breakfast technically in bedroom" on your next little slumber party hookup.

(R) I'll reminisce over Gordy's lickety snorts fondly.

(L) Who?

(R) Him. Ravishing your corns there.

(L) Oh. Really going to town, isn't he. Gordy, you sure? Wasn't it Joe-Bubbly or something?

(R) Well, honestly no, I'm not too sure. His attention is pretty easy to come by.

(L) Where's Drew? Isn't this your guys' little bondy wee-wee time thing?

(R) Well when you put it that way, mm—

(L) Couldn't stoop to "Oui"?

(R) Almost did, but thanks for the out. Actually he's off covering for me, or for that skeezy crock of butt-boil runoff—finally quit, so it's just us two and the owners.

(L) They ever even slink out of their doomplex anymore?

(R) Depends on whether they're feeling like being begged or threatened, and if I guess right. And, Li, really, doomplex?

(L) I know, even for me, right?

(R) Especially for you.

(L) Yeah, I hear you. Do we have jam?

(R) Why? Oh, seriously? Maybe in the backyard picnic toolbox. You want some powdered sugar for your orange juice too?

(L) The rest of the world is fine with jam, country boy. Is Trina up?

(R) No idea.

(L) Not really like her, is it? Come to think of it, I didn't see much of either of you after the first act of King Ralph. Did you two just, uh, unfurl mad fatties in the clamspace or what? What?

Holy knuckle sweat. That's about as wobbly a wicket of cylinders primed to misfire under his oily brow as I've seen.

(L) Wait now, nooooo. I think I've got half a morning-after pill squirrelled away, but it might be molly.

(T) Ah, Christ.

(L) Morning!

That's right, eat my chinny schoolyard grin, Miss systematically vetting roommate candidates on lowest casual-hookup probability.

(T) Inspiring show of restraint, Rob.

(R) I didn't, really. Shit.

(L) Well I'm inspired, but I'll only babysit if Rob sends me trout-face shirtless selfies with my window in the background.

(R) It's never just regular old dick pics with you two.

(L) So. Just so we're on the same page, I get the hallway bathroom now, right? Now wait. Why, aside from being completely wrecked, am I remembering this so patchy? Did I somehow tune out a bunch of stoney winkey gropey couch stuff?

⟨T⟩ No, I got up after that weird champagne domino banquet scene to change out of my work clothes. Rob was coming to ask us to turn it down because he was sampling our neighborhood, mockingbird?

⟨R⟩ Nightingale, I think.

⟨L⟩ Uh-huhh.

⟨T⟩ We were both too fucked up in that two-foot hallway gap not to sort of inadvertently grope in passing. Or, well not that much passing, except later both of us more or less passing out around second base.

⟨L⟩ I've heard better cover stories from toddlers for chocolate handprints than that white-hot dung spatter. You Amorites, you.

⟨R⟩ No, it really was a pretty odd, half-baked ordeal.

⟨T⟩ See? What a gent.

⟨R⟩ Yeah, yeah. I saw you ogling my resplendent rump downy.

⟨T⟩ Ugh, sure. Can't argue with downy.

⟨R⟩ But, in the spirit of being the outnumbered hairy person at the moment, and peace in our times, I'll venture that holding second is an amenable outcome for post–three-footer roommate hallway encounters.

⟨T⟩ Maybe Li's the real hero here for soldiering through King Ralph.

⟨L⟩ Oh not at all, I might have to rearrange my whole top thirty-eight.

⟨T⟩ Good. I can be alone with my regrets then.

No, no tittering from this corner. I always take my malformed three-fifths of a waffle and complementary foot gnawing in a crisp stoic haze.

(T) Oh, before I forget, either of you still up for that thing at Annie's friend's later?

(R) Sorry, can't. The community demands my hearty blustering at fourteen-minute intervals.

(L) What was it anyway? I probably should be getting an early start tomorrow.

(T) Oh, I forget. Free oversugared spritzy drinks, testy socialite gentritus and a few locals. Maybe ingratiating over some frothy burp of a professional milestone. And maybe costumes, I think.

(L) Wow, fun.

(T) What's early tomorrow? Can you cancel?

(L) Trip back home? I think we went over it pre–three-footer. Long layover in Oklahoma on the way. Hopefully for Sunday slosharoo with a few second cousins.

(T) Ah shit, right. And you're seeing Kate and Paul?

(L) Of course, might rent a car and go there first. Or, first before home and after the slosh. You know what I mean. Cousins don't count.

(R) I believe that's on my family crest.

(L) So, can't cancel anyhow. You really need me out past last call, or what?

(T) Huh? Oh. No, no, just this girl from work's in the Secular Society and she's been twisting my arm to do Sunday morning chess in the square.

(L) Sounds like an underworked emo lyric. I'm not too up on the early-morning counterculture these days.

(T) But, yeah, just fishing for an out, I guess. My excuses have been running so thin it's getting awkward.

(L) Sorry, been out here too long without the old family death rattler. And I got at least a trunkload of shit that

didn't make it into the two suitcases I've been living out of
the last year and a half.

⟨T⟩ Oh yeah, right. Well, good luck with the big transmission.

⟨L⟩ Cute. Yeah, we'll see.

How long ago did you realize that relationship with the hot
gin and cherry you're nursing didn't really have wings? More
of a slide-whistle plummet off the nest? I'd be the last one
you'd want to hear any of this from, but see that funk between
the eyes I've got doing its little tremolo? I promise it means
exactly what you need it to. A wholehearted "ok, sure".

Decidedly no assent or general acknowledgement of whatever yoyoing-plates, dank-attic-corner-chest mankid topic it
is you're hoping I've secreted some remotely comparable frac-
tion of butt-sweat and brain wheezing over, and certainly
not in its most avatar-bedecked forums for jargonal mastery
of a toy world the author clearly hadn't constructed with
permanent occupancy in mind. Nope, sorry guy, no gush.

What will your invite-only vlog hear of this face I'm
making? Totally missing the mark with forthright naivete?
Cheery yet demure slow-mo hairpin removal enthusiast? Blind
firing duplicitous angst? I'd take that. But realistically—let's
say granting you plus-nine eloquence with your afterparty
goatskin bowler on—overbearing calm? Maybe teetering
on militant cosmo-tautological primordial overlord fearing
atheist with requisite white-lipped irony tone-deafness? No,
sounds too vogue for this degree of deep-set smug.

Yet you still look listened-to. Maybe some of the inadvertent ESP's sticking. Then it's subtext and whatever else
you've left me to sift through, with some serious lead-footed
expounding past my full popped-knee perturbed disinterest.

Finally that spark of realizing you're capable of reading
me a bit, between your tooth-skimmed breaths and my duo-
syllabic angling. It's ok, we all remember our first brush with
the mystical prowess of the remotely cogent and typically
considerate. No, I promise it doesn't get lonesome on this end,
lent ears are a stable commodity. But your unprompted juke

to verging on offput blimpwittery does make me wonder if I'm better off diversifying. Well, it's a chore getting guarded about it. And prattle this tinny and inane is certainly taking some sort of piss, as they kind of say. More impressively disgusting the longer it goes, but it does always run out.

I wouldn't worry yourself too much, chum, let the sound of your own surly droning carry on as a lighthouse to the mighty paddleboats of your mind's achievement-trophy case.

Yes, small talk would be an improvement. Everybody's mood falling in over weather and cheery circumstantial gossip, can't beat it. Easy to overdo it, but let's blame that on the times. Smack in the age of prescribed innovation and we're more prone to dysfunctional taciturn lapses than ever.

Not that I wouldn't mind getting a little deep, but lately it always seems to hatch as a cumbersome opining ritual. All very political, though we're mostly only half-pretending the bizarro punditos earned the stance they're not supposed to take on the facts they forget to intone. Yeah, sure, somebody's lonely grandma reads the checkout stand rags religiously. Yes, yes, damn shame, and a far cry from your flavor of spew, which only dips its toes in the nutso tub now and then for a provocative hypothetical. True, true, the moderates are keeping up with some laudable hat-holding tack, but you're right, better not point to pragmatism too seriously, certain taboos are worth malignantly withering for. Oh, I see, just straight into what you're passing as a version of shop talk? Thanks anyway for leaving me longing after some breezy assumed rapport with at least a conciliation of some dry technical trivia.

Ah, but enter the austere video technically game cloner who introduced himself through an upturned ancient NBA all-star game collector's cup. Mid-nineties, judging from the complex Maytag patina. So, Billerer, then? Burgmur? Strummond? Some sort of consonant taffy. Well step on in, I'm starting to remember your smooshy auto-didactic touch on about any subject beginning or middling with "ph" or otherwise floated without a unanimous gag response.

Sure, you are more agreeable than anyone else in arms' reach, so do tell. Oh? Not much beyond the opener there, huh? Hm, a heady gulp of warm asphalt-roof runoff to tarten our cohort's marathon piss trough. Almost had me hoping for some dissertation on the inevitable market mechanics of holographic tabletop gaming for arthritics. Who's gonna sit around another six decades spamming Zerg lurkers with a mouse, right? Certainly worth stewing unemployed over how easily someone more perseverant than you could slap together a proof of concept, eh?

All your comrades in inevitability conjecture are so dead set on the old standards? But not this nerd boldly renegading into cavalier hypothetical greed. Ok, how about I swerve off the impending nerd-credential chest-beating causeway with a friendly glass-in-hand salute and step away with however much smile can inkle through my sloppy overcranked taut restraint? Salut.

Hm? Ok, sure, why not three back-to-back. Well yes, it is nice to immediately meet your favorite anecdote, but when all you've got is hammer metaphors, everything gets screwed. No, my nod's not the delirious waggle you probably knew better than to expect. Yes I'm aware my hands are a dead giveaway, but hell at least a third of us thought it was supposed to be a costume party, no?

Well, in a perfect world then. I'm off with the implied four magic words. "Stay. I go drink." Here's to the consoling view of the disproportionately lush Cerwin–Vega's who brought me so much support through this trying time. May the memory of their prowess be not overshadowed by the mystique of their having been fit through the front door somehow.

Six mingled and not a one shimmying that white-knuckled inch on the eight-foot limb of asking how any part of the last couple decades went for me. Great damn day too. C'mon, nothing wrong with jumping in like cronies and burning out over that summer-camp camaraderie kick, straight to those ponderous sophomorisms till sunup.

Oh, Trina and Anne in overwhelmingly adorable sister near-clutchiness mode? Move over, friend starts with G and your irreverent, assertive, extra crispy blouse, sanctuary privileges invoked abreast forthwith. My day? Oh Anne, you shouldn't have. Damn great in fact, barely did a thing and still coming to terms with the splendor of it. I'd beam harder but those last two goobs might misread joy over a butt-snugglable friend and her clammy but happy-to-be-out sister as some coy raucous.

Out with it, Anne. Oh no, I definitely don't mind you starting in like we're all already leaning in and nodding. Hell, I did desperately elbow in after all. Onto your third serious girlfriend? Queue sloppy surreptitious eyebrow to Trina. Four a.m. ground-rule double at some crashed sorority-yard sludging was last I heard on the de-turtling front.

Started fast. Good for them. Never have tried that myself, and getting to think it's fine enough knowing when you know better and otherwise taking advantage. All us sods thinking initiative means paying the bills. Ok, she'd been about poised to air a canned, but heartfelt, fealty proclamation.

Full stop, maybe remembering me or Trina's grim re-countings of alarmingly shallow clinginess horror, or just the pervading un-hipness of the moment, probably. Walks herself back a few thoughts, something strange and oddly wholesome about it, rarely done that neatly from such a tell. Bravo.

Still, a little too reined in now and it only amplifies what's got to be on the odder side of relationship belly-uppers. Yeah, ok, occasional dicey vibes aside, the exigent other's a romping good time and speaks up like thinking twice is taboo. Then comes the dreaded other day, ten-plus dates in, already about as gaga as it gets, and the girl lets on she's maybe a bit shacked up, pregnant, and not so maybe also trying to break things off with the pretty-much landlord after an admittedly ill-conceived arrangement.

Trina spits up three bucks' worth of Lizardo, lime, and gin, all's I can muster is a coachey hummph. Anne's not phased, just itching at it. Not especially hurt or going for some cracked waif poutiness. Just two parts genuine discombobulation, one part unapologetic lust, and a little prickly gherkin of loathing swimming on top for letting it out that clunky despite herself. Which makes sense now that she's pointing at the frizzy purple-cum-blonde in the swirly aqua Marc-or-something knockoff, and point-blank ogling Billerer.

The same who, it happens, blew her savings on eighty-dollar haircuts and recording gear for baby daddy to-be, who DJs two nights per average club-ownership duration, and gloms through the rest of his time grooming free-to-play RPG avatars, mastering culinary disaffections, and grinding down his wits on aggregate sites only distinguishable by their ad catalog. A marvel, really. Probably clinically depressed on paper, but perfectly conversant, noxious, and attractive.

Anne cuts the gawk short, tugs us back around before frizzy starts pretending not to look back.

(A) Mr. and Mrs. Brettley or something Runnel. She's about half sure it's not his, and that he'd leave if she kept it either way.

(L) God help her if he doesn't. He's been chatting me up. Little booglets of charm here and there, but he'd probably see no problem paying child support with gift cards and crates of Code Red.

(T) I don't know. Seems just as likely to go full-on goof dad like your average homebody hipster post-thirty.

(L) No, nonono, that there's all the makings of a new breed of bropank deadbeat.

(T) Hm, yeah, ok maybe. What's actually her name, anyway?

(A) Ewha. After a subway stop in Korea somewhere.

(L) After a subway stop what?

(A) Named.

(L) Ah.

(A) Her parents met over there doing some expat humanitarian work and stormed the gates of the embassy to have her there. Cab broke down on the way back home, so they did a little pilgrim march to the metro. A few dozen college girls got on with them and went dead quiet the whole next six miles or whatever it was.

(L) Yuhwuh Runnel?

(A) Ee-wah.

One of those rare uninhibited open group stares. Bitchiness and morbid curiosity both in order, but either Anne's done venting or was already more or less resigned about it, and the girl looks ready as ever to rubber-to-glue it. Actually looks about ready to somehow gracefully mount the cabinet

grand, summon a Sam, and sultry us all to quivery little bits.
Gotta say I'm doling out kudos to all involved for poise except
bropops. Pity points deducted for Ewha's masterful denial
thinking he'd pan out in any sense. Good kisser, maybe, I'd
say seven-to-one against though, considering in-grown esteem
that thick. Suddenly foggily intuiting an Ewha with a finally
moderately tamped needful crotch syndrome, having planted
through enough kicks to the head throughout the ordeal to
just wait for him to flake off naturally.

I could sally on over and pick up his passes where I left
them off while she must have been on the can. A little
charitable ammunition to Ewha's camp for the bulge's sake?
Nope, it'd require a paradoxical degree of drunken confidence
and tact. Hm.

(L) Wanna bum-rush her trying to casually explain I'm
cousin Chuerlinneh fresh from a borderline creepy damnation
and hellfire retreat and I caught you staring and you told us
she's your squash partner?

Almost carnival clairvoyant sibling synergy drawing both
of them into one long cockeyed deadpan. Trina breaks first,
with her patent choked contralto huchghuck gurgling.

(T) Squash. I like it. Like it can't not get tetchy.

(A) Fun. What's the safe word?

(L) Cropdusted. Also the approach tactic.

Alright. Turn and show. Pinch Trina, can't poke her
without losing face. Cue ruing, or abandon it with an eyeroll
over some perceived dealbreaker? Could just sell it with
a half-stumble toward the liquor nook and a what-the-hell-
was-I-thinking-anyway cheesy glance back. But, farting with
intent, you don't just throw that away. Ok, dial it back on
sympathy for Ewha's looking blithe, despite herself. Drop the
creepy hellfire bit and no false names, too small a town anyway.
Keep the squash for a light tetch. Maybe a thin-lipped dose
of racquet-centric banter will accelerate the flaking and score
it a good deed.

2

Six days for that first twinkling of reverse homesickness to kick in while back in the hometown. Fine by me. Would've been lame if it'd come sooner, but nice anyway feeling it hit over a would-be ten-day budget recalibration imposition turned sitcom cuddle romp.

Are short vacations tacky or is that the scoffy underpaid freelancer in me? Maybe the proud recessionists who couldn't afford non-couch-oriented vacations until our late twenties don't tend to waddle around with as much of that wincing tourist diligence. Still gotta dream for that little beat-off path of our own. It's introverts who travel well, come to think of it. Eat that ostensible misnomer, bloggos. Or extroverts probably deserve more blame for the tourist traps at least. But do your eggings-on anyhow. Mm, the world listens well from the battered old chenille La-Z-Boy in all its turquoise melange profundity.

Already at about eight bowlettes a day of Bertos sauce and not a trace of heartburn. Thank you Mom for stocking that old favorite milk-like multi-grain swill. And real tortillas. Say what you will about our rampant opportunistic bull ticklers and the perennial droves of snowy-driveway-disenfranchised hard apples, the natives here are generally, what, king snakes at worst? Take the imports and don't complain. I did, and

left, but let's continue to assume usually no great stink is
made.

Could be road rage even started dying out here first. That
110 breeze does sap pretty hard, but maybe extremes tend to
distill to a vague camaraderie. Old hobo lost in the crosswalk?
God bless him. Hope he finds a nice shady squat. And the
land of the split-second honk. "My good auto-mate. I'm
nearly dozing myself, but what's say we roll on through, no?
No sense us basking out here on the asphalt any longer than
needed, now. All nicely re-rubberized and soporific or not,
there's much finer AC up off the foothills, I can attest." Well.
Better cap it at anachronistic deportment encounters. Must
be past 11:30 already. Time to play Spaniard and be one of
the slightly less brain dead come supper.

Ohgh. I can tolerate daynap sickness doldrums, but that's
way too startling a dream to neatly waft me down into the
standard funk. Was it Kate? Mountaineering? Ohh right.
She wanted to pull off some digitally hexangulated loop that
equated to making our dotted trail on the map more of a
samba than a few sashays, while statistically ensuring the
highest views from the most angles with the least effort. Was
she saying it and I was measuring it digitally, or was she
waving around some Star Wars pen? Must have been the
pen, I never visualize anything so well awake, and don't know
why I could expect dream-me to either. Jesus, I need to leave
the house.

Thrilling to have gas money to drive a couple hundred miles
on a whim, or a three-day-overdue drop-in with whim-like
planning, as the case may be. Especially in the family space
box. And a new one since last visit, at that. Sliding doors
have their market, I guess. Cars got all transformery looking
the last couple years, didn't they? Insectoid? Way too much
eyeliner at any rate. This one must have just made the
holdover cut. More of a rubber baby curby jumper, but still
that trim sets it damn near nifty for a mom tin.

The classical station's still so much better out here. Shame.
Always less tame in a respectable college town. Time for early

aughts indie mix anyway. The weather's momentous enough for Khachaturian, but this leg of the drive wouldn't feel right without a little cat's cradle on the heartstrings just like the last fifteen times. Need to de-numb from the happy tinny AM oldies binge back in the city anyway. Hell of a balm on a scorcher, back when I was but a jangle in granpappy's coin purse and sad songs were still peppy, dammit. They sure haven't stopped flopping out the milkiest crooners as dogma dictates and only dusting off the odd Alley Oops and Sunny Afternoons just barely enough. The deep cuts station might still be on that T-Rex kick, but there's no way it comes in at all clear this far out of town. Nah, give us your blubbering, self-vindicated, Elliott Smith acolytes. Remember us our brand of angst, ye converse waifers.

Paul's office looks neater than it used to. More questionably tacked or otherwise hand-pressure mounted glammy fine-art posters of no discernible taste spectrum, and an addition or two to the punked-out legends of nobly curated pursuits. But somehow now it's finally worked up the nerve to blow a few wistful spit bubbles on dorm-room fare. More tomes past bulging to a carefree, sneeze-topple-ready overflow across his bonsai ramshackle sine-warped shelving endeavor. More loaches and greenery in his trademark 50 gallon bowed-front security bubble, maybe fewer knickknacks and other vagaries otherwise. Kind of nice, finally seeing it sober. But, papers stacked neatly in places. Very unseemly. And only half a hamper's worth of emergency dresswear going stagnant by the rubber tree, some even haphazardly folded. Either he's getting laid or his yogi is on sabbatical.

There's no way the senioritis case out front remembers me, too flustered with hold-button training last time. Good on Paul making sure she knows anyone our age and mildly assertive is welcome to the love seat of his wild, longing-out-the-window-to-frat-party-sounds days. Mmm, that gecko pink and seafoam weave. I could maybe still name who each joint burn belongs to. And still smells like that half a New Year's cake never got plied from the pillows, plus the old deep-set Mario Kart sweat.

Associate Professor still on the nameplate. "Seniority over
Assistant Professors, in all but job security," or was that
Loyola?

Now, will the 40-minute block scheduling tide drag dear
Paul in, or do I get the privileged catnap upon the coveted
old fifth roommate. Ah-hah, both of them. Conspiring to
bedazzle me, when all I wanted was a hoarse eight-hour "been
missing you too" shoulder cry. Christ, why does Kate look
like she could impregnate an ox?

(K) Jesus Li, you look too young, it's pathetic.

(P) Ugh, yeah, turn away. Please take this the wrong way,
but you could try to smile more. For the wrinkles.

(L) Awww, just hungover. But Paul, it melts my heart
you can still spin a misogynist maxim into a little bite-sized
chuckle patty.

(P) You know me. Don't I get some long-lost musketeer
love too? And didn't you guys see each other a few months
ago?

Oh, sweet Pauliaboo. It'll always be too much work to
bother worrying much about you. Never failed following
along to the deep end in your floaties. Kate's so much more
fragile than you've ever picked up on, and I'm too insensitive
to not have nearly derailed whatever's actually memorable
from all our unconditional drunken gay pacts. It's nice
anyhow having you checking over us all being so happy to see
each other. Each worrying our respective new neuroses won't
let us stay so good at hyper-intimate dorm-pal soothing. But
Paul, you're still so certain, so seriously hapless, such a
wholesomely and devotedly half-baked dilettante, never a
prick about it.

(L) Fine, Paul. Two years is long, sorry.

Ah, Barbasol, Old Spice, Heinz, that'll do. From
biochemical-amorism to comparative metallurgy, and back
through time beyond via a veritable East Asian pharma-
copic interpretation dabbling use to an "oh God did all the
other passengers just appear" landing in early spear and

feathered-hat age Caucasus hegemonic network modeling or however he calls it. More ambitious than us two, I suppose, given a respectable library in walking distance. For all the bitching about tenure, I never heard of such a pulp-blooded bookworm having too much trouble getting a middling college gig. Myself excluded—guess you can't just pin a syllabus on compulsive exception-taking.

(K) Oo, my workshop. It's like a complete nightmare right now, you should see it.

(L) Right now?

(K) Yeah, we've got like, three hours right?

(P) For me, yeah.

(K) Alright, c'mon c'mon.

Yes, let's keep it fleeting for this spot. Only so many minutes in the den of perquisity before the whole virginal salve sensation starts numbing everywhere a cheap party drug wouldn't.

Quite the glow. At least eight monitors, only one or two less than ten years old. Literally green, most certainly e-waste interventions, and probably about as energy efficient as hanging it all f a windmill blade. Must not make color profiles like they ud to.

Off she goes, so how badgering through an explanation to Paul of the five s she's hopping between to composite decent 3D renders vo solemn but dying to frolic young woman ten-footers a young-blood mortgage-company-owned low-rise. On the foyer, one for the, what this hell is it... Portico? ngling at each other through the marble-swirl glass wa aking up all the LEED-certified space-breaking flourish ld be one of the more glorifiable eras to become a sculp me to think of it, despite all the gunky plaza heaps att otherwise.

The Easel of Ages s erect. Funky new one next to it, overlaid with jun Rack of power supplies and controllers carefully cabl nblemished, but squeezed off behind a kelp forest of improbably stacked, perfectly un-alike terra cotta accoutrements for a proper tinkling of Luddite disdain. Giving up on Paul and seeing me wondering, she goes full beam and pops the workshop door open with all summonable John Hammond-ine majesty.

Christ, three robot arms with freakish roto-tool hands and all. Sinister by right, though the candy stripe neon blue and purple decal work does give it all a nice fuck-all verve. Ghastly rotted sawhorse bearing an undue load of what appears to be buckets of live cabling precariously ivying through the gantry.

(L) Like a little tree house just for rats' nests.

(K) It's a rescue.

Smattering of decades and exhibitionist cladding in the wiring. One of the arms apparently running randomized circuits with a mister around a three-foot clay woman in a timeless high-collar robe or dress thing. Mid-stride, hands just happening to have crossed behind the back, looking up to one side a little weirdly like a bird's flying at her. Her sister's a light wood, ash maybe. Deviant frown, wild half-lashed eyes, one arm bent in front holding her shoulder, calmer lips, same hips but leaning back, aimless and satisfied. Both look pretty much done, all tendoned and everything. Shoulders and feet still a little blocky, mouths and cheeks still a little creepily gummy.

(K) Behold.

Slips her hand in a goddamn tension-mounted power glove and the priciest-looking servo gets to mimicking. Drilling holes for, planting, and apparently UV curing little carbon-fiber eyelashes on little sister.

(L) And how on earth was this poor monstrosity not de-commissioned to its proper resting place? No under-rug deep enough?

(K) Arrangement with the materials department on real-time replication materials of comparable quality to the origi-nal.

^(L) Hm?

^(K) I let it run all night, doing machine learning cubism from seashells and driftwood to fill out our pledge for some new touring AI museum thing.

^(L) Wow. Making friends, huh?

^(K) Made the happy mistake of forgetting to change out of a low-neck blouse before a fundraiser for the User-Interface Design Initiative, and got drunk enough to have ended up an unofficial mascot or maidenhead or whatever.

^(L) Figurehead?

^(K) Yeah, what did I say?

^(L) Something a bit more hymeny.

^(K) Ah. Well in their case, I think either would apply. It still took much more schmoozing than I'm proud to admit.

^(P) And God knows how much very loosely debatably misappropriated grant money.

^(K) Plus about eighty percent of the regional Warhammer club's operating budget for testing and design of a holographic rig for their pen pals. But since somebody swiped my seven dirty dwarves out from behind Paul's aquarium and cemented them into a little nook over the drop-in clinic's water fountain, it's been pretty much cult-like.

^(L) Lolly, Horny, Sleazy, Gropey, Busty, Rumpy, and Dick?

^(K) Aww, you remembered.

^(L) Well you're such a big fish they put a waterslide on your back.

^(K) Mmh, the dean's doing her best to spread the word I have a perpetual need for sweaty sophomoric companionship but should only be solicited under the strictest bowing and scraping protocol.

^(L) Eeish. So, shoulders for last?

(K) Yeah. Can't settle on strong or rounded. Angle's all weird too, this one's going at knee height, baby sister's perched three stories up. Here.

A CAD-vomit bible of any conceivable pedestrian perspective at any conceivable time of year and day. Her meticulousness teeth finally came in. Glory be.

(K) Lucy looks too glum around Christmas and Easter so far. Ruth's more consistent, but gets all demon-looking at peak hours if they're rounded and too slutty if they're square. And meanwhile all I can focus on is dabbling in micro-pointillism on the brocade in her tube top.

(L) Who's it for?

(K) Nobody.

(L) Nooooh.

(K) Mm. Some run-down municipal administration office complex that's pilloried in a twenty-year zoning quibble, with good shade and foot traffic.

(L) The holy grail. Will the wood hold up?

(K) One of my most zealous oglers is doing a dissertation on spray-on nanosqueegee-based lacquer. Says it'll give her a good fifty years at least.

(L) And how old are they so far?

(K) Maybe about sixty-five working days, not counting prep.

(L) Leaving time for?

(K) Avoiding Paul's cooking.

(P) Hear hear. Plus she's been chatting up strangers at basketball games.

(L) You're a changed ascetic.

(K) I can admit I'm starting to like it here.

^(L) And just twelve years in. Wait until you see the water tower.

Sorry. Aiming for a prickly tousle and timed it out too much like a wet furry slap. So chronic wanderlust's apparently not terminal with a decent enough whirlpool to slosh in. That is encouraging. What was it worth running from anyway? Gnashingly bland and supportive parents? Certainly passed for terminally restless popping up that summer as the staunch, shy-by-gruff next-door neighbor to us gum-butt undergrads, with no relish in the all-but-seldom trips to the Mongolian grill and all the other eighth-year senior poverty frills. Startlingly lucid even with me chaperoning her down through the most precarious acid foibles. Then setting the most wholesome little figurines you've ever seen out of a box at craft fairs for six bucks each between patchy junior college gigs, which was moonlighting either way. Remaining severely unimpressed through a recession's span in the more decrepit hipster enclaves doing stints at haberdashers to save for materials. Then, corralling her to a first exhibition of mostly awestruck-passerby Pinterest screenshots of her park bench carvings to overnight relatively gainful tax-funded hermitage. Which was what, five years ago? Jesus.

^(K) I mean *here* here.

^(L) Yeah, sorry, dumbstruck at you two's lofty airs. Not even a strong hunch they won't get torn down?

^(K) Hm. I'd have to let you see it in person. I doubt it. Lucy's a risk, maybe. She might get trashed by some shitheel sooner or later. Ruth's corner is perfect. The most ignorable spot I could've dreamed of. Nobody'll remember anything else having been there.

^(P) Some hobo or old coot won't miss his clammy old blank wall?

^(K) Well he's my audience then. You think old coots go for strong shoulders?

^(P) Could you do one of each?

^(K) I'd sort of planned it that way, but they started converging and its pretty much too late now. There's an issue

with Ruth's neckline and both their clavicles are too well-defined already.

⁽ᴸ⁾ Which one means more to you?

⁽ᴷ⁾ God, I don't know. Maybe Ruth. Shit. No, it's gotta be different expressions.

⁽ᴾ⁾ Last resort?

⁽ᴷ⁾ Uh-huh.

⁽ᴸ⁾ Who gets the one you planned?

⁽ᴷ⁾ I didn't, just wanted them the same. Some tense extreme between grief and childbirth.

Not even the dewiest sarcastic residue. Well, means something to her. As far as I know she wouldn't know much about either, but what of it?

⁽ᴸ⁾ Is there any expression that doesn't cover?

⁽ᴷ⁾ Huh. Yeah, good point. Let's call it something like: early-stage placid mourning and a touch of midwife's diffidence.

⁽ᴸ⁾ Does sound delicate.

Stack of creepy dollish masks in each hand, most looking practically blank anyway.

⁽ᴷ⁾ Paul. Hold.

⁽ᴾ⁾ Yes'm.

⁽ᴷ⁾ Ok, Li, here. Dimmest ones on Alibaba.

Wow. Never saw a penlight this measly looking that didn't fall out of a Rice Krispies box.

⁽ᴷ⁾ Slow circles on Ruth please, good, yeah. Hold on, let me get a good hobo perch.

Three effectively lucid minds set on abstracting for permanence' sake. Neat. Occasional grunts against her cheek to go for dusk, or try number six. Must be numbered on the back. Full hobo slouch, only half-propping her head up when we get warmer.

⁽ᴷ⁾ Screw it. Number four on both, keep 'em wide set.

⁽ᴾ⁾ And the shoulders?

⁽ᴷ⁾ Strong, maybe a little hunchy if I can cheat it.

⁽ᴾ⁾ Sounds good.

She hates it.

⁽ᴸ⁾ Not too much compromise?

⁽ᴷ⁾ Lucy'll look weathered but dignified, won't need as much surprise or discontent in the face to really sink a gaze, which I'd have found a way to fuck up anyhow. Aughh. They're doomed to a few clowny shadows a day regardless. I went too far before picking. Shit.

⁽ᴾ⁾ Ruth's the one up overhead?

⁽ᴷ⁾ Yeah.

⁽ᴾ⁾ What if the lips were just a little more drawn, like she's taking a deep breath? Like, grieving mother above, holding back tears. New mother below, still in ecstasy.

Goddamn Paul. Takes a village idiot.

⁽ᴾ⁾ Too much?

⁽ᴷ⁾ No, made my day Paulmo. Been starting to have recurring blur-face dreams. I might end up owing you a few weeks good sleep.

⁽ᴾ⁾ You know, despite our ostensible lack of history, others in my position would read that as a veiled lash batting.

⁽ᴷ⁾ What, would they? I'll give you a tiger balm face rub if you're that desperate. Thanks, brat.

⁽ᴾ⁾ Any time.

⁽ᴸ⁾ If the terms are fair recompense, I know what makes him sleep.

(P) Uh-oh.

(L) Well I was gonna say three vape hits and a George Carlin special, but now I'm afraid I'll go to my grave half flummoxed and consternated if I never know what you uh-oh'ed about.

(P) Cherry Garcia and furious masturbation?

(K) Liar.

(P) Ok, you got me. Nine times out of ninety I fall asleep one PJ leg off, book flat on my face and my balls draped over a gently cradled groinery like a cape. Nobody ever barged in on me back in the day?

I would love to be a little more gullible, just so this sort of thing sinks in the extra bit.

(K) Paul, there's probably some fourteen-year-old out there right now, kneeling at his bedside, praying for a hero like you to abandon what really matters, and, for his sake, start writing Dr. Who erotica fan fiction.

(P) The book thing's half true, honest. A few times a year at the very least since I can remember.

(K) What book?

(P) Doesn't matter.

(L) Neat.

(K) Yohh, little baby Paul capey pee-pee leg.

(L) So then are you gonna sleep ok without the requisite eighteen hours of creative fury?

(K) Yeah, probably. Been at it all day already anyway. Feel like seeing where they're going?

She wasn't kidding about the spot. Dreary, drafty, everybody skittering along through, wishing they didn't remember it was saving them half a block every day. Nice little cafe anyway. Wasn't here before. Don't remember when I picked up on

Kate's favorite zen thing of the striking views more often being from across the way, but she's certainly gotten it down to a science.

Paul must be six minutes further into his elephant-in-the-ivory-tower rant than he realizes. Something on open-access research. Aren't there half-assed inroads already? Unbeknownst to the present dissertator. Serviceable attempt at a softshoe segue to our current whereabouts, if mostly an interjection into me and Kate's practiced inattention.

A duo of sunbathers in the park catty-corner. Swanny buxom mare and chipper tagalong. A drifter setting up on a bench just out of leershot, much too self-assured a swagger and too absent the huffed-out or crackhead vibe to be a local. Fixes up a seat for a well-traveled pair of homemade bongos.

⁽ᴾ⁾ Math and technical mastery take years and years, sure, but to make an analogy, how can you cultivate great art if the museums are ala carte?

⁽ᴸ⁾ Huh?

⁽ᴷ⁾ Artists don't need museums, cities do.

⁽ᴸ⁾ What's the sell here Paul? Aren't you galoshing into the old kiddie pool of idealistic mandates?

⁽ᴾ⁾ Nope. My point, esteemed peanut brickle brigadiers, is that the tangible, pain-in-the-ass flaw means some poor startup unterwhiz can't skim through the eight hundred articles cited to get to the twelve they need without, what, fifty grand in library fees?

⁽ᴸ⁾ Is that how it works at all?

⁽ᴾ⁾ No, probably not. I don't know.

⁽ᴷ⁾ Ok, crying shame registered. What's your panacea of the week?

⁽ᴾ⁾ Oh I've got at least three in my to-be-blogged notes.

⁽ᴸ⁾ Wow, how many more pages of notes until the big debut?

⁽ᴾ⁾ Irrelevant. Maybe a fowl-swoop memoir to be blurrily snapchatted at my funeral.

Bongo man's honing his warm-up thumps with an impressively tactful deadlock-stare at the two civilly exposed perfect butts. Grossly underestimated his leering capacity. He might be misjudging the jarring effect of a live rhythm on our beat-machine cradled ears, but the tone's muted enough to pass for an eighty-dollar Bluetooth scepter. All-in-all, a welcome counterpoint to the taut abandon of the tanners. Paul's got a supposedly urgent email and I crack Kate half a nod toward the tableau. Only so many haphazard serenades these days.

I'd wager a full etymologically correct 90-second moment before Paul or either sunbather clues in. Nope, much too generous. The tune hits a make-or-break moment, could've vamped it, shifted sideways a bit, and prompted whatever amounts to a prone shrug. But he's doubled down, head-on, full toothy beam, popping each four like he forgot the one. The girls don't need words for this grade of write-off, though tagalong is already too sun dazed and senseless of propriety to really mind that much. Good for her. Not enough sway to hinder big sisters' recursive-scoff bustle, but cool enough for a sidelong half-curious guffaw.

The culminating now outright mild huff prompts the requisite chatter. Towels ceremoniously refussed, and the three of us are just far enough to play dumb. Anyway, Kate's too entranced for niceties. Ahh, big sister's got a little Lucy to her, cool one's definitely a Ruth.

^(L) Strong shoulders?

^(K) One round, one strong.

^(P) Strong clay, weak ash?

^(K) Uh-huh.

3

July? 2nd at least, MMX4.

Dear Terminal-Glaze Induction and Masturbation
Advisory Apparatus (formerly John Stamos affection
repository, Vol. 32),

Old roomies making me drunken jelly. Really
though, envy of some sort. Fuckin love 'em. Tow
it: Pauls' academia and/or eco-terrible rant on
overdue obvious "non-tomfuckery", the 8-napkin essay
transcribed as promised:

- Etch-a-sketch paper or something, you
  uncompromising dweebs

- Biosphere caliber fishtopias

- Atonal questionnaires in double-blind clinical
  trials, you sneaky pear-headed wimps

- Transparent thin-film nano-eclair emulsion slide
  film-looking video screens to "subversively
  render the legions of god-awful powerpunts more
  nappable".

- Spidey mace can. (Extant?) Fire extinguisher /
  low-grade active "jerkhole" deterrent.

- "If you build it [AR goggles he is certain don't
  exist yet] they will 3D pong [expected mantra
  chorus]"

- Ball-point stylus with little ratchety
  rollingness [mumbled expletives, ~3 min]
  dinky clipboard slabby TVs up to 19th Century
  standards.

This local digital void thanks you Paul. Duty
conceded with eyelids at a new droopiest-while-typing
record.

In affable haze, yours, Compy dearest,
Li

Back in the city for the Fourth. Downtown's extra coppery,
to a cell-shaded saturation. New blood, largely pedestrian,
not quite openly marveling at the tinge for what could be
the first time since the recession that Central and Van Bu-
ren looked any good. Woolly cloud cover, dense enough to
trip to on whippets and Josta, flirting back up along South
Mountain and off to somewhere more commitment-oriented
about precipitation.

Wrong. Comes in full, rounding along the long east stretch
in Washington. Sunset dies out faster than I remember ever

seeing. Dust rides in on the wind, not flagging, nice mealy Baja doft with a bright Pacific finish.

Hard enough now not to pretend the last three days weren't a buddy bender. Pulling over to an NPR special on Ebert's voiceless years through the dust-storm proper gets me all pepped again anyway for the promised send-off at Angie's. Who'd have thought she'd have finally clued in that sustaining guests without ventilation, drinking water, or remotely hygienic habitable surfaces does actually become stilting? Now she's flopping out omelettes and puttering over outdoor brick-oven cocoa seating coziness between bong gripes about the boneheads running her ragged at whichever mega-firm it was.

The day back with mom and Deb was a rollick at any rate. Nice to get out of the little boomer nook in time though. Dowdy sort of Christian Science vibe to the subdivision, but one of the sad few well-elevated spots in the clay shingle sea from which you can't catch a decent grand finale or two in each cardinal direction. And Christ is it blooming along the 51 into the 202. Curving along the Salt they're damn near overhead. Five scurrying bozos out on the defunct rail bridge. Very smokey work. Strange thing rounding toward the lake doing 75 into in a pack of gleefully distracted drivers with poor time-management skills. One of too many anonymous automotive solidarity poots.

Caught the first heaves of the climax in the rearview. DPS wranglers all sweating their taints off at the jumbo rubber-neck herd. Mandatory detour out to Hayden but it gets me the best bits of the real final squirt from McKellips. Hm, drive-through patriotism. Probably couldn't put a stranger vibe in traffic. Friday-nighters and minivans all out in concert one hour every however many years.

Well screw not showing up back at Angie's house twice as wired. The burrito shop beckons. Temper my gid with soggy adobada my dear compatriots, condolences on missing the hoopla.

Hello three a.m. sofa-gelled and just now half-asleep phone buzz. How long since I last swore off couch crashing? Well kudos anyway on feeling too lazy to bother driving a solid six hours out from a halfhearted bubbler hit.

Angie must owe something to the newly verbose old roommate for this whole prim and tidy shtick. May, was it? Shit, not Meg for sure. Well, whatever wasn't clicking on the domesticity meter's looking proudly ditched by now. But still quaking a bit in the shadow of whichever gap generation gave pink-gravel interiors their three-decade reign.

Must have been more than half dozing, now some dada trench warfare on the homefront dream's coming back to me. Jesus. Tidbits of the suburban hellscape de jour being particularly shellable.

Ok, eighth ring. Hm, who? Kate? That's a good few years' lapse on the bestie bosom o'clock confab pillow-wracking spool of dry, metered, ever-so faintly manic rants. Always seemed she got an ounce of self-aware cheek out of it. Last one had gone from near sleepy to a pleasant mild flabbergasting all before I'd really fully answered. But ok, let's see, she'd been still a little elated figuring out certain training wheels had been knocked loose all along. I sure as shit didn't mind. Call me anytime, yes dammit. But wrangle one too many grating monotone bouts in the dark on a pot-empty stomach and the ground rules don't have quite the traction.

Still on the sheer bombed-out trauma wavelength, the new facepad's delicate buzz was bridging my dream brain to one of those death-whirler 800 rounds a breath battleship guns from off deep enough in the Papagos to lend a grisly moan to it.

Something stickier about this dream overall. Yeah, the eerie gradual plod. No four-inch front-page proclamations. Just the hesitant fickle stumbling into calumny, and too muddled on all sides to be about much but race, or overwrought greed, all getting the backseat eventually to the rote numbed-out scavenger class and their tin-tooth cronyist dandylords. Too clearly too many losers to blame some consensual phenomenon. Nothing like a little Nostradamic ick to wrench me near sober at least.

Sorry love, but something tells me too many people take this kind of call and wish to all they'd rolled over on it. Buzz buzz, tap click, oh what a releasey trick.

What'd I have in mind drifting off anyway? Oh, the

sprout. Nine days home and I don't once think back on
my transient splay of furniture and tepid-scented yarn eight
states away. Then suddenly I can't get over meaning to have
somebody water the picked-over basil pot with the mystery
sprout in the corner that I found growing out of the bathroom
sink drain.

Goh, fine Kate, but you're getting extra thick grumbling.
No outright irritability—too easy. Just pure, sudden, interrupted pothead slumber.

(L) Mm?

Pitch perfect. Please let a note of it color the crisis at
hand, dear. I'd hope by now she's equipped for a pang or
two on amplifying my hangover-to-be.

But it's all some scratchy muffle, oops. Either a prostrate
Netflix butt dial or she's tied up in somebody's trunk. Well
shit, that's a discrepancy I won't be drifting back off to gently.
Long shot for trunk-bound with mostly gueraffe-art dinks
and nano plasterers in her circle lately, but she does rarely
skip a chat with the itinerant odd duck.

(L) Kayyy-it.

(K) Hey.

Near-breathless, near-whisper, more edgy than panicky.
Shipping container maybe? Ambience is muted outdoorsy
for sure. Something on the order of a sparrow ghosting in
around a cupped hand. Voices too, maybe. Not tense if so.

(L) What in the fucking lord? Can you talk?

(K) Mmm. Hold on. Yes, now. You hear me?

(L) Sure, yeah.

(K) I'm on a roof right now. Big commercial one. By your
dad's house. Ass of the super Kmart where the old Harkins
was. Putting up gargoyles. Saw a security guard's hazard
lights and dropped one right on the Chili's apostrophe. Cops
are here but don't know what the fuck.

(L) Jesus.

(K) You have a ladder?

(L) No. And absolutely not. And I'm at Angie's anyway.

(K) Shit. Do you have your dad's garage code still?

I do. Yes. That's what, 20 miles away. No eyedrops or hair ties and, let's see, one sock still missing. C'est la Bohème.

(L) Christ. Have you considered the dimensions of my backseat? It pukes out mike stands halfway down the driveway.

(K) Then put it like skis or something. Jesus Lianne, do you know what adjunct faculty means?

So slathered in rhetorical-cum-condescending I'm nearly without a can't to even. Must be too used to the soft-spunkin' reflected wit of full-brooded hipsters.

(L) Yes?

(K) Indulge me.

(L) Good bail-money connections on what can easily be spun into a token madcap saccharine civil disobedience cocktail-hour knee-slapper?

(K) Well, in all fairness that's not unlikely. But you know I hate diet.

(L) So, you want me to be your corn syrup?

(K) Pretty please. Kidding aside I could be terminally fucked. No cutesy blogs on cavalier Professor Banksy junior unmasked while cajoling the troglodytes. Just screwed down a few pegs to pottery classes at the community center.

Well that is about as rationally distraught as I've ever heard her. Pretty endearing, come to think of it.

(L) Dammit Kate, fine. You realize it'll take me like an hour at least?

(K) Yeah, ok. I have a book on my phone.

^(L) I was wondering why you sounded so postured.

^(K) Wokka wokka. Just please get here before sunup. Come up on the fountain side, where it used to go through.

^(L) Right.

Morning to you too officers. Truly a fascinating intersection, dull as it may seem. Once one of the deadliest on the map, now a marvel of punctilious signal work.

Ah, you've surely marked the dear old family uprearer making its casual, but I assure you, well-secured abutment from my sunroof. Turns out there's truly no better time to clean Grannie's gutters than Saturday at 4:30 a.m. Sunrise on the shingles and all the choice monsoon windfall lemonade I can keep down.

Loose dingbats huckin crap at a poor apostrophe? Preposterous notion if you ask me. Ah, well, looks like the civil engineers even gave us pre-dawn idlers a thought. Looks like green means toodaloo for now.

An airy, warbled whistle that wouldn't pass for anything more organic than a battle-pocked nerf tetherball. Indistinct and non-human enough anyway.

Wow, straight overhead like a bad Escher mirror-me spitting into a pond. Relatively poised after half a night on a big-box roof. Ticking her chin, but I'm too disoriented to, oh, there's the little beast. Darling little Alfred E. Neuman, Milton Berle mix, though appropriately more grim than either. Toes curled over a jut of sheer architectural malice. Easy odds no one officious enough will notice it for years. Goddamn marvelous. And back at her peeky frothy eyes, and a world class shit-eater buried by the ledge. Curdles up a doughy, extra dipshitty wink and starts whistling "The Candyman Can" while I set up.

Such a relief driving back this time. Life decisions on a flightbook dot whatever page always have that looming impotent

misery to them. Some bits of home are doing the nagging tug
a little harder this time. Then I wake up tingling with my
arm smooshed under a kidney and a half-dream of a frantic
hooting carnival organ still ringing out clear and I'm readier
to call it a premonition than make any sense of it. Yup, pack
in tomorrow, drop by the U-of on the way east. Abandon
the stormy notion of Skyping up a subletter and humping
around the snake pit another few decades. At least it's almost
all grown up now. Might as well let the trees fill out and
the suburbs melt back down a bit to a more shapeable pus.
Hopefully reclaiming a little of the old hick twee and a better
bromide balance in the conversation pool.

John Stamos Affection Repository, Vol. MMM,

    Sentimental title reversion as this is likely my
last entry. The motel staff are clearly piqued for
their tainted blood ration in what I suspect to be a
bi-weekly offering to whatever lives under the pool
drain. Great wi-fi though. And the shower and the
door latch both worked in the second room they gave
me. The more first room was surely a test of my
divinity. Admirable how the staff hid their concern
at my meeting the challenge. I shall heed my summons
with propentious grace, oh humunculan Nefertiti of
the what I imagine to be a deep end. Alms be in your
honor, wield my lithe cocoon twixt rending maw and
talon with all the exonerable compunction of your
algaic station. Rest this weary blaggart's ruminant
spirit.

    But seriously Compy, it's just a smidge glassy
across the board around here, concierge down to the
provocatively clad ice machine attendants. All sorts
of half-drawls lotused away to a sonorous highway

nouveau.

Stopped in and saw Kate on the way out. Cocoa
and apricots over her roommates' e-funk psycha-twang
practice. Made some more-than lighthearted overtures
on holding me back. Probably misreading a "let's at
least hook up once while we're clearly not old yet"
vibe in her doubling down on the familial bit and
spousey rump thwops. Wouldn't rule it out entirely
though.

Had one of her poor grad student minions whip me
up a parting gift. A deceptively toy-like riding
bow with an honest-to-God plunger tube and paintball
feeder mechanism. Forgot I wasn't flying back and
made sure the poor sod designed it to fold up into
a tabletop wire easel. She wouldn't let me read
the note on it in front of her. All it said was
the name of a guy in Ashfork who could brew me some
army-declassified three-day mildly psychoactive
stupefaction mace cocktail. Christ. Craft fair
networking I guess.

Beyond me how to make any non-felonious use of it,
but good on her remembering my letting slip that whole
pre-teen self-taught archeress phase that led to a
spate of pigeon-chunk unearthings which earned the
neighbor's basset hound gastrointestinal notoriety.
Well, here's to new fedoric heights.

The wood seems a cheaper grade than you'd think
possible. Something about a deal with the Materials
and Design cross-consortium seminar conveners in
exchange for any new laminable and/or printable
stocks the tolerance guru's iterative pet brain deems

lattice-like.

It's one of those squat Mongolian numbers. Gives
the easel setting a bell-like look. Kate must have
done the elaborate fretwork around the plunger /
canvas tray piece, or, hm, the superfluous rivet holes
make me wonder if I'm in possession of an abandoned
Shakuhachi flute design. The old hand-carved
near-regift. Can't complain with relief work like
that.

And after the whole folding, loading,
pretend riding and aiming routine, she did her
Stimpy-forklempt bit and pretend-rummaged out from
her junk drawer a bony looking ocarina with mostly
hot-glued valves and the better part of a bubble gun's
innards. "It's a prototype" she says. In honor of
the time we'd accused Paul of being a sheepish pisser
and he'd recanted with his off-kilter frankness that
it kept his legs unsprayed (the whole desert / shorts
conundrum. Something about the rest of the world's
shorts-wearing men misting their shins with, I believe
it was "glib insouciance").

Or more to the point, years later he'd admitted
to passing out during his new favorite drunken ritual
of spliff and sit-down pee. And, as is now lore, he
woke to a chirp-drumming of the leaky intake dripping
on the blue-gray tile, which, as he never fails
to recollect, was the only tasteful square-foot of
flooring in the entirety of that dim two-bedroom hovel
you only still see in abundance near college-town
railyards. As Kate then never fails to interject,
having been summoned as chief witness at the time,

it was random, or precisely non-repeating but with
an uncanny diatonic tendency, by some means hopping
around a twelve-tone melody like the mockingbird of
bad plumbing. In his toilet fugue state, Paul tested
throttling the drips before making a recording, only
to find the tuning had been a miracle of delicate
calcification.

At any rate, I'm now in possession of the worlds'
first hydronic flutophone. Runs on a 9-volt and
a tablespoon of spit in a pinch, but she says you
need ice cold tap water and a dash of talc for
that gleamy dulcimer ring. So far I've given it
my best Gillespie-ing at the expense of some jaw
cartilage, and managed a few resplendent splurts. Her
zitwit operating instructions were so unrelentingly
cheeseball she either got the right sound out of
it once and was too drunk to remember, or there
is actually some hybridization of reed/flute/brass
embouchure going on that will take weeks to clench
into. I do see why she only demoed it unstopped with
a whoopee cushion rigged to the mouthpiece via what
I'm reasonably sure once belonged to a special-order,
borderline unwholesomely tight fleshlight aperture.

And the kicker: she's spent the last four months
sending Paul late night gee-wow links to all things
hydraulophone related. He should know better than to
assume she'd have subconsciously or otherwise lumped
his toilet epiphany in with the clever and curvaceous
but ultimately moog-sounding water-fountain keyboards.
But he's always been too dear and presumptuous of his
friends' intellect to catch on to this depraved a con.

    Hm, no, the thing has to work. Too many atomizers
and perforated membranes and neatly strung ceramic
beads to be a worked-once-maybe effort. Lord. It's
probably worth at least a half master's thesis alone.
What she's playing off as drooly nerd leverage appeal
must be more like a budding polymathic clout. Which
I'll take to mean she kept the manual dippy-cryptic
on account of some wunderkindic timing well beyond me,
and out of respect for letting the muse have a first
real crack at a polished one. Which leaves me with
the option of risking lockjaw for bragging rights, or
waiting for a gleeful Skype lesson where they coolly
demonstrate what a no-brainer it was all along. And
Mom wonders why I keep forgetting Christmas.

    So long, dear repo. Should I succumb to pillow
spores, or be consecrated to my inexorable fate as
the effectuate transmutationary tribute, commiserating
the hospitality deity on her inscrutable letting of
all that sanguinary guile that once stood abreast
brochure racks of yore. Should I befall such a fate
twixt these surprisingly comfortingly starched fibrous
loins of our lady and hereagain twixt her hour of
the pilgrim's drowse and the diesel and ethanol-tangy
grey dawn. Yes should such betwainery sever this
transitory bliss, and just so short of your most
assured siliconic metamorphosis so brusquely deemed
singular, may any cognitive benefits parsable from
these 'strokes... may they be your heart's trellis,
compy, and its beacon of all talismanic directive.
    -L

4

Finally back to the crisp, dewy balance of deep lush valleys and sprawling outlooks. Where the last bastions of proper burritos have their rare mingle with quality brisket and catfish. Oh, how daffodilic the something or other specialty poplars are in late summer. Whatever I'm waxing does not boast well of my off-brand remedial-scouts pastorality badge. Mea culpa Mithrandir. Maybe I'm shell-shocked from one too many metaphysical faux-cunning debates with fledgling botanists.

Still, can't fight this hunch the word "azalea" must have meant "ooo, sounds pretty" throughout most English-speaking cultures for more decades than however long since it made its first full-color glossy debut. Oh, don't get glum, Lijo, you're not even in the county yet. Here's to catalpa and rubiaceae and hepaticas, and all the fen and tussock to boot. God this heavy air smells good. No fellow window crackers in 30 miles either.

The sleepy, lanky anti-smug neo-hip hyphen-worthy proletariat still holds a healthy delegation in the outer ring. Good, their urban counterparts are already edging back into sensible pants and flattering tops. Ok, favorite part. Walk right up with keys a-jangle, pray the betta and the succulent menagerie didn't jump for it, and brace for Rob's daily garlic plumes under whatever forever-in-the-shower scent Trina's got lingering in her third of the square footage.

Greeted with a first good look in full daylight at the bread loaf mutt, who I see now is on the more quizzical, pitiful side of the Jack Russell or Shar Pei gene lottery. You were here last year on something like a three-week squat, weren't you? Well, fresh dog is always good. Means the place should've been kept as clean as a pet hotel, which for us is iffy, discounting Rob's immaculate two-foot perimeter around his Ikea low-rider queen. And my desk, not counting the drawers or the fifteen-cable footrest.

I knew this dogs name, and recently. Rob's ex's, or sister's? Damn, they're hard to tell apart, though it seems more to do with a few too many rooftop forty-and-a-blunt all-nighter confessionals (to his credit, post-dating Rob and the ex disembarking from their seven-year scarring match) than any uncanny physiognomic sameness. Still. Weird not to know if the dog is a familial or a floundering obligation. Well, Jarl, is it? No, Jacques? Jorge? C'mon you skittish nut, judging from the bearable garlic sting we've got hours before Rob's back. Best get re-acquainted.

Yes, I am aware your balls are the intact and well-groomed coin purse we all lost bets on that one time, clutching gingerly while impersonating our favorite celebrity on a budget in the produce aisle doing mental math on pluots per pound. Thanks for the reminder. Jingling coin purse, ohh right. It's Gene or Eugene or something, yeah? Hoh, hoh, now he's the licky loo. Sorry guy, I think dog saliva was somewhere in my New Year's manifesto. Wow, ok, toes can be an exception if you're that emphatic. Anoint away, Giblet. Gibbles? Why does anyone think leaving you alone all cooped up in here is fair? You could clearly hack it on the outside, we both know that. Inexplicably feline poise, wolfish mange, and rakish squiggliness.

Well G-man, who knows, maybe your great grand pips will putt around in radio-flyer sized robo cars by their own neuromoderated volition. What kind of voice transmuter would you go for? Thick Peruvian accent maybe? But with the bulk of your twenties in Toronto or Minneapolis, for that little buttery lurch here and there. You'd definitely be the one-to-three-word statement type, pulling the "still a dog but appreciative of the specificity" vibe. "Caution: off-brand tobacco; minor chinchilla mistreatment; dyed-black denim jacket, third owner. Prognosis: low alert, medium growl."

No doubt that sea change that would end up more jarring for us hind-walkers, eh? All our wubsy misconceptions on the bounds of primal reasoning thrown to shit with the snouts on the collective knee, asking politely for seconds, but without so much pepper if it's not too much trouble. Hm. Well, all for best, right Geeno? Dolphins probably get the beta privileges though, bud. Then the primate geeks would make a big stink and elephants will be sending smoke signals before you get a say. Sorry boobae, we're doing the best we can. I can't say you seem all that worked up over it.

Pushing well-over thirty. Carrying a dog, a forty-pound suitcase, and an effectively heavier by unwieldiness muck-shined old pinkish nylon backpack in little kitchen circles with heels popped out of my shoes and muttering about animal hegemony. If adulthood's a chunky blend of eight and eighty, I'm on the right track.

Alright Growlerly, let's see what kind of flappin in the breeze operation we've got runnin here, shall we? Styptic stick and a plate of brownies on the counter—still chewy, fair enough, but I recall your being a kitchen-table mountain goat of sorts, no? Back door open, screen door locked. Gonna call that a plus depending on the garbage status, which is... wow, only a nominal offering of pocket-pressed leaves of wrappers and receipts. Eerie. Rob's not trying to get laid if he's dog-sitting. Trina wouldn't bother with any housework if she was. Maybe Drew made his annual pilgrimage to the dumpster. Clean toilet. Noon on a Friday and no one is stoned or unemployed on our couch. Holy Mother of Gorgons, we really are hitting our well-over thirties. But Drew shaves electric, so what the hell's Rob doing with a braidable beard and a styptic? If he shaved anything above the neck he owes me fifty bucks, if memory serves. Which means... a new job? If so, a moment of silence for the staff picks shelf at Reed's Books and Discs, may your inevitable desecration be staved at length by Rob's standing champions.

That's it, G, there's too much red-lettery in the air. Better unwind these highway-shot nerves and take it in. Let's just go in and set this shit down and find your leash and see what this town's been trying to pull without me.

Oh, fancy meeting you here Queen Staffanstorp. But I was just about to—oh, with my clothes on? Well someone's glad to see me. What's that? But you never told me your sheets liked it a little dirty. Screw it, letters stay red longer up in the hills or something, right? Oh lord, not the infernal pensomnulate prosaiccups. Fight it, oaf, you know the kind of warped dreams you're in for. Mmmh, but there was that one with the fiery Romani hodgepodge string ensemble doing dueling musettes and Mahler with the electric klezmer brigade and somebody's poor philharmonic trying to fill in the missing bits. Or, no, just give me some old bat humming tooraloo over a washtub. Nobody needs an eighty-piece after that much driving.

Whuh, windy highway wave-pool effect. Freak leg twitch, check. Bi-weekly terrifying pillow-half-inhaled palpitations, ten-four. Auguring short-term neural cache with childhood drowse subroutine number four: cartoony astronaut meta-physical soliloquy with interspersed sensations of corporeal demagnification. Dilating splines. Auxiliary sensory check reading proximal dog, self acceptably bathed, erratic fridge hum three clicks under neurotic threshold, passing motorist frequency locked at mildly reassuring. Bladder on 6.8 hour standby, well within this exhaustion tolerance but let's make a note of it for next time. Easing into manual for low-grade azimuthal tuning. And, calling it green, quick slip to deep with any luck—looking like a bidirectional haze of adolescent cruelties in a sugary re-hash at worst. Fine work everyone, let's just leave the paperwork for the night shift and get a few rounds in at the duodenum before the rush.

5

Good glorious heptatonic subdivisions, it's the feted Tuesday Balkan Folk discourse again! Not sensing much new to the table this go-around but a reinvigorated abandonment of steering wide of long-form redundancy. Ok, a hastily recollected morsel here and there, a smattering of new YouTube bookmarks not painfully slowly dug up, but nope, nothing meaty. Well it's arguably a pretty filling standard queue and they never need a... third ladle? Second saucier? Overattentive proprietor, maybe. No pride let from this nook of the humble cafe patio's cramped railing window with inexplicable utility-post dunce table I laboriously forged into the debutante dunce table it is today.

Rob's losing his footing. Time to move on to the virtues of the few living flag bearers of true great funk and their recent remotely head-bobbable efforts? Too late, Rob jukes to an ambush grilling on Drew's creative output of late—nearly taboo in these parts Rooboo, but you got me piqued. Parry, thrust, and scabbard kick Drewly. This is your daily dignity amongst ambivalent friends at stake. Ooh, bravo, puffed

up into a deeper slouch. Well bud, you did lay out that
butt-warped moleskine on the table before any of us got here.

⁽ᴿ⁾ So, how far along is she?

⁽ᴰ⁾ About the fifth trimester now. The looks I get from
the lady at the stationary store went from doleful to outright
abjection. I went in and ordered some nibs I probably won't
need for another three years.

⁽ᴸ⁾ Woe be the page to the ascetic.

⁽ᴰ⁾ Damnit Li, don't make me start taking dictation, I'm
desperate enough for that to sound inspiring. Last time you
got me going I ended up starting that etymology blog.

⁽ᴸ⁾ Come now D-ber, my flow only wants the best for you.

⁽ᴿ⁾ Eugh. So, what is it mostly at this point? No more
misty sixth-century doomscapes?

⁽ᴰ⁾ No, no more. That alternate spacetime shit is such a
madlib. The physics on it feels so threadbare anyway.

⁽ᴸ⁾ Who cares?

⁽ᴰ⁾ I don't know. The poor metaphysical zeitgeist is a
slave to the whims of the mathematical elite.

⁽ᴿ⁾ Jesus. Distill that onto a bumper sticker and watch
the world squint. Sooo, thick with the prose or what?

⁽ᴰ⁾ Sure, sort of. Largely narration from conflicting aura
thingies. Disjointed but hopefully intimate.

⁽ᴿ⁾ So, like a horse and his rider in an ESP-off?

⁽ᴸ⁾ I'm on the edge of my ass already.

⁽ᴰ⁾ No, more like collective consciences of neighboring
countries having a few beers.

⁽ᴿ⁾ Conscience?

⁽ᴰ⁾ Mmh-hmm. Not hive mind, nanny mind.

⁽ᴸ⁾ I'm sold. Is it good?

^(D) A little. At this point I feel like I'm tossing buckets of varnish at a tree trunk.

^(R) Well fuck. Try kerosene?

^(D) Nah, burned enough trees on it as it is.

^(L) I'm lost. Is varnish like paint?

^(R) Uh, literally or figuratively?

^(L) Whichever is less humiliating? Fine, both? Never mind. I quit. Motion for dismissal.

^(R) How do you not know what varnish is? You post woodworking glamour shots like they're eighteen-dollar dinner selfies.

^(L) Yeah, I know, come off it. I just thought it might be a more generic thing than I was thinking originally.

^(D) Hell, maybe it is. My fault on the piss-poor analogy. Anyway, the thing just feels forced in all the places I was expecting it to.

^(L) Deep, man. So any new side projects wriggling up from the mud for a first bask?

^(D) Ah, yeah, I guess. You know the day after you left, one of those schlubs from Jynkles sat down right where you're sitting and roped me into doing a five-minute sketch for their big new belly thumper.

^(R) "One of those"? Aren't they as motley as an NES ice hockey team?

^(D) Forgot my glasses that day. Could've been two of them, taking turns, honestly. I think it was the one who sounds like an old detergent commercial.

^(L) So *doing* doing or writing doing?

^(D) Writing. Don't think their egos or what's left of my shame would ever conspire to have me grace that stage.

^(L) But it's so neat and slippery with fry grease.

44

^(R) Heard they're in an old butcher-shop turned gallery now, actually.

^(L) Moving up. Then how's it coming?

^(D) Done. They might even get some of the jokes well enough to overcome their chronic hypo-comic-timing-ism.

^(R) Ooh damn. Are oh tee eff ell, meyan.

^(L) Well? Can you spit some of it up or do we have to milk you for it? I learned a good privacy swaddle from a young mom at the airport last Christmas.

^(R) Yeah, he is looking pretty cheesed up. You sure it's crotch-compatible?

^(L) Don't see why not. Okay Drewie, remember I only carry lube because I'm allergic to Vaseline. Any mention of arid biomes or chilled cake-batter taffy is grounds for summary expulsion forthwith.

^(R) Minus two points for expulsion, Li.

^(L) Ah, damn. Okay Dee, there's only so many times you can spray coffee though your nose at us before we have to get your septum checked.

^(D) God, so much for this shirt. Taffy, Li?

^(L) Sure, sandpaper is too damn hyperbolic. Okay, take us there. Plastic beer cups are all a-crinkle, the sound guy cues the non-ironic power workout jam and dims the lights, our players sexy-frown jounce on to a Brookstone thingy light show, t-shirted in a red-to-indigo gradient after a titillating ordering mishap. Semi-blackout. The onlookers stifle their Natty Light burps in collective awe at such sheerly deflated hope. Annnnnd, lights more fully up...

^(D) All right, all right. Hold on, I think I scrawled a draft on one of the back pages here. Mm, okay, it's set in a prison yard.

^(R) I love it!

^(D) Thanks Rob. Okay, there's four inmates passing the time. A big scary one, let's say Guffo. His two cronies, uh, Bilkins and Kurt. And poor Dern Pete who's a little slow. Ok, some crucial stage direction here. They're trying to tell jokes, but in a sort of reverse knock-knock where the punchline is always popping a thumb out the mouth and sticking it up the butt while doing a raspberry. Got it?

^(L) Yup.

^(R) You had me at Bilkins.

^(D) Okay, so Guffo says, "How do you hail a cab in Wichita?" then does the thing. The cronies love it, Pete chuckles nervously. The cronies follow with "What's the best way to shower at a truck stop?" and "What's the difference between a radiologist and a submarine captain?" to the same effect, despite Kurt not really getting the idea, which makes poor Pete even more nervous for his turn.

^(R) A subtlety only the Jynkles could make sing.

^(D) Good point, maybe I'll go with the baby hippo line I had originally. Anyhow, all eyes on poor Dern Pete, who takes way too long, then lights up with "How do all racist jokes start?" and a spirited pop-n-plug. The guys are seriously nonplussed, Kurt says something about being conceived to a racist joke, but Guffo eventually lets the matter slide. Then, in the same order, we have, "What's the secret hippy handshake?", "How did the Wright brothers check their windspeed?", and "How does Ross Perot check if his dentures are in right?" with escalating jocularity.

^(L) Wow, must be lifers.

^(D) Yeah, another fine nuance for our troupe. Pete, again frozen, then blurts, "What was JFK's favorite beddy-bye song? Happy birthday Mister—" pop, plug. After a tense silence, Kurt and Bilkins open up with "Does your mother know you desecrate the memory of renowned historical figures?" et cetera. Guffo boils over, shanks Bilkins (who takes it like a champ), then points the shiv at Pete saying something about Bilkins knowing he had it coming, but that Pete's next one

better make them all smile like they got a big red firetruck on their fifth birthday or something. Pete quivers, then says, "What... does... it... seem... like... when... you have... to... go... but... there's... some... others... outside... waiting?" After an excruciating belabored pop–plug, Pete preemptively cringes into a ball practically, but the others just one by one start crying and form into a group hug. The end.

(R) Wow. Have they ever done one with an ending before?

(D) Oh stop it, you.

Well call this my little social saddle, what a moment. Still a bit alarmed by the whole soporific profusion of unincorporated greenery. Siren's call to a cactus kicker. Ultimately there's a lingering sweetness to it that's more dizzying than anything, but the old unobtrusive corner spot has got me a view of a mother and her mid-teen son, somewhat adrift from the university-tour circuit, stopping their survey of the first eighteen rings of the train stop's brick terrace. A few deft utterings smothered in familial nuance while bowing together over a map and phone, with stray locks absently mingling in the wind like that whole Avataradactyl thing.

Then we have the impressively discrete gaggle of girl geeks, clearly imbued with one too many late-night cast-party pacts or DD/40k coups, but refreshingly a few heaps less insular than us old tube-sockers. And, of course, they break obliquely around the carelessly browned and toned summer-job-on-the-lake boys bumming the dive-bar patio, hunched over a smorgas of the finest local three-dollar entrees. One poor kid's got his inner Tony so plumed up for his undiscovered Maria it's nearly too much for him to ogle, chew, and grunt assent to his hearties' opinions on septic packaging all at once.

But it's getting on to that time of day where the bus drivers only seem to stop for visible symptoms of heat stroke, and the questionable abrupt cutoff of injected downtowntrification half a block south lends a more palpable dreary note to the view. What was it, eight low-rises and at least thirty-six boulange/patis/lingerie/confett-eries? Well, the thinning murmur puts Drew at ease at least. Let's see, drop the till for two slow looks around and they're back to unspoken primacy mores.

⁽ᴰ⁾ Sure, sure, but that's all some new flavor of forcible repression. I'm talking about the tinfoil hatters losing ground to more subtle actors.

⁽ᴿ⁾ But not subconscious.

⁽ᴰ⁾ Not really. Whether or not it's pseudoscience to implant thoughts of any effect. I mean unwitting cells of trolls catalyzing certain critical social debates before they're ripe. Letting people talk themselves into astroturfing just by forcing a few obvious hands.

⁽ᴿ⁾ Uh-hm. You know some of us simpletons just watch our embarrassing injury videos and call it a day.

⁽ᴸ⁾ You're saying our tweet-addled thumbs are becoming susceptible to some nefarious leaky kairotic hindrance network?

⁽ᴰ⁾ Yeah, sure, let me think. Yes, that's essentially what I said in a horribly deformed nutshell.

⁽ᴸ⁾ Thanks. And it's still the tired and true melting away of the bulk of our defensive will to the point of careless submission argument?

⁽ᴰ⁾ Sure. I know, plenty of plain-old evil abounds to make it lame worrying about some Illuminati'd marketing intern ensuring a particular unpublicized isotope of tooth whitener kills off all our last vestigial Neanderthal-dominated zygotes or what all.

⁽ᴿ⁾ I don't think the geneticists are quite there yet, bud.

⁽ᴸ⁾ Well, sooner or later... But what do we do, bolster our internet ramparts with counter-trolls spamming dadaist soliloquies and lengthy eighth-grade essays somehow spinning every debate into love being quintessential despite all these gawl-dang modern trappings?

⁽ᴰ⁾ Fight pacification with obfuscation?

^(L) Geh, when you put it that way, I can see why there's been so many frank-to-a-fault war heroes. Holy miasmic mind cloud, Bundtman! Where does it all stop?

^(D) Preferably by the end of this sentence.

^(R) Hoo, this beetle's got a stinger.

^(L) So, ok, you're saying there are, ehh, retroviral marketing agents among us, most of them none the wiser?

^(R) Let it die, Leeho. Please, I already had my lunch beer.

^(L) Yeah, sorry. Well at any rate, your new literary bent passes my audit. But I might miss the pouty narrator man-Smurfs and all that cozy Murakamic longing.

Ah the snippets our rear-guard duly hip overhear at the grownup tables over yonder. Strut on, wee self-reverent drip refill loiterists, how near you've come to gleaning the whole fehcade.

^(R) Mm, and Peckinpah sex plus with all those extra last-minute role reversals.

^(L) It's like your pen has a fatal entanglement with badly transferred mid-20s film stock.

^(D) Yeah, yeah. So how's your work anyway, Li? I assume someone's financing your marathon pajama sessions on the back porch?

^(L) Steady. Mostly six-block jogs, really. Taking Friday mornings at that verging-on-outright-seediness chain cafe up by that place with the really good pastrami. So, so-so, I guess. Well Rau-Bau, care to join the elective personnel review round-robin?

^(R) Care to? That's a tough one. It would take awhile.

^(L) Maww, proceed with all due protuberance.

^(R) Fine, but that sauce talk gets you the short version. Let's see, there's the unmentionable franchise serfdom gig, then the same dream job in the wrong decade DJ gig for the same hands-off holding-firm cabal that still only chimes in

for the monthly dehumanization chat to keep things running on... uh, to keep, uh the old engine knocking? Hell, I don't know, they still never said anything about my thought-I-was-quitting rant over an initially inadvertent mashup of, shit what was it?

⁽ᴰ⁾ Oh, it was gold, I remember. Partridge Family?

⁽ᴿ⁾ Hmm, no, Hansen and Harry Nilsson braided into a sort of basis, with Roger Hodgson and the Monks comping and Klaatu and Captain Beefheart trading fours.

⁽ᴸ⁾ Really much of a departure from your 3 a.m. slot?

⁽ᴿ⁾ Horr dee hurr hurr. No, I don't typically drop so much liquid scat in full view of the FCC or any other acronymical body.

⁽ᴸ⁾ So either your overminders don't listen or they thought letting a tantrum go neglected would break you somehow?

⁽ᴿ⁾ Shit, for all I know they took it at face value. Got some cryptic fan mail over it. Believe it or not, this county's insomniac delegation is a bit on the cagey side.

Rob's little fish-lipped head toss lands perfectly over one of those oddly common pedestrian syzygy thingies with three people crossing at near-right angles: our tireless barista who told me her name once, something like a Becca or Lily—Liza in my book now for all that heartfelt humming; a hitch-stepped dude in full busker regalia, a late-season hack, presumably; and Trina, chucking her phone with a chummy poised resentment.

⁽ᵀ⁾ Hey loves. Rob.

⁽ᴸ⁾ Missed you hon. Stuck here all July?

⁽ᵀ⁾ 'fraid so. The long-stay crowd loves their salsa.

⁽ᴿ⁾ Any more injuries?

⁽ᵀ⁾ Probably. They always half-ass the warmups and end up more and more grimacing and clenched. I'm starting to doubt that spouses should ever really exercise together.

^(D) I'm with you on that. We never got ice cream without a weirdly taciturn family bike ride. Don't ever tell a kid to hurry up for sprinkles unless you're holding up a jar of them.

^(R) Aww, but your folks are such sweethearts.

^(D) Yeah, sure, they're fine. I'm saying I've got to err on the side of humbuggery when it comes to co-ed family routines involving heavy sweating.

^(R) Fair enough. The family that sweats together...

^(D) Ugh, don't.

^(R) Oh, you totally set it up.

^(L) Frets together?

^(R) Ooh, that's even better. Wait, oh man, Partridge Family? Frets? Did you even?

^(L) Didn't even. All you, buddy.

^(T) Thanks Rob. Am I drawing this out, or you guys having more, what are those, toddies?

^(L) Iced Vietnamese-bean sludgy glory. Deep off-menu stuff.

^(T) Oo, the cocoa-butter one?

^(D) Yup.

^(T) Okay. Three? Two?

She makes me feel klutzy just skooching her chair back. The world needs more dance instructors scraping up savings to finish their master's for the fifth year in a row.

The busker's set up nearly close enough to high five and he's tuning a shower radio to some top-forty, four-note lamby crooner. Ungrafittied light mahogany... Ibanez? Sir, I'm fairly certain we're downwind and your musk remains at bay. If you're not moonlighting I may have to find out what soap they're using at the bus depot. Ha! Knew it, tear that junk pop apart. Kick some dirt at those airwaves, man.

(L) You guys seeing this?

(R) Jesus. He's got his pinky and thumb crossed.

(D) Why am I suddenly compelled to abandon my day job, creative pursuits, personal convictions, and fiduciary relations and hunt elk with a cudgel till my knees give out?

(L) Mmhmm. Like a rarefied aphrodisiac that makes your pubes grow like bamboo.

(R) I feel like I'm reading a good book that's a little over my head, and my favorite movie's on TV, yet I'm processing both as if they're part of the same saga.

(L) What's your favorite movie?

(R) Could've told you five minutes ago.

Don't know how long Trina's been back, hard to say if we've been tucking our interjections in at twelve- or sixteen-bar intervals. Her setting out the second rounds and sliding back in is accomplished with a heightened sense of performer's solidarity, easing us all past the awed titter we'd thought our holding down the stoop had earned us, dwarfing all prior skooches as skirmishes.

Hail to the ringer, then. Whichever municipal arts' center keeping you fed is getting shorted a matinee worth twice their annual wine and cheese budget. Performances this strong usually lead me on halting epiphanic bouts. Nibbles of lucidity probably overdue from years of neglecting the morning crossword or meditation. Or joint, for that matter. Not here though. No resolutions, no sudden grasp of unadulterated pettinesses smudging my wellness beacon. Nope. His fingers just aren't sparing any grit, no mirror holding-up or whatever I've been taking as that sweet requisite factor between a toe-tapper and a face-melter. No, he demands both. Maybe Bird could have foretold of such twiddles in his less cohesive waking moments.

Probably did. Dearest holies of blues and rock gods, a prophet is arrived, with impromptu tenderizing of our daily bread. We bow our heads that he may have not forgotten those in need of butter. There it is, or more olive oil let's say, much more on the twangy succulence side. Brought to the brink of resounding applause from four crummy schlubs on a dead afternoon in the touristy neck of Third Street.

The background jam starts its fadeout chorus, actually not as feeble a latter-day wannabe Madonna belter as I'd guessed. One of those playfully produced world-house-funk hits that for all its demographic slathering has enough pluck to end up in the regular fourth-hour wedding reception rotation for at least a half-decade or so.

The reverie's so stupefying, our customary owlishness fails us for once. Some poor ten-year old girl's been hovering by our cranny a brave twenty feet or so from mom, whose lips and brow are cross-curled in a bemused recognition of her encouragement's minor misfire into a social bramble too thick for the girl's undoubtedly authentic laminated name tag and tastefully sheathed pamphlets to have any effect on her confidence. The boys are still crushing on the ringer as he drapes a few painstakingly ragged arpeggios under the fade out, but Trina's seen the girl too and leaves me with an "aww" face nearly audible in its own right.

(L) Hey. Doing some pavement work yourself?

Oh God. She's flopping on the deck and I'm offering San Pelligrino.

(L) My name's Lianne. You're out here with your mom?

( ) Yeah. I'm getting donations and you can get a ribbon, even just for a dollar. It's for research.

(L) What kind?

( ) Orange.

(L) Great. I'll take four please.

Can't be certain I've ever handed anyone an uncounted wad of ones before, it does have a nice seedy camaraderie to it. And, miraculously kept a five left over for the virtuoso that I manage to paw across to Rob, who's nearly too forklempt for the salutary saunter to the guitar case.

Then two kicks under the table from Trina to check my oversatiated verging on demented lippy grin and collect our awareness strips. And I'd nearly convinced myself a little catch-up work session was just the right way to round out the afternoon.

6

Kathryn, dear me,

Your encrypted VIM macro wizardry has befouled my trusty old off-grid beater as instructed. Hell of a grep cypher. Do I take this to imply a fresh notch on your D20 from the math department? Hope you've enjoyed scanning the spirographed FFTs of this here. Crypto's so much better with a little analog trim, eh? Protocol's still sound if it's all under the same one-use pads, I hope? May be wasteful using a pad just on the instructions, I know, but it occurred to me it might not be obvious that the prize file was concentric deconvolution params.

You know, it makes someone like me feel loved to get a shudderingly disjointed letter in the grand old

best friend's handwriting with an enclosed gift card
to a nonexistent discount jeweler's in the boonies
that turns out to be a geocaching mecca. However,
brotip: maybe pick a slightly less trafficked
one next time? There was a sweet old Finnish guy
still signing the logbook when I tripped the first
drone--didn't mean to, I was just trying to act
natural and tossed the card in the box like a good
little cachite thinking you'd left me step two
scribbled in the log. Poor guy looked like he missed
last week's Buck Rogers when it started spooling out
the RFID stickies. Wouldn't worry though, I made
something up about a pesky younger brother hacking
my phone and surveilling my geofun to spoil it with
taunts of ludditry.

I'm thinking my heartfelt exasperation at those
there chilbins dern underappreciation for a good
old-fashioned crowdsourced GPS lark carried the lie
far enough past the language barrier to take. Anyway,
I made sure I heard his car start before smooshing the
sticker and gift card around. Hell of a two-factor
solution, Kay. Again, given that two years ago
you didn't know a Blackberry from a dongle, I must
register my dubiety at your surely ill-gotten gizmo
prowess.

The second drone's payload I shall treasure
eternally. As a flouting of our now most surely
secure channel, the inventory stands as:

1 pocket notebook w/heavy-grain hand-pressed extra cloth-ey
paper cover of swoopy, sloppy watercolor design work in
Kindergarten green, background stripes in freeze-dried puke
yellow, and little diamond-headed stick figure borderwork.
Contents are, namely, 16 formatted one-time-use, handwritten

grep-script-obfuscated cyphers.

1 shoe-box-sized 3D printer with operating instructions in
Mandarin, Indonesian, and Bengali and 3 spools unmarked
polymer.

1 Lemon Sunrise Yankee candle with USB drive embedded at base.
(As if to blend with other wholly inconspicuous contents.)

5 Satchels kooky pictogram-marked powders.

1 Bag sharpie-coded asst'd springs, clips, screws,
supercapacitors and var. accoutrements.

1 culinary syringe

50 plastic sheets, bizarrely capillaried and perforated.

3 two-ounce bags mixed Jelly Bellies.

I don't know how long your friends think this
underground skynet of theirs can go on without some
grade-A spooks breaking the door down on D&D nights
far and wide, and I'm a mite flummoxed there aren't
payloads of greater import to your jediacal droogs.
On the assumption this is a beta-phase morse along, my
gratitude at gopherdom.

The little meltbot is chugging along at this very
moment. How thoughtful of you to have it print out
the assembly-instruction obloid last.

God forbid a roommate should barge in on me in a
witches' circle of what appears to be a disassembled
spring-action vibrator/sewing kit combo without
plausible deniability.

An upgrade? And I was just getting the hang
of terrorizing the local beer can population
with frozen nerfette balls from the paci-bow.
Alright Celebrimbor, you've remotely procured me
a hand-baggable collapsing-grip jumbo-BB-caliber
burnball pistol. Said doodad chambers the recommended
trial salmon-egg round on unfolding, cocks with
an ambidextrous rotary action over the bulbous

back-chamber, which houses at least 30 rounds-with
optional large-intestine style surgical tubing
bandolier of six braided channels in a lemon wool
cosy with creweled number munchers. In all, resembles
an implausibly compact battery-powered hair dryer.

What kind of dark alleys do you imagine we're
facing out here? You realize the neighborhood
watch is two octogent vets vaping cannawax on their
porch and calling out passersby on their 50-dollar
tattoos? This itch/whip/buzz/stick/poof theory of
graduated incapacitation is intriguing anyhow. Am
I going to blow up my vacuum making these? Are the
urchiney electrodes some sort of nanohazard? Do I
just pincushion them in or scrape them around the
supercaps with a makeshift mini rolling pin? Maybe
those deadly baby-corn-shaped corn cob skewers? That
or a dollhouse curtain rod.

These instructions are so far from foolproof I'm
starting to fantasize about the IKEA gummo as the
disrobed Bob Vila my mom always dreamed of.

From the molds I've cooked up so far, it's looking
more like garnish/fizz/splat/calming mist for my
deterrence palette. If this is all rooted in our
perennial discourse on the highway patrol vs. the
Devil's Rejects in assorted heavy-crockery-based armor
at close range, let me assure you I find no assurances
for either side of the debate here. Or is this a
"holy water, clove leaves, silver shavings and white
oak" sort of thing?

The feed selection dial does lend a sense
of this being a particularly well-thought-out

prototype, but I stand miffed that you neglected my long-standing dead-foot/crotch-gong/flip-gut school of supersoaker gunkatta. I must assume the schema for the piezo-timpanics and nauseant rounds are en route.

Ok K-bo. Marginally more serious now: assuming the dark alley thing as pretext we can call this the most circuitously ethical funneling of tax-based grant money imaginable, but please do keep in mind what sort of rumors are gracing your padawans' bong circles. Yes, Counter-Urban Animated Sculpture and Design is a great cover, but make sure it's not all applied mayhem majors on the roll for Christ's sake. Bribe some Art History dorks with glass-blowing lessons if you must. Please, pray to the adipose mons for guidance with all duteous fervor. Bye iloveyoutakeyourvitaminesbye,

The Estimable Li H. Jorowsky

P.S.

Please advise on the superstitious protocol for having your shoes pooped in by an unidentifiable small mammal while leaving them on the back porch to air out from a floam hermeticity mishap.

(D) For all we know, it could be the last operational AM/FM simulcast station with a main street sidewalk view.

(L) Were there ever any others?

(D) Hm, come to think of it I may be mistaking Do the Right Thing for deep-seated Americana.

(L) Tell me about it. I also often say things that are completely unintelligible but are said with the right helping of conviction to elicit a companionable wince.

^(D) Yes, it's a movie, sorry. Seems like a no-brainer anyway. No coffee for you yet either?

^(L) You know I knew something was off. Or wait. No, yes. Way too much in fact. Seems like hours ago. Just that I had enough gluten and lactose-rich treats to put me in a relative narcotic state. Mm, nothing against non-leguminous, anti-endospermic curd-like beet-sweet treats though.

^(D) They have come a long way.

^(L) Yeah, oh and oatgurt parfait, it's been too long. Think we can pull a Bloom Room run before the thing?

^(D) What is it, 1:20? I don't know. But yeah, if we end up pushing it, I could just go get us all take out. Pretty sure Les's just got me logging clips anyway. Is that them?

Anne's more than a few shades flashier than I'd have pegged her having the gall for, but it suits. The counter-bobbing guitar, stretchy jacket, and Trina's cheeks leaking out sib-glow from under the deep-set deadpan all spell out a more singular air than ought to be palpable this long before lunch. Certainly clashes with my unshowered wandering in from a protracted breakfast over vintage Kung Fu dubs on YouTube to a near-hallucinogenic hypercaffienated tipping point of jerky sedantry versus fresh air and fulfilling loosely recalled social obligations. Worth it sampling the espresso maker at a decreasing-volume gradient anyhow.

^(L) Yup.

^(D) Wouldn't you say this calls for a little pomp? Did he even acknowledge us yet? Doesn't he ever look up from grumbling over that three-week-old sheet of copy? It's been like a solid six minutes.

^(L) I don't know, in that seat he catches a nasty glare this time of day. Always squinting.

^(D) Alright. You gong the windows, I signal the unstopping of the orator's pipe?

^(L) I don't know if Rob's got any stoppable pipes, but I'm on it.

From the look of it, the zoning goon finally axed the spiffy old Bose wedges from their perch. To which Rob, or less likely, his institutionalizable but for scissory good manners and undue wealth boss, got out the one-inch flat bit and put a hole through a surely inadvisable, largely mortar cross-section of the exterior brickwork, then mounted them close enough to their former home to deliver the familiar click and hiss of Rob putting the feed through, albeit now with an old tinny tube-megaphone effect. My gonging might be carrying through on air—the foam-lined studio between us and Rob may as well have been rigged by a recovering Dr. Teeth roadie, these days at least down to just huffing glitter. But Rob banters on, unfussed by our dicking.

(R) That was "D. Lady of the Lover Night and Her Drawn Foot" by the Erogenators. Off their unnumbered EP "Friends with Bohner Futz". So rare a track it's never been de-clouded to any known media. But fear not, faithful capacitive cadets, we're always six clicks ahead at KBLI. Any song dump your mobile OS can't wrap a GUI around is fired up on our state-of-the-art, refurbished, unbranded, purportedly multi-core tower and waiting with the bristly, lovable poise of its digital woodland kin for you to call in and realize you can't remember the song titles to any of your indie faves released in the last nine years. But wait! Hold that nonstarter, we have another block of some especially mandatory messages from our local sponsors, followed by some person sitting in front of me playing music or something maybe.

(L) What do you call that, puppy dog basting eyes?

(T) Probably just halfway between lunch and early-afternoon breakroom rips. And please, nothing food or pet related this early, Li.

(D) I'd go with resting duck face. Coming?

(T) Yeah, hold on. My shoe's still all weird. You feeling alright there, scamp?

(L) Oh just all peachy tits and you name it. Maybe a little crusty, even for a, what is this, Sunday?

^(T) Probably.

^(L) And if my whole right side starts arrhythmically spasming, go home and kick the coffee maker, it's probably just some quantum decoherence.

^(T) So I should expect more marginally coherent tongue fuckery?

^(L) I prefer soupy prattle.

^(T) Yes, yes you do.

^(L) Thank you.

^(T) Alright, can we please go in now? I've never seen Drew fawning like that before and I'd never forgive myself if I let my sister fall for an aspiring avant-garde sci-fi sentimentalist while I'm out here hearing you and Rob both bullshitting at once.

^(L) Aww, their babies would be wholesomely underappreciated by the turgid masses.

^(T) Oh Jesus, is he curtsying?

^(L) Well, her boots could pass for medieval.

^(T) He's actually rocking with his hands behind his back. I didn't know anyone really did that.

^(L) Yes he is. Wow. But let's admit, far more adorably than anyone would have thought.

^(T) Li, please.

^(L) Yeah yeah, he's probably half a kerfuffle away from abject floundering without our help anyway.

Rob's really improved his robo announcer voice. Almost a fully graveled transformation into Stephen Wright fighting to stay awake on a moped. It's either more bassey inside or hiding his face behind the cue sheet is backfiring and making us all compelled for a good gawk and titter.

^(R) That's right folks, set 'em up at Keester's Rockhouse Funpub, where pinball's always two-for-one, pitchers come

with pool, and arcade games are free after eleven to all tipping customers. And while you're at it, why not head down over to Shirla's All-U for a three-phase colon-care expedition, or recalibrate your chi in their Yelp-acclaimed sensory-invigoration wombs. "A positively addicting experience" says one of their dearest...

Uh-oh, the copy fails him. He's said it as an adjective, and they've meant it noun-ized. Think, man!

[R] ...enthusiasts. Shirla's is the senspiritive sanctuary for discovering your daily center, or just a joyous retreat for a heart-to-heart with like-minded lovers of life.

Stupendous, but for the faint molar gnashing under the coyote and birdcall bumper.

[R] And. Now. Back to the—Oh except Wait. This just in buckarinos: Jumble's burger crew wants you to "Both it!" You say "Both me!" and that they will. Any two of any items on the menu are free... for both-ing. Forget "I'll just have a" and get both-ed. Can't decide on cheeses? Both 'em for one! Milkshake flavors! Patty squash-ins! Both in one or both separate, it's always for the price of one. That's how to Jumble's, so come on down for "both" meals of your choosing, and get a double both-er same-day loyalty discount.

And that's our hourly beloved spate of paid local advertising, folks. Be sure to tune in next hour, where at least two of the same ads will be read in a different order, one will have up to thirty percent altered text, and one may be omitted entirely depending on the clearing of a check by our derring-do production staff.

In the meantime, we continue our sesqui-terminal "pledge to end the drive"-athon. Now, normally we'd be taking our traditional "shut up and spin" paid requests this hour, but we've got a brain de-icing treat today. "Free tickets or some crap" you say? "Text-in driver's trivia" you grumble with a knowing smile? In fact, no! There's a person here with a guitar instead. She calls herself, by her name, Anne Tierney.

How about you introduce yourself, further, Anne, and maybe strum a chord or two so I can text a picture of our levels to our sound engineer down in McMurdo?

⁽ᴬ⁾ Hi Rob. Hi Tri-County area until the signal fades at sunset.

⁽ᴿ⁾ Hoyo! It seems we've harrusled up a local. And I hear you've brought a fellow creative type for some set-inspired brush- and/or printwork as you play?

Oh, slurpy shit-soup grimy fucking bastard fucks. Of course I was so expertly coaxed in and politely deferred the only other available seat, which happens to have a studio mic clawing over it.

⁽ᴬ⁾ That's right. I believe she also goes by her name, Lianne Jorowsky.

⁽ᴿ⁾ Well hi there Li N.

⁽ᴸ⁾ Bueno.

⁽ᴿ⁾ Now, the contestants have drawn switches beforehand, but in case our listeners at home aren't familiar with the provisions, we have invited a panel of impartial wonks to critique both the aural and brushy work at the end of the hour. The runner-up will be politely but firmly asked to re-evaluate their notions of what constitutes a complete waste of time, space, energy, or spirit-force of their choosing.

So it's a Globetrotters–Senators deal then. Fine, you snide little snots. Suppose it serves me right practically never listening to my roommate's radio show. He probably pulls this sort of shit every chance he gets. At least I don't need to wait till the next break to ask about the cheerfully lumped-up sack of discount drug store crafts-and-toys aisle chaff everybody's been averting gazes from, plus the Seussian pile of assorted garage-sale quality arguably paintable media under my seat.

⁽ᴿ⁾ Layn, care to elaborate on your media for the folks at home?

⁽ᴸ⁾ I'll be revisiting my nymphic phase with high-gloss posterboard and food-safe modeling clay, using a deep-smear hand staining for heavy-residue strokes.

⁽ᴿ⁾ Astonishing. The subject?

(L) A propped-on-couch vestigial totemic of my mother's late terrier Merle, limbs askew, with coloring in the spirit of Ute needlework.

(R) Oh gush, you've made me exhale studiously. Anne, sounds like you're the one to be beating. Alright ma'am. Marm. Budgies of the fennel. The prevailing clump in the hourglass is forthwith to be shaken loose. Simulated livestream video simulcast is up as always on vid dot posepot dot share slash rumbuckle pepper fourteen, letter-oh, eight pee aye en tee bit dot ell why slash whatever our call sign is. Somebody within a hundred yards of your nearest speaker-repair hovel probably remembers it. Also probably there's a homepage. Donations of replacement strings and grown-up art supplies will only be accepted by non-family members on first-name basis with contestants, and only within twelve minutes preceding the first TBA tie breaker thumb-war break.

Well, devout haughty yule-logs, all further ado astride, crimp your hearts and butter both sides. Ignore my exasperation as a fifth hurry-up wave goes unheeded to what appears to be an heirloom twelve-stage tuning and finger slickening procedure; find the nearest available sympathetic shoulder, stool to strap to, or rare pungent hard candy of 'ere to pique your sentimental glands, and allow me to overtly stall for, just, ok. Now songs from Anne Tierny and her silent twins.

I guess that's what he'd call tweaking a rookie's nerves. A few bars of that clipped, purring vamp of her solid opener and he's onto his saggy bloodhound loll bit in case she makes the mistake of looking his way for support. Maybe she has, I'm already lost in it, she's done some serious polishing since that last ambience-for-waddley-loos slot at the street fair. The general effect's perfect: melody is sparse, dark, even bordering on grim, with grounding strums but mostly a struggle for dominance between upper-fret flourishes and a smokey deflowered Disney waif chant. But with our dippy grins still wearing off, she's got some giddiness seeping through and it gels into an eerily lighthearted romp through crippling wants and apprehensions.

The portrait's at least on par with its forbear, the result of one of my first encounters with "fuckin hydro, man" and the consequential overdrawn schmaltz. A tad more nobility in Merle's off-recipe Scolorky heritage this go-around.

Rob winds down the hour with a saucy imaginary blow-by-blow of the judge's remarks to the effect of Anne's having fractured our inner snow globes while I clodded my way into the annals of purple participant-ribbon holders immemorial with great potential for future aplomb.

(R) It seems Li-hem, your piece at once dutifully strives for a neo-classical insouciance, while honing a rambunctious post-cubist niche of its own. Would you agree?

(L) I'm sorry? I dilettante quite get what you were asking?

(R) Ya ha! Art begets snark, as us devout hip know all too well. And with that dangling nugget of distilled something-or-other, dear purviewers, I must lead us back to the un-nethered realm of prerecorded performances and bid our guests a bye-bye. Thanks again to Anne Tierney and Lee-Yam Yourassgleek.

(A) Any time, Rob.

(L) First one's always free for you, Rowbow.

(R) And how. Well folks, that's it for our locally sourced portion and any foreseeable pledge-able content for the next four to thirteen weeks. We assure you our operatives are no longer standing by. Genesis is next, guess the track name and mail it in and we'll send you some stickers maybe... And ok. Clear. Thanks for not cussing at me Lijo.

(L) You owe me a week of dishes, dickwattle.

(R) Deal. So is this shoot still at three-thirty? I've got a stack of surprisingly palatable face melters all punched in and cross faded to cover the rest of my shift, but I haven't heard back from Tad and he's starting to come in later and later.

(D) We can go wake him up, I'm gonna stop by Bloom's anyway.

(R) Cool. I only need like a minute to lock up.

The studio's stuffiness is already outweighing Anne's well-earned afterglow. Trina's herding instinct flares and we're merry-banding down fourth, giving Drew meal orders and cash with martial efficiency, parting ways as neatly, and slapping backs on set having hardly skipped any real beats.

Despite the requisite indie film set haplessness, the amorphous swirl of three or so ingenues at the helm seems to amount to a rough grasp of how one ought to operate. From the blocking, it looks like we're transforming one of the few less-than-pleasant throughways in town into a passably grimy alley for a culminating encounter in some sort of grab-fu noir with a dash of paranormal effrontery.

On our end is an attempt at a live-synced, ostensibly unimprovised score, with nine or so unrehearsed musicians cordoned off in the old travel agent's office that reeks so deeply of unmitigated municipal plumbing disputes that the drummer and his groupie-cum-auxiliarist are chain smoking without objection. Our busker from the other day is on lead, still fully bedraggled, and garnering a hell of a lot of deference from everyone else, who seem to know him on sight. Apparently my ringer-dar's in check.

We've all eaten or shared away our zesty vegan slurry, sound-checked and re-checked to Rob's satisfaction, and run through the beer-stained charts to that of the twiggy, mega-haired composer/bari-sax guy before any lights have gone up. Giggers' pride in being low-maintenance, I guess. Something in the lull gives Rob the gall to realize he doesn't have six hands and delegates me from second-chair in the ominous woo-ing chorus to sole boom-op.

Fair enough, I've got no qualms on bearing my early-onset spinster jangleceps full tilt. May get all goosed up by it anyhow. Film sets are so damn hormonal to begin with. Can count on a real four-star rubbey dovey later on if I want, and not with that dazed, pervy consolation-run feel like after standing around with some gawking bros at a chip and dip and bad autopilot DJ jamboree.

The keyboard player's doting on a Franken-Rhodes, with maybe only the bridge, tuning-fork looking soundy-rods, and some of the crustier coils left from the original. He's managed

to miniaturize the action with crossed hinge springs just for
resistance, hammers hanging straight down between them,
and the rods seated in a well-gabled bloom of RC-modeler
grade 1/12 scale hydraulic pumps and controllers fitted to
backflow valves, with a single eel-looking, ooblek-filled bladder
as a damper, against little shoed tentpoles supermanning out
from each hammerhead.

Upon inspection, his name is Mehan, or Harry for short,
which is biblical as far as he knows, and he calls the machine
Togar-Raph, which is also biblical and whose onomatomy he
is much more familiar with.

(L) I've got a friend back home I wish you could meet.

(H) Musician or has a tinkering problem?

(L) Associate Professor of Interface Design, Eurasian
Archivism, and Textile Sociopolitics.

(H) Wow. Whatever kind of tinkering that takes I can't
imagine.

(L) No, no. He's mostly a slob. If I remember right, he just
thought it'd be a lark founding the cotton gin restoration society so he'd get the longest nameplate in the interdisciplinary
college.

(H) Does he make his own IRL-amajigs?

(L) We've honed his cocktail napkining skills over the years.
When the stars align he blacks out and we farm out the designs
to undergrad machining shops to be carved up exactly as
crudely as drawn.

(H) An exercise in catering to a client's mediocrity?

(L) Mm. And a bookish drunk client with no clear mar-
ketable intent at that. We usually tie them to ornate ballon-
animal phalluses and leave them sticking out of his mailbox.
The pedal-powered metronome we actually floated in through
the chimney.

(H) Jesus. Who's this diabolical "we"?

(L) Oh, just me and our other poor interfacier's tormentor. She's a sculptor. Also tinkers I suppose, but trades commissions for heftier tech favors lately.

(H) Neat. Which makes you?

(L) A victim of theoretical math. Typesetting and compositing for second-rate astronomy journals at half the guild rate in exchange for laughable oversight.

(H) You know I've never met a scab before.

(L) Hush, there's paid musicians in the room. You've just never met an honest scab.

(H) What? Wait, who's paid? I better fire my agent.

(L) Lured you in with promises of free pizza and pot discounts like the rest of us poor saps?

(H) More or less. I even wrote the damn thing.

(L) Our contract? You know I've got to say, your unspaced en-dashes are not sanctioned by any known style manual. Or do you mean the score? I thought that was beefcake over there.

(H) Nope, neither. The script, actually. I was stuck on another story loosely inspired by poor old Rhodesy here. Found this madcap gooball on my bathroom counter one morning under an empty eight-dollar Malbec.

(L) Imagine if it had been a five-dollar bottle.

(H) We'd probably be in marching band uniforms. There was a lamely consistent mix of live-stage direction and camera placement notes, but Doug over there had come in at some hellish hour from a particularly soul-crushing softcore shoot, read it, and he'd already chalked up a beat sheet in toothpaste on the mirror.

(L) Ahh, so you're running one of those artiste assemblages my bridge group keeps telling me about.

(H) 'Fraid so. I hear they're about as common around here as duplexes.

(L) Yup. Pretty soon they'll start hawking food stamps outside the stationary store, mark my words.

(H) Heard last week the didgeridoo teacher had a line down the street, while the poor old junior bricklayer's clubhouse can barely afford to keep its kiln hot as an Easy Bake.

(L) Utter shame. Least you've got the gumption to stuff that boojhee bopper full of some sensible hardware.

(H) Yah. If there's wires there oughta be tubes with it, s'what I always say. It being the family motto from since electromechanical bygones immemorial.

(L) And a fair one at that. I don't know if we ever settled on anything except "for the love of God, please not in the house".

(H) Sounds like my kind of paradoxical crochet mantelpiece.

(L) So this gnarly gadget indirectly spawned our current endeavor with another pet project on hold? Were you a software developer in a former life?

(H) Maybe an international hurdy gurdy spokesman moonlighting as an organ grinder.

(L) Ooh, unconscionable. So then you got this idea from the pet story in question?

(H) Hah, no, not the current one, but good guess. I'd tell you all about it but I know too well when Doug's hair sucking is verging on frantic.

(L) Ah, thanks. Better get out there and post my stick. That's how you say it, right?

(H) Good way as any. You might save your friend over there some serious stink eye if you get her off the phone on your way.

(L) Good call. Pleased to meet you Harry... Gurdyson was it?

(H) Close. Barber.

(L) Oooh, hence the disparity from the given.

(H) Ya.

(L) You know I never met a Barber.

(H) Many women haven't.

(L) Hm, you got that one written down somewhere?

(H) No, the puns usually come my way.

(L) I can imagine. Good to meet you Mr. B.

(H) You too, see ya.

Well Barber, that's a cordial handshake you've got there. Didn't hold back expecting the femmy dead fish. Or is there an art in softening it to a subtle come-hither cue I've been tomboying out on? Shit. Then again, nah, don't misrepresent grandpa and all that.

Anne's not in mouthing range. Shame, could have distracted him for a good old middle-school telepathy ruse, complete with a flashy wink and float away as she drops the call mid-sentence. Hm, not even close enough for a pushy glare, and of course now she compounds it with a third-degree aural shielding hunch.

Damn, halfway over to her and somebody else's glare stuck. Better tread lightly, that was a perfect specimen of the kind of flat goodbye that makes you miss flip phones.

(L) You look like someone who's been getting laid regularly. What's your secret? Apple butter toothpaste?

(A) I wear an extra pair of panties to properly saturate my crotch chakra.

(L) Now why didn't I think of that? Beats nosegays and Kegels I bet. Ok, I'm sorry, I gotta pry. I was on instructions to get you off your phone and now I'm irrevocably piqued how a lunch-hour radio star could get so seriously pissed so quick.

(A) Just got fired. The owner's niece said she'd sub for me and blew it off. Sounds like she lied about it or is actually that spacey and incapable of self, ah–

(L) Fault recognition?

(A) Sure, and Boss Hogg is too keyed up on his feudal righteousness for me to even want to bother setting things straight. Guess I gave niecey the cadet's benefit of the doubt.

(L) Noble. Well goodbye toddler seats and sour cream cups, eh? You ok on rent and shit?

(A) Not really, no. I'll be out looking for something shittier tomorrow or pulling teeth with my mom.

(L) A gee-you-know-I-always-pay-you-back-lickety-split loan?

(A) Yeah, pretty much. Which is true for all but the last one.

(L) First case of ramen's on me, then.

(A) Thanks Li. I should be alright.

(L) First case of Natty Ice then.

(A) Ugh. Yeah, I'll hold you to it.

(L) Now if you'll allow me a question. Would you say that's Rob's pitifully underdeveloped version of a stink-eye, or more of an aimless all-comers glower.

(A) Can't say. Definitely something non-committal to it. I'm gonna go with a "get out here and look bored with me so they hurry up with the lights" strain.

(L) You may be on to something.

(A) Better go see to him regardless. Looks like he's hurting without his late-afternoon nap.

(L) Yeah, you're right. Poor thing. If it gets rough out there watch for my boomer's morse. Left elbow is dot, right is dash.

(A) All I know is SOS.

(L) Should suffice.

Alright Rob-o, your faithful ding-a-ling vaults the precious

inches of rented dolly track with foam-capped pike expertly
balanced for its next sonic rout. Her stolidity unbesotted by
the merest driblets of distemper. Sheer, indeterminable poise
at your whim.

(L) If we talk softly and shake our heads a lot, you think
maybe it'll flip down some subliminal dicking-around switch?

(R) Doubt it. Ike's regulars are PA-ing on some FX ghost
show thing out by the lake.

(L) Which lake? You realize there's like twelve in biking
distance?

(R) Really? Doesn't everybody just go to that one with
the floating nookie huts?

(L) With the poop hatches? I think the EPA finally shut
those down.

(R) Too bad. Well anyway, we're stuck with some day-
blazed juniors from the conservatory and a couple of Ike's
die-hards from his MiniDV days. Everybody's doubled up—
prop guy's pulling focus on rollerblades, reflector girl's getting
an iPhone helmet cam, drone operator kid's doing traffic control.

(L) Christ. Might as well put him on the police scanner
for good measure.

(R) Oh, by the way, by the logistical virtue of your belt
recorder, I'm bequeathing upon you deputy band leader du-
ties.

(L) The fuck?

(R) Yup. I gotta man the deck and I couldn't dongle up
the built-ins, and nobody brought walkie talkies. So. I say
"speed", you give a four-count. Or wait for Ike to call action
maybe. I think he still usually just mumbles "yeah now".

(L) And the actors watch me tap my toes?

(R) No. The kick drum, high hat, and upright's E-string
are synced to little green LEDs on the drone kid's old laser
tag vest. Keyboard dude rigged it up.

⁽ᴸ⁾ Yeah, he's got a pretty otherworldly skillset.

⁽ᴿ⁾ Gugh, you know that's one of my gripe words.

⁽ᴸ⁾ Sorry, I left my self-censorship brain chip at the homestead.

⁽ᴿ⁾ Aggggh, stop!

⁽ᴸ⁾ What? I'm just dissembling my prattle a notch to keep abreast your societal hyperacuities.

⁽ᴿ⁾ Wow. I'm finally starting to grasp the whole kryptonite concept.

⁽ᴸ⁾ Dang, sorry. Would you say I pushed all the way past can't even to just plain can't?

⁽ᴿ⁾ I think it's a service to the species not to dignify that remark.

⁽ᴸ⁾ Don't cliche your way out of this, mister.

⁽ᴿ⁾ Fine, maestro. Please forgive my stooping with you.

⁽ᴸ⁾ Damn straight. This baton prods one way, bucko. Outwardly. And woe be he who chafes these fine callouses with an insolent flex of his cheek fat.

⁽ᴿ⁾ I'm. Fuck. Just going to go back in now. I will keep backing away slowly and speaking softly until you see that I'm not a threat.

⁽ᴸ⁾ Hey, why so quizzical, broheme?

⁽ᴿ⁾ Please, no more.

⁽ᴸ⁾ Fine. We'll just have to sublimate this like likeable-minded individuals would do on their instas.

⁽ᴿ⁾ Don't you dare, uh, grilfrin.

⁽ᴸ⁾ That's all you got?

⁽ᴿ⁾ Egh, misfire.

⁽ᴸ⁾ Yeah, well? I'll double-dog your ass any day, boy-man.

Aw, dammit, just like him to smirk away inside with me

shouting filthy innuendo-sounding jibes over a suddenly quiet
and ready to work swarm of geeks. Guess it's good enough a
christening for whatever follows the mucking around phase.

(T) Hey, dingwad. You're either muttering Rescue Rangers
or Carmen San Diego, and it's a little disturbing regardless.

(L) What? How can you hear me? What have you heard?
And who?

(T) You're holding a three-thousand-dollar microphone.

(L) So it would appear. Wow, these wraparounds are so
light I forgot I had them on. Wait? Am I on the monitor?

(T) Just mine until Rob needs a sound check. And poten-
tially anyone else with headphones who's bored.

(L) Oh, shit. Well you know I've always had an unfulfilled
next door neighbor soup can–string phone bestie fantasy.

(T) Despite daily cell phone use?

(L) Yeah, too remote, doesn't do it for me. But here I'm
definitely getting that up a little bit too late naive defiance
vibe.

(T) Wow, what a rush. Are all your fantasies so vanilla?

(L) Keep in mind I was raised by touring musicians with
advanced social science degrees. Milquetoast is something of
an unholy other for me.

(T) You realize whispering it into a shotgun mic still counts
as saying it out loud, right?

(L) Whatever you say, Jiminy. How's Annie? She mention
the shitty boss thing?

(T) Mm-hm. I'm not too worried. I've seen her take it
worse on worse jobs.

(L) But it's a bit habitual, no?

(T) Nah, not really, or only to her credit. She's just too
honest with your average fuckwit dick manager.

^(L) Good for her. Average dicks are so self-inflated anyhow.

^(T) Oh God. And I beg to differ, Cujo.

^(L) What's that? Bigger the fitter? None too big to fill?

^(T) Golly cumdrops Li, do I detect an overripe little celibacy streak hobbling its way off toward the 35th-floor balcony?

^(L) Oh, that ooze ball jumped weeks ago. Got snared on a crane or something.

^(T) And stuck worse for all the little wriggling?

^(L) Yahh. Caught myself tearing up to Pat Benatar the other day.

^(T) Sweetie. Never listen to Pat Benatar sitting down.

^(L) I was in bed.

^(T) Oh no.

^(L) Eating peanut brittle.

^(T) Oh dear holy mother of salty wombs, this is worse than I thought. And I'm not sure for how long, but Rob is clearly eavesdropping.

^(R) Sssshhhh.

^(L) Aghh! Cans off asshole. You got your levels.

^(R) But you're my only link to the great alley beyond, Li.

^(L) Off! There's four heads and counting bobbing over the sync-signal thing. You can go twiddle your dongles till you see my armpits, Rob.

^(R) Awww, c'mon.

^(L) Off.

^(R) Fine, fine.

^(L) He playing nice?

⁽ᵀ⁾ Yeah, far as I can see. So what's at that bottom of it, Li? Libido weirdly firing at all hours as usual?

⁽ᴸ⁾ Sure. Never better.

⁽ᵀ⁾ Crippling introverted tendencies resurfacing?

⁽ᴸ⁾ Uh, what's the yardstick for that one?

⁽ᵀ⁾ Let's say, how many books and movies did you finish last week?

⁽ᴸ⁾ Mm, no more than nine.

⁽ᵀ⁾ Jesus.

⁽ᴸ⁾ What? They were all really good, and I probably had strep.

⁽ᵀ⁾ Fine. Let's see, diet? What did you eat for breakfast?

⁽ᴸ⁾ Yogurt with raisins and a dollop of molasses. Remains of an orange, and drippy kale eggs with some generic stocking-stuffer hot sauce.

⁽ᵀ⁾ Shit, you win. I'd take drippy eggs over my last grope 'n snore caper.

⁽ᴸ⁾ There was some week-old Danish rye from Chempton's too.

⁽ᵀ⁾ Ooo, stop. Not here.

⁽ᴸ⁾ Wait, it's coming back to me, I found a bag with two dates in it while I was cleaning up, so I cut them up into some sunflower seeds with cocoa and peanut butter.

The rare Trina titter alights from afar with its chalky iridescence.

⁽ᵀ⁾ Madness!

⁽ᴸ⁾ It's all true. Had there been powdered sugar on hand, you'd need more than a pair of Marshalls to avail my victual carnalities.

⁽ᵀ⁾ You know Halloween's still a ways off, hon.

⁽ᴸ⁾ What a stabbing reminder.

Well, she's now hit pinched aristocratic whinny. Uncharted waters.

⟨T⟩ Ok Grampa Munster. The head dude's gotta go through the changes.

⟨L⟩ Getting vamped up or just staking a few piercing licks? Don't be cryptic now.

I'm so soupy on the dismount with that one I think I hear her fart to hold back a chuckle. Introvert that, hon.

⟨T⟩ Oh fucking Lord. Anyhow, please never switch to oat bran and instant coffee.

⟨L⟩ Shouldn't be a problem. Rob, s'that you? I appreciate the courtesy grumble.

⟨R⟩ Of course.

⟨L⟩ Armpit time?

⟨R⟩ You guessed it. Remember to droop it back toward Ike between takes.

⟨L⟩ Roger wilco, Rowrow. Skipper's mumbles at your layzhure.

Christ, Ike's a madman. If I didn't know his smoking habits better, I'd think he was gauging the angle of the sun and cloud cover probability for an ideal mixed-light window. I hope he's weighing in the fairly sluggard-skewed crew, and our pendulous savant attention spans, sharpened on grossly off-demographic pop-tart and Easy Mac metabolisms.

Maybe he's got something prescient bubbling up anyhow. If it's not a knack at seizing a decent moment, he knows when to offer it a meaty after-church handshake without getting caught up in the niceties. Lucky I'm standing figurehead on the dolly's improvised sidecar, the rest of the crew's footwork's shaping up to be as intricate as the actors', with reflectors fanning around on cue like overzealous Busby Berkeley stagehands.

Must be my new tinkerer acquaintance who set up the little denuded mechanical metronome necklaces to eerily waver in proportion to the altitude of the Wii-mote fouled bell of our emaciated maestro's horn.

Something about all this chintzy production value's got olive garlands in all our eyes from take one, but apparently the 85 wireless signatures need a little warming up to us. Thank God the drone's such a turd that Rob won't be the lone emissary from the reviled kingdom of the un-fudgeable hum. Another six false starts and the cornet guy's gonna need reconstructive jaw cartilage implants.

(L) Deputy count-off-er to Monseigneur Rohbly, come in Rohbly.

(R) They're about to call it Li, What? You're off speaker.

(L) Maybe we oughta keep a vamp going between takes? I look for skinny's nod and count three then two beats quiet?

(R) A two-three-four ungh, ungh? Hm, yeah I like it. I'll float it with the slick wig.

(T) Uh, sorry to interrupt, but did either of you two consider that the man could be a mite bit touchy about his conducting style?

(L) Often. But that much wax on that much hair bleeds "voyeurize me".

(T) I'll just pretend whatever you were trying to communicate there was abundantly clear.

(R) And he does eat like a horse. The pants are an assertion of his hyper-metabolic brain if anything.

(T) Derisions, derisions.

(L) But pray, m'Treeny. Can we not also love our derisibles?

(T) Oh go hark ye loins.

(L) Can't say that'd be a change of plans.

(R) Ok Li. Herr Direktor Emile likes the idea and the bard's on board. What's the holdup out there?

^(L) Uh, terse shots fired at Ike from everybody but us. It's looking like the forehead mopping's now piggybacked a battery swap and infuriatingly overdue back-focus check. Be a dear and put us chatty chums on a private line for the five, would you?

^(R) If you say so. At least try to look like we're troubleshooting a hiss or something.

^(L) Sure shore sir, over and innit. So, I guess if we wanna play nice you should tell me a joke? Or a story or something?

^(T) Mmhm, ooh, ok. Remember that girl Ewha?

^(L) Anne's mom-crush? Yeah, why? I recall feeling an overwhelming social pressure to stick my finger down her throat.

^(T) Yup, that one.

^(L) What? Did she discover broponk's nascent goofdad tendencies and panic?

^(T) No, actually, you sort of called it right at the time. He tried to break it off on a late-night drive back from Arby's.

^(L) While she was?

^(T) Still is, yup. Five and a half months at the time.

^(L) Yow. I've never regretted farting on somebody before. What in the seedy flying fuck was he thinking? Then again, I've never been on a second-trimester Arby's run before either. Did he not know about the bi-thing?

^(T) Nah, I don't think that was it, least not o– overtly?

^(L) Ostensibly?

^(T) Ah, sure. No, well, I did get most of this from Rene and Julie, but apparently it was just the same old "I'm not cut out for it" tripe.

^(L) You know, in his case I'd say that's unexpectedly mature.

⁽ᵀ⁾ Ugh, yeah, I don't know. I mean, he holds down a job and doesn't appear to screw around. Or not enough to get gossiped about.

⁽ᴸ⁾ Not as much as her at least?

⁽ᵀ⁾ Right, well, who knows. Anyway, he gets enough of his schpiel out for her to get what he's trying to do and she just floors it. Blasts the radio seven hours straight to her grandma's cabin out somewhere halfway to Little Rock. Chucks his phone out the window when he gets all pissy, then chucks hers right after for good measure.

⁽ᴸ⁾ Holy mother of sheep.

⁽ᵀ⁾ Yeah. So she swerves out through the tall grass in the backyard, pops the hood, rips out the intake lines, wobbles up the stoop and grabs the cabin key from whatever hidey hole and just stink-eyes him right on inside, knowing there's enough ice cream and deer steak and canned goods to make it through to an al fresco delivery if need be, all without a word on whether she really wants to sweat him out, or just keep him shacked up for his rightful share of the suffering.

⁽ᴸ⁾ Wait, this was...?

⁽ᵀ⁾ Two weekends ago.

⁽ᴸ⁾ Whoa, I could have drove right past them.

⁽ᵀ⁾ Did you catch the storm?

⁽ᴸ⁾ Ah, no, I think I beat it here then slept through most of it.

⁽ᵀ⁾ Well, they got hit hard in the cabin. Power goes out. There's a little backup jenny but it'd gotten soaked and shorted about as fast as it kicked on. And they didn't want to risk using the gas, so they're sitting there in the dark, eating beef jerky or cheez-its or whatever, and the storm's too loud to sleep or talk their shit out or anything.

⁽ᴸ⁾ So they're just taking turns fuming and averting awkward lightning-lit gazes?

^(T) Exactly. So eventually it calms a bit, and they start nodding off in their presumably rustic but not un-snuggly cabin chairs, when there's odd voices on the porch.

^(L) Bullshit.

^(T) No, no, real shit. Just odd, like familiar but out of place.

^(L) Because of their ecto-phantasmic displacement?

^(T) Nope, because of their Amishness.

^(L) No shit!

^(T) Yup. Couple brothers and an uncle or something. Turns out they'd camped the porch before, always seemed to catch a big late-summer gusher walking between the last podunk bus stop and the greyhound station in the next town over.

^(L) The hell were they doing in Arkansas?

^(T) Not sure exactly, maybe a particularly devoted and immobile quilt customer? Something tells me they'd skip the carpentry shows. All I know is it was a regular business thing they could handle with backpacks or what do you even—rucksacks?

^(L) You'd never imagine them carrying them anything but with their hands, huh?

^(T) I guess. Anyway, after the necessary freakout and humble apologies at assuming the place was vacant, the whole "not a romantic getaway" vibe starts sinking in and Uncle Hezekiah just flat-out tells them they're about to bring a screwed-up kid into the world and they'd better rope some couch cushions around the deep freezer while him and his nephews see if they can put the jenny on cinderblocks.

^(L) Quite the gentlemen callers.

^(T) Yeah, woof.

^(L) So?

82

^(T) So? So the men all slept in the living room. In the morning, baby daddy made a pile of hashbrowns while the boys hooked the power back up and uncle fixed the car without being asked.

^(L) Isn't that Amish anathema?

^(T) I guess the fix-it instinct trumps. Or some exigent circumstances clause. Shit, Rob's doing that muppety floppy thing with his hands.

^(L) Gah, shoot it down. The DP's got Ike in some sort of ego embroiling hold.

^(T) 'Kay. On your head be it. That was about it anyway. Bro dad went full fuddy over the whole thing, like he finally had a fateful night to tie it all together, without noticing that it was making mamma-to-be whatever the opposite of cloud nine is, wishing she'd let him off with his roast beef and cheddar.

^(L) Oof. Makes you wonder the price society pays for rearing people that easily awed by a little frankness and pragmatism.

^(T) Oh, like you wouldn't treat having a wizened Amish dude knock on your door in a crisis like seeing a double rainbow.

^(L) Yeah, ok, rainbow in the sprinklers at least. Shit, now I want ice cream.

^(T) Tell me about it. Totally off-subject, but Rob was just showing me pictures of this what he called gastro pimp food-truck hermit—some old eccentric three-star saucier on sabbatical—who was tuned in the other day and just rolled up and politely demanded an interview. Rob being Rob just says sure after some tacit beard-guy squinting ritual and him and Drew are suddenly slobbering through a fifteen-course on-air flavor trip through mini-salads, a freeze-dried Vegan stew gingerbread house, hand-blown microscopic parsnip and chanterelle faux roe hand rolls, and miniature Hungarian chocolate-shelled cottage cheese fingers.

(L) So a Wonka incarnate in a cross-country ice-cream truck?

(T) No, full menu, the entree was bean and cheese burritos with no frills and respectable salsa.

(L) Wow. The sky must start falling wherever this guy goes.

(T) Rob said they were the best part. The only embellishment was a little palette of Lizano, Tapatio, Cholula, and La Guacamaya circling little dabs of a nice pasty sour cream and a simple chunky guac.

(L) Sounds like the man deserves a jingle, or a ballad maybe.

(T) Or a bat signal.

(L) As a freelancer, I suddenly feel inclined to organize a parasitic caravan around our nation's truck-bound culinary minstrels.

(T) Ha, our unfettered data enterers and graphic designers circling their Jettas on the prairie for fish tacos to a punkadelic kumbaya.

(L) With big-top Sunday services at Our Sacred Menagerie of the Upholstery-Deep Crotch Sweat.

(T) Aw, that's sweet.

(R) Uh, I only caught the last, like, six extremely perplexing things you said. Li, please note the dancers melting on their marks and Herr Direktor's eyes on the monitor and the pinchy finger motion thing.

(L) Right, thanks, on it.

Wherever Ike's been scouting leads is certainly a step up from his usual blandly pissy dorks just barely dragging the scene through one misread after another. Granted it's no dialogue today, but with a little sweat over the jitters, they're making excessively multi-camera dance combat seem old hat enough to actually sense some acting beans dribbling through.

I guess miracles really do have their seldom showing-of-ankle on a budget of favors and peanut-butter crackers.

Lucky nobody out here's paying any attention to me after the count, because the whole aural conduit thing is trippier than I expected. The band's just trading fours now between takes, and the ringer—now known affectionately by all as Lewis—is just battering around it all as he pleases.

I better double check my horoscope if there was anything about getting carted up and down an alley with an unusually purposeful ten-minute jam in my ear while two heaving, spirit-gum curdled Grease honchos kick-snare-counter-jab-throw-block-ball-change to the gunkatta bridge then quick but subtle shift to the silhouetted last chorus and the lucky shale-shiv stab to the leg for the hero to scoot just as the errant baddies finally catch back up.

⁽ᴸ⁾ Y'think twelfth take's a charm?

⁽ᵀ⁾ I think the poor guy push-brooming the softshoe sand between takes is about to have to call his mother, or pretend to.

⁽ᴸ⁾ So that's what all the delicate dirt tossing was about. I thought it was a puffs of kick and punch dust deal.

⁽ᵀ⁾ Yeah, just like old saying, "I really kicked the dust out of 'em"

⁽ᴸ⁾ Are you accusing me of inventing tropes and/or combat phenomena?

⁽ᵀ⁾ Ayup. I mean do you ever see that happen? Non–bus-cushion related.

⁽ᴸ⁾ I've heard it's where demi-wargs draw their life butter: especially the ones with the party-popper zest obscuring their crusting stains of pre-Turn slobber. You clearly haven't seen enough Westerns.

⁽ᵀ⁾ I think you missed a hyphenate there. And aren't they nano-vamps or something?

⁽ᴸ⁾ Euhh, the hero's a vaccinated regenerative zombie out-law, the bad guy's a reconstituted wizard avatar thing with a sprouting spore-conscious.

⁽ᵀ⁾ Right. You know I think maybe I saw something sprouting in that slow take with all the strangely intimate twisty kicks.

⁽ᴸ⁾ Oh? I thought it was one of those boxer hug things. Better check the dailies.

⁽ᵀ⁾ Do I spy a C-stand getting pulled down?

⁽ᴸ⁾ Yeah. Tight-lipped guy nods are zippering out from the epicenter.

⁽ᵀ⁾ Oh, thank God. There's been an unwholesome measure of skooching in toward Annie.

⁽ᴸ⁾ Well, sister bear, you know talent can do that, right? From out here she looks fairly serene about it, or perfectly oblivious.

⁽ᵀ⁾ Uh-huh. I'll stop swooping when I'm dead or she's, let's say two-and-a-half kids deep, or equivalent thereof.

⁽ᴸ⁾ I hope so, you'd be way too good a cockblocking ghost for anyone to compete. Mind if I join?

⁽ᵀ⁾ Not at all. Oh gross, please hurry, they're already trying to talk shop.

Weird how the trials of siblinghood seem rooted in a pact of misreading each other half the time. Maybe creepily synchronous twins or whichever monozygote litters are the cosmic norm and we're just a freakishly dissonant outlier.

Whatever carnal skooching was going on, it's frothed up into a full schmooze circle around Anne and Lewis, who's deflecting as neatly as Anne's soaking it up.

Both are offered seats in beanpole's combo without a whiff of ado. Weekly paid gig at The Bup and all. This sets me and Trina's hover recon at full tizzy. Mister Barber must be taking this as somehow directed at him, his practiced fretting over the Rhodes is abruptly unimportant, and he's got a purposeful stride for an awkward number-offer written all over his petrified doughy stare.

⁽ᴸ⁾ Hey, don't look now, but what do you think of the keyboard player?

⟨T⟩ You mean the guy who was torturing himself not to openly ogle you for the last ninety minutes?

⟨L⟩ Mm-hm.

⟨T⟩ I think you'd better save him making a spectacle and go give him your number.

⟨L⟩ Nahh, just like that?

⟨T⟩ Oh, for Christ's sake, yes. Please, before he starts naming grandkids.

⟨L⟩ But, shit, Trina. The turtley ones are always so cute when they squirm.

⟨T⟩ Ugh. I'm sure it would boost his confidence so much to hear you say that. You do realize you're biting your lip? Normally I'd say crossing the line, but it's a sort of Stimpy effect.

⟨L⟩ Maybe I'll disarm him with a rump-bump shuffle all the way over there.

⟨T⟩ It'll sure keep his finger off the trigger. No better way of saying I only put out on your parents' couch.

⟨L⟩ Oh stop singeing my, uh, seasoned curlies? No...

⟨T⟩ Dehumidifying your lower larder?

⟨L⟩ That's the spirit. Yeah, stop and let me swoon my way into it for once.

⟨T⟩ For once what? When have I ever gotten you laid?

⟨L⟩ Exactly. Can't you just stop egging me on a minute and say something cold and discouraging.

⟨T⟩ Ok now you're floundering. He's eyeing that keyboard case mighty hard. He probably thinks your name is Leslie and is too preoccupied with getting home to feed his ferret to be worrying about what you think of him. And he's really on the fence about those velcro Jordans, but you know, just for whippet night and gardening.

⟨L⟩ Yeah, that's the stuff. Ok, ok, don't wait up.

7

2014/9/2 8:04 p.m.

    HashTaggart - Hey.

    LiCanSam - Heya. Get my crypto-jams?

    HashTaggart - Yeeh. Let's never do that again?

    LiCanSam - Agreed. Running thin on favors from the

comp phys depo?

    HashTaggart - More or less. I'm feeling obligated

to start downplaying the whole avuncular tech-vixen

arts prof angle.

    LiCanSam - Oh? Seems like it had an edge on the

old angry hungry stoner approach.

    HashTaggart - True. Still feeling about ready

for a dowdy sage phase. Something tells me it might

actually improve my sex life.

    LiCanSam - Which is?

HashTaggart - Diversionary? As in diverting the bouquet of misguided overtures academia office life has to offer. Plus a few less than shameful trophies from punk show outings with some of the lit and sosh gallies. Dunno, I'm ironing and darning like you wouldn't believe.

LiCanSam - Hahahaha. You what now?

HashTaggart - Aghh shaddap. Started as some self-sufficiency or anti-consumerist pretense. Now I'm just enjoying it.

LiCanSam - Creepy. Also ridiculous. You already work with your hands you know.

HashTaggart - Less and less. That's probably the problem. Still cranking out showy new figures, but getting all caught up in the sourcing of lacquer and shit. Hard to find a rythm.

HashTaggart - rhythm*

LiCanSam - Sounds rough. Yesterday I had to refund a job because I wasn't polite enough noting that the client had constructed the figure captions in his submission to Scripta Chemica like an overzealous MOMA curator.

HashTaggart - Eeek. Probably some karmic necessity not taking his money.

LiCanSam - Spoken like a true ivory tower-ite.

HashTaggart - Yeah, yeah, my work is infinitely more fulfilling than yours on every applicable level. Happy?

LiCanSam - Charmed ;-{´-|====[

HashTaggart - So anything new? Besides shit clients?

LiCanSam - ...maybe. Took home an engineer pianist from a film shoot the other day.

HashTaggart - Oh?

LiCanSam - No, no, you're gonna make me schpiel. Not sure if I have it in me.

HashTaggart - Good or bad schpiel?

LiCanSam - Probably good.

HashTaggart - Then gosh forth Philouza.

LiCanSam - Ok ok. Let's see, he saws, solders and codes well enough to make Paul really jealous.

HashTaggart - I like him already.

LiCanSam - What about Paul?

HashTaggart - Oh Jesus. We'll ease him into it. And?

LiCanSam - And he's on the nice guy side, but no clingyness red flags or anything. Kind of easily put off, but not such a dick about it at the same time.

HashTaggart - Dreamboat!

LiCanSam - Hush.

HashTaggart - And have you...

LiCanSam - Don't you start ellipses-ing me, missy.

HashTaggart - Fine. How's his bedside filigree?

LiCanSam - Losing no points on the makeout count. Pretty rambunctious for sex, especially sober sex. Some kink undertones I think, but like a hermit prince sort of thing.

HashTaggart - So more toward the E. Edward end of the Gray spectrum.

LiCanSam - Huh?

HashTaggart - More Spader in Secretary than 50 Shades.

LiCanSam - Ahhh, I get it. Yeah, exactly. But
let's assume more of a sucker for hip-highs than dead
worm enclosures.

HashTaggart - But?

LiCanSam - Not so much but yet. No butt to speak
of for that matter, a little funny around the chest.
Almost matronly in a beanpole way. Maybe it's his
posture, dunno. Carries it better than your average
nascent beer belly, that's for sure.

HashTaggart - Matro is so in.

LiCanSam - Ahhah.

HashTaggart - So he booked it after first hayroll
and you tattooed another notch on your sacral
thermometer?

LiCanSam - No actually, we got to talking about
cooking. And he's just shyly recalling pleasant
experiments with seared kale and sausage salad abreast
a red curry that's really his aunt's turkey chili, but
you know, always a hodgepodge in his kitchen. And
I say something like "working on any other dishes
lately" which could have come across as a sadly dusty
innuendo by accident but I don't think it registered.
Anyway, irrelevant, uh, and yeah, he just flouts the
social risk of telling two kale stories in a row, and
gets all procedural about baking salmon in a wreath of
roots and most nameable members of the cabbage family.

HashTaggart - Just what was on hand, of course.

LiCanSam - Of course. And so it's lavished in
some tapenade and wine and honey fun, and he realizes
while he's preheating and flipping through the custom
streambox thingy that he doesn't have a respectable

sauce to go with it, so he throws together what sounds like about a half-gallon of fresh herbs into a little creme tartar thing from scratch, with about every ingredient you'd see in the salad dressing aisle, but fresh and hand mushed.

HashTaggart - Sounds mushy alright. Where's the kale?

LiCanSam - Oh yeah. It was clamshelling the fish, along with some shitakes and "those savory orange ones with a weird almost minty aftertaste". A few minutes in the oven and he picks up a bogey on the olfactdar, but with some clever tong work, the offending under-coated leaf is extracted and the dish is saved.

HashTaggart - Did he proceed to pour melted peanut butter all over it without breaking eye contact?

LiCanSam - Well recall I wasn't actually there. But I'm sure I wouldn't have minded.

HashTaggart - Ah right, you just made it sound so, so real. And he's an engineer?

LiCanSam - Yup

HashTaggart - Shit. You're making me hungry, horny and depressed all at once.

LiCanSam - Hah, wish I'd told him that. Nearly asked him to turn around and start over from the beginning.

HashTaggart - Then?

LiCanSam - Then he made us patty melts and cheese fries. Or was it kohlrabi, turkey marrow, porcini, all risotto-omeletted and inside-out raviolied like an astonishingly glutinous uramaki? One of those, I forget. Is it Tuesday?

HashTaggart - Oh my God. Your pupils are probably bigger than your belly button right now. Where's the hidden But? Please.

LiCanSam - Did I imply a But? My bad.

HashTaggart - Dammit. Please, something.

LiCanSam - But but but... but I've really had to stock up on kale?

HashTaggart - Thin ice, jerk. You let me brag about trophy punks.

LiCanSam - Transcript tells a different story, ma'am.

HashTaggart - Since when do I not downplay my conquests. Get real.

LiCanSam - :) glad for both of us then. And our third leg? How's he fare? Still pretending not to fawn over all his inexplicably chipper and unblemished grad students?

HashTaggart - No, he's in workshop mode. Formally requested an adjunct slot with the Phys Ed school to test a new team water sport he made up. Dean of the Lit. department's started sliding old Speedos under his door.

LiCanSam - Weird, Rob slid a pancake under my door just before I came out to visit you.

HashTaggart - God, do they just raise them in summer camps or something?

LiCanSam - Well, in his case Tacoma or somewhere up there I think, so more or less. So what's the sport? Compressed helium roulette?

HashTaggart - Oh fuck, something with torpedo toys

and goalies and wall bounces and a YouTube video on converting LCD 3D glasses into blackout facemasks for some offense/defense marco-polo thing.

LiCanSam - Oooo, with little submarine pings? I'm vaguely recalling some stoney rant about his sophomore salad days sneaking the Magic club and the theater geeks into the country club lap pool with a pair of duct-tape goggles and breaking down all social barriers.

HashTaggart - Sure you're not thinking of that nerf-buckler flag football fiasco?

LiCanSam - I recall that being a genteel time, rudely upstaged by a keg.

HashTaggart - Well, anyway, he's probably already line-itemed grant money to fly you out here as a referee.

LiCanSam - Aww. But, Kboo, doesn't this at least mean matching one-pieces? Haven't we gone long enough without knowing how that feels? Feats of unprecedented lung-capacity coordination? Taxpayer-funded submersible electric headgear in no way intended for personal safety? Smacks of an opus to me.

HashTaggart - Ok turbo, I'll pass it on. I'm sure there's no risk he's avoiding work or channeling his emotional shit into a new creative low.

LiCanSam - Well imagine how floored we'd be if he was twelve?

HashTaggart - Hm, but will he ever top the mix-n-match celebrity Guess Who board?

LiCanSam - Aww, I still have mine. And you're one

to talk anyway. You two have been brooding over some
fairly dank cauldrons lately.

HashTaggart - I know. It's not good. I'm
lecturing on fumes half the time. Enough caffeinated
forthright dreck to keep it perky, but my eyes are so
fizzed out the dramatic pauses are turning into creepy
librarian squint naps.

LiCanSam - Yes Kate, that's not good. And with the
way you used to pass out?

HashTaggart - Yes, I'm aware. Sorta feels like
holding a dump in too long, except the only release
would be everyone packing up quietly and dimming the
lights on their way out.

LiCanSam - Well that does complete the librarian
fantasy. You sure this hasn't actually happened?

HashTaggart - Oh it's way too tantalizing to be
real.

LiCanSam - If it's any consolation I just pulled
two 40 page jobs on cold rooibos and a stale edible.

HashTaggart - Jeesus, go take a walk after this,
ok?

LiCanSam - Sure, sure. So is pioneering water
games really that out of step for Paul? What's
between the lines here, K?

HashTaggart - No, same old Paul, more or less. I
don't know. Guarded around me a little.

LiCanSam - So like a decade-plus of platonic Paul
batter hitting the griddle?

HashTaggart - Wow, no. And that's as disgusting as
it is senseless. Maybe a nap before that walk, yeah?

LiCanSam - Already tucked in and curled up, bawdy.

HashTaggart - Good. Sounds like you may be beyond standing and reasoning capacity.

LiCanSam - Well, you're beyond beans and spilling capacity, jerk. Sorry I take most of that back. You're a perfectly capable jerk.

HashTaggart - Hm, there's a faint zinging sensation in my gums. As if there's someone I know six states away who's stoned off their ass, typing themselves to sleep like some bad emo concept disco opera.

LiCanSam - Stall stall stall, madmsmslle., and I'll have to start postulating. That's what you cackameemians do all day right?

HashTaggart - I'm all ears.

LiCanSam - Each time Paul's debatably unsavory juices boil over, your own creative output is usually somewhere between an idle and an outright wallow.

HashTaggart - What?! When do I wallow! I say poppy and cock to your slanging, Liyo.

LiCanSam - Oy, much apologies deary. Never said you'd been an outright wallower, just those times when your work was mostly having us video you destroying your prior weeks' work in usually startlingly uncathartic ways.

HashTaggart - Ah ok, sure. But we'd never have forged the Meltiplex otherwise.

LiCanSam - Hm, I'll give you that. But anyway, my point is that Paul's madcap crap might be tempered into something a little more focused if you let him play boxing coach now and then. Maybe he's lost without a corner to shout from.

HashTaggart - Uh-huh. And how do I go about this

stupefyingly figurative task? Us hanging out together
ends up at an 18 pack and NHL '95 well more than
half the time. Which, it's probably safe to say is
not regularly followed up by periods of staggering
productivity for either of us.

LiCanSam - And how often does he beat you at NHL?

HashTaggart - Gee Doc, tough to say. Maybe 1 in 5
times? Genesis wasn't his home turf.

LiCanSam - Aha! Lies! I've seen him crush trolls
at NHL who had double chins deep enough to tie their
ponytails under without seeing the knot. I think I
scored a goal on him once after like eight years, and
he flung the last of his Easy Mac at me.

HashTaggart - Oh God.

LiCanSam - And don't pretend you're not essentially
married on most other counts. When's the last time he
really went full bouffant for a future Mrs.Associate
Professor of All Things Panderable?

HashTaggart - Aggghhh, Li, no. Leave the pebble
of obviousness unturned, I'm begging you. There's so
much joy in subcritical sexual tension.

LiCanSam - There's a pun in the air involving
control rods and meltdowns that I will now
respectfully neglect and insist you turn those 18
packs into moonlit forties along the canal.

HashTaggart - Dammit, fine. You know me and Paul
had that handful of bumbling Four Loko hookups, right?

LiCanSam - You mean the halcyon days of our
shimmering youth? Oh yeah, rings a bell now that
you mention it. Let's see, there was a prolonged
period of me pretending not to mind you both pinning

me with three-word secret pass-along messages all sappy with the last night's hair twiddling, which gradually devolved to equally sappy irreducible signal flags carefully maneuvering you out to unmushy waters.

HashTaggart - Odd, I just remember a few awkward lunch dates and you managing to roll your eyes and shoot me chinny bro grins at the same time.

LiCanSam - Got one aimed at you right now, dawgly.

HashTaggart - Ok, aside from the fact that I take it as a point of pride and personal safety that I've almost never followed any of your remotely serious advice. You're perfectly right, we're functionally married to the point where I know how his snoring changes by season and which porn he's too devoted to to keep from popping up in autocomplete. It's not exactly a bolt from the blue here Li.

LiCanSam - But that's perfect! You've been comfortable with each other's bullshit for years. You've even borked a bit without screwing up our sacred Beat-Lover's Trio. But now you're settling in for a nice Sunday roast and avoiding eye contact with the gravy boat. The poor little giblets just crying out to be washed in little mash potato tidepools. Giblets of love KT. Giblets of sunshine and backyard blanket sex. Anyhow, food for thought.

HashTaggart - Asshole. I'm laughing a fair amount. But still: asshole. Don't get your hopes up. Now he's starting to go gray there's a new prim and comely adjunct lolling at his door practically each week, with two coffees and a flimsy pretext.

LiCanSam - Ha. "Why Baristas Hate this Perfect

98

Trick for Snaring the Office Hottie". I have trouble
imagining him not falling flat trying to flirt with
someone who's actually read half the outdated psych
texts he scrutinizes us by. Wouldn't know what I was
looking at if he wasn't such a putz anymore.

HashTaggart - Yeah.

LiCanSam - Mm, and speaking of flimsy pretexts.
Come visit? There's plenty of stagnant crannies here
begging for gremlins and 8-bit mosaics.

HashTaggart - Tempting. I'll see if I can
piggyback with the design geeks to a maker conference
or something.

LiCanSam - Cool, and sorry for the breakdowns and
diagrams and shit.

HashTaggart - No, it's ok.

LiCanSam - But at least pinch his ass once in
awhile or something, so he doesn't go sour.

HashTaggart - Can do. Thanks for compounding my
worries with a stark reversal.

LiCanSam - Anytime. Well, my leg's asleep all the
way to my knee and my eyes are sort of twitch-fighting
their way shut.

HashTaggart - Eyywhh. Don't work so much Li.
Nighty-night. Miss you much.

LiCanSam - Thanks Kayo. Byeeee.

LiCanSam - Love ya.

[HashTaggart is now offline. Your messages will be
seen later.]

$$8$$

Whatever this performance-induced trance thing I'd expected
to grow out of halfway through puberty maybe finally deserves a moment's scrutiny. I suppose ironically unattainable
through Trance. Maybe dancing does heighten it, but the
more profound moments are mostly seated. Guess that speaks
to the sensible magic of Jewish rites. Couldn't ever really
pin down if it's just my flavor of the universal tuned in /
zoned out sort of deal, with an excess of some flailing ADD
pompoms. Let's see, definitely must be live, on my ass, usually gazing somewhere off stage right, can't be too bright, or
verbal. Bonfire complex maybe.

I wonder if they have a real sense of how tight they've
gotten in what, two and a half weeks? They must. There's
something bolstering the cool from getting too much ego
barnacled on. Just the bassist throwing spazzy elbows, but
they're well-earned. Not a drop of the old campy spit-shine
slop. Mood in every beat, tempers flaring or racing or clashing
in check. And they ride it all out without some how-dee-
dingading coda. All the satisfying bubbly glut waiting back
in my earbuds just went stale, except maybe the choicest
Schubert and pals which suddenly demands prompt revisiting.

Now how'd I overlook the glossy, honest-to-God rosy-
cheeked tugboat adrift on the stool that never quite settles

in between the bar's short end and the booth-waiter's
requisitioned two-top, often actually teetering. She ought
to be the perfect chalky antidote to my lolling, but she's
betraying that nearly voiced hum of meandering into
mesmerization. So unadulterated it's quenched my whole
cerebral flit parade—let's hope for good. Well, good for her
anyway, and whatever pinch-swab-twittle mobile OS habit's
being floated as mildly worthwhile. Probably only defraying
some noise a little calmer and more fully than whatever my
roach-eaten SCSI ribbons lead to. It's all so invigorating
I'm going to compulsively check my own phone in solidarity,
without loathing.

    LiCanSam - Rob. Stop digging around for patch
cables and get down here. The band has teeth, sound
may carry. Probably to Japan and back, backwaters and
all.

    Rowbspyr - Instant universal appeal? So
post-hipster.

    LiCanSam - Fuck 'em. My face is melted, my heart
is what? Blushing? and it's not even happy hour yet.
I'm all cortexes go man, without any cheap heavy-drug
aftertaste.

    Rowbspyr - Congratulations.

    LiCanSam - Overselling it?

    Rowbspyr - Wee bit.

    LiCanSam - Well you get the idea. The timeless
Talente Disproportionante retold.

    Rowbspyr - Which ends in?

    LiCanSam - Mm, realistically? Low-key and amicable
parting of ways after a handful of club contracts
and inevitably slightly off-genre festival gigs,
with a bit more payout than any of them are used
to, but a consolation of soiling disproportionately

post-menopausal panties.

    Rowbspyr - Now there's a fine example of how some people come to shudder at the use of certain words. Ok, how does it end non-realistically? What do the near shut-in former roadies and booking agents say to VH1?

    LiCanSam - All the makings of a six-decade supergroup but for the untimely spiraling of the flappy-armed bassist into a tame but critically uncool trainwreck.

    Rowbspyr - Tame trainwreck? I think you've out oxymoroned yourself. One example please.

    LiCanSam - Uh, like snorting nutmeg and watching Amelie backwards to In Rainbows while blogging about 19 to 22 year-old men's rights? Or blogging in general, really.

    Rowbspyr - Ouch, but fair enough. I vote you dub it lamewreck.

    LiCanSam - No, too syrupy. Couch scion?

    Rowbspyr - Fun, but off the mark. Right-lane tailgaters? Death-grazers?

    LiCanSam - Like they gently but firmly contemplate mortality under a fierce, uncompromising Autumn sunrise over a cup of stark, bone-jingling unsweetened barley tea? Also good, but we're straying.

    Rowbspyr - Better write it off as a fool's errand. I got a long ad break coming up, and some sinister Sunday phlegm heaving it's wobbly rear micwards if I don't act fast.

    LiCanSam - Ok crumb bum, but if you're needing an excuse to dip out early on Drew, flappy's bird is looking mighty rufflable over by the bar.

    Rowbspyr - Ok poosquirt, thanks, maybe.

    LiCanSam - PEEESS.

Sorry flappy, but I'm gonna have to put my money on your next six or so girlfriends having about as much respect for your professional demeanor as you do for their low-key gym ware drawer. Of course when they're eighty, maybe they'll finally hear that one Mingus solo that always drove you nuts, over brunch with a dinky grandkid or two, and realize you were the only one who really had something going for himself.

(A) Hey Li. You're looking more aloof than usual. Were we that off?

(L) No, not at all. You guys took me to church despite it being essentially my Wednesday. Exactly what I needed, in fact.

(A) Thanks. It's starting to feel like we really got a set together.

(L) And then some. If they keep letting you sing like that, people are gonna start forgetting the other names on the marquee.

(A) Whatever you say, ma. I guess being broke and hungover is the only way to really find your sound.

(L) Desperately broke or just pitifully broke?

(A) Just pitifully, but desperately hungover.

(L) Ok good. As fine a recipe for greatness as I ever heard. Just keep churning that hollow ache into whatever old son'rous lather you had going up there.

(A) I don't know, an aspirin smoothie and six hours of some show I kept hearing about three years ago sounds pretty appealing at the moment.

(L) Fight it, Annie. Ma needs that communion processional and dear leader over there looks about ready to give the go-ahead on drink rations for the second run.

(A) Bwuhh, please no words that close to rum.

(L) Usch. You're worse-off than you look. What's your secret?

(A) Drinking ten times too much, but only about half as often as people would expect.

(L) I see. And I thought I'd go to my grave never knowing how you keep so fresh and miserable.

(A) You know my dad used to say, "Flattery will get you mole hair".

(L) Wow, was he speaking from experience?

(A) Sadly, yes. So what's a not-so-girly Sunday drink that doesn't involve citrus or tomato?

(L) Drawing a blank. Or, let's see, just ask for the first red liqueur you see with soda.

(A) Alright. What if there's nothing red?

(L) Slide down the rainbow, hopefully no further than Chartreuse.

(A) Got it. Thanks Li.

(L) No sweat, hon. And I mean it about these guys. It's a damn buttery groove and not like anyone's hearing in any studio, not lately at least. I say ride it, but don't forget you're the one that'll be getting the drinks sold around here.

(A) We'll see. Some of these guys have actually been paying their bills on this and a couple Memphis gigs a week.

(L) Good, then you're in the right company. I'm just saying I don't wanna see you plating mozzarella sticks again once one of these guys gets talked into giving it all up for a loving home and fulfilling career.

(A) Too late. Groveled my way back into a Wednesday shift at Salsinas.

(L) Oof. My condolences. Then at least plate those grease rods with all due angst and perfidy.

(A) I'll assume that means what it sounds like.

(L) Good call. Me too.

(A) You want something?

(L) Sure, thanks. Second cheapest beer they got, in honor of your arguably gainful employment.

(A) Deal.

I could read into that brow-bristler smirk for weeks. Fold this equivalent Christmas and Easter in the nosebleeds sinner into your parish, Apollina. I rescind my phallic communion for the time being everlasting. Or until Harry texts back. Shit, it's been over two days. Where did I leave it, hmh, "You betcha sir," shit. Like a housewife who finally worked up the nerve to set up that doily stall at the flea market.

( ) Hey, you ok?

Agh, accosted mid-wallow. Flappy's groupie. I'd wager us having met and one of us being too plowed to remember. Let's see, ponytail and high-contrast undead pallor makeup? No way. Shit, maybe.

(L) Yeah, no, just wishing I didn't text like a tipsy grandma.

( ) Ha! I always get this feeling mine are secretly filtered by my skeezy old Econ teacher after I hit send. It's Lianne, right?

(L) Yeah. And, I'm so sorry, we met at the shoot, or?

( ) No, it's ok. Jen. From what I hear I was all silhouette and hoodie in that last part and we had to leave pretty early from the afterparty thing. I don't think we really met, just heard Rob griping about you hogging the open channel.

(L) Ahhh, yeah. They did that slo-mo closeup of the maggots and grime spewing out of your knee when the good guy juked left.

⁽ᴶ⁾ Yup. Wasn't really the big debut Tom talked it up to be.

Tom equals flappy. Flappy equals Tom. Flappy Tom. Good. Memorized. T-something.

⁽ᴸ⁾ So's this his idea of a date, or are you as weirdly fascinated with intense live music played to pretty much empty rooms as I am?

Aww, she's damn near smitten. Here I was, making her out as forty-proof cinna-bubble on color coordination and hair frigidity alone. All red and black, with a yellow bracelet. Shit, king snake, no wonder.

⁽ᴶ⁾ No, not really. Says he's got us a table on Ed's roof if the weather stays nice and if they finish practice with enough time for table-service and all before the first set.

⁽ᴸ⁾ Ed does that?

⁽ᴶ⁾ Just for old friends apparently.

⁽ᴸ⁾ Damn, I bet the view's spectacular up there.

⁽ᴶ⁾ Hope so. But you know, I've hung around a couple times like this when he was in different bands and it practically drove me nuts. Like, the songs were always catchy and neat but it was like an old dogs, old tricks sorta thing?

⁽ᴸ⁾ Uh-huh.

⁽ᴶ⁾ But I'm really getting into it with these guys. Maybe it's like they're not reaching for it so much, like it's better if they follow the sound but not like stomp after it, y'know?

⁽ᴸ⁾ Yeah, actually, I think I know what you mean.

⁽ᴶ⁾ Cool. I usually feel out of place trying to talk about this kind of music. Tom's got all these cool records, but his friends get all wrapped up with weird nicknames and genres I can't keep straight. I mean, it's a little ridiculous to even try half the time.

⁽ᴸ⁾ Eh, I wouldn't worry about it so much, it's like baseball cards for pot heads. And present company excepted, most of the newer stuff usually sounds like interrupted seagull sex. If anything in Tom's collection actually keeps you awake, just throw in a name or two and they'll probably go nuts that someone who showers regularly has any awareness of their drool-warped liner notes, or they won't have heard of it and it'll embarrass them into getting out from under their best-of lists.

(J) Ha, yeah. Good advice, thanks.

(L) So you mind me asking what you do when you're not expanding your tastes at four-thirty on a Sunday?

(J) Like, for work?

Huh, genuine concern over clarity, zero apprehension. A bona fide peach. Dammit, I thought I'd get a rapport going without getting all obtuse.

(L) Yeah, sorry, I often speak more clearly after a drink and a half, but it's been a long week.

(J) Oh I work around politicians most of the time, so I'm not really sure who's making sense half the time anyway.

(L) Aha! So you're an aide or...?

(J) No, just doing grunt work for the public affairs show that goes out to a few NPR affiliates.

(L) Weekly State and Local with Eric Karnauer?

(J) That's the one. We tape in the city so the commute sucks, but I try to take a day a week working from home when I can.

(L) And you get to meet the heartland's finest dirtbags and muck sculptors?

(J) Mm-hm, my boss had to super awkwardly ask me to dress like a schoolmarm even in summer so they'd stop slobbering in the green room, which is fine by me except it really is way too hot. The building's like, eighty years old.

(L) So then you dress to the bangs off-duty, out of sheer primal necessity?

⟨J⟩ Yeah, sort of. You think it's too much?

⟨L⟩ Oh, no no no no, I mean for the best fish in fifty miles at sunset with a private lakeside view? Hell no. I'm probably a little jealous, my work has the opposite effect. I sit around praying for a good excuse to wear pants.

⟨J⟩ Freelance?

⟨L⟩ Yup, politely nudging hoity toities of all walks into communicating intelligibly. And squeezing pictures around some too.

⟨J⟩ Doesn't sound so bad.

⟨L⟩ Well I can run around being nearly poor wherever I like. Not too bad, all in all. So, you come from a long line of PA's? Or just moonlighting while your portfolio matures? Why do I get the sense you're brimming with unalloyed poise and bravado?

⟨J⟩ Heh, usually feels like I'm brimming one way or another with this bra on. And I did do a lot more dance not that long ago.

⟨L⟩ Mm, that's gotta be it. You didn't hang up your jazz shoes for good, did you?

⟨J⟩ No, not quite. Some of my friends in the city still rope me into doing their black box shows when I've got time for it. Had to skip the last few though. Turns out there aren't many slow news days in election years.

⟨L⟩ Ugh, I bet. Hey, I've always wondered something about dance, maybe you would know: It seems like ninety percent of the time most of the dancers are doing pretty much the same thing, or there's one or two oddballs with everyone else swirling around them. Is it, like, sacrilege to have everybody doing something different but still looking coordinated, or is it just a huge pain in the ass?

⟨J⟩ Um, the second one. I mean synchronized swimmers do some pretty amazing sequence stuff, but you would basically need everyone to have crazy solo chops and perfect rhythm.

⁽ᴸ⁾ Plus a stoat-tempered choreographer with half his hair pulled out and a Winston one-hundred glued to his lip?

⁽ᴶ⁾ I'm not sure what a stoat is, but yes.

⁽ᴸ⁾ This is most certainly inaccurate, but I imagine they're somewhere between a badger and a wolverine, but much more graceful.

⁽ᴶ⁾ Ah, ok. Yes, plus he'd probably need about eight Tony's and a rehearsal hall with a live-in philharmonic.

⁽ᴸ⁾ Well shit. I was hoping I'd stumbled on the next big thing in physio-rhythmic science.

⁽ᴶ⁾ Hey, who knows? I can pass it on to the board for the quarterly review, but they've been doubling down on step touches and hip curls since the recession.

⁽ᴸ⁾ Thanks for the tip. You know Rob's been grumbling about hitting the eight-month zero-party mark. If we get one going you think you could rustle up a dancer friend or two to help keep butts off couches? Trina's always saying she will but never comes through.

⁽ᴶ⁾ Of course!

⁽ᴸ⁾ Cool. I'll spark the ceremonial fire under his ass so he has the required fuss-hours for his playlist. Hey Anne! Party at my place a week from Saturday?

⁽ᴬ⁾ Hell yeah. Maybe I'll get some of the pooters to show up.

⁽ᴸ⁾ Do it. How's the drink?

⁽ᴬ⁾ Not bad. Bitters and some blood-red pomegranate thing. Here.

⁽ᴸ⁾ Ooh, tastes like I'm seeing my first R-rated movie, but on the beach with a leather jacket for a pillow. Oh, uhh, Anne–Jen, Jen–Anne.

⁽ᴬ⁾ I think we've met a couple times, actually.

⁽ᴶ⁾ Yeah, it's been awhile. But I didn't think I ever heard you sing back then.

(A) Nah, probably not.

(J) Well I love your voice. I feel like nobody sings like that anymore.

(A) Like a tipsy church choir director?

(J) Hah! No, like, I don't know, like there's nothing wrong, or no, like you're not shaping anything and just having at it. But still really punchy like I wanna bang my steering wheel to it.

(A) Thanks. I guess not giving much of a shit at the moment helps. Guess I'm finally taking up the family legacy. My dad's been wearing sweatpants at Thanksgiving since Reagan took office, or Carter maybe.

(L) Smart man. Oh, uh-oh, I'm being buzzed. Looks like my sweet grannyisms fermented into passable flirting. Excuse me while I turn awkwardly and act bored and indifferent.

(J) Don't mind a bit.

(A) Go for it, Grams. We're not even here. Get that old inner Woolworth's all bedazzled and, uh, fence the great turgid acres.

(L) Ok ok, I'll take it outside, barfbutt. Bye-and-nice-to-meet-you if I don't come back in.

(J) Bye!

Marks on the taut deadpan, Anne. Wouldn't have thought I'd ever see you that giddy off a few sips of nothing much. Big sis's gung-ho side must be rubbing off. Or you're finally claiming some diva due that you had the better instinct not to milk too soon. Oh, come on, damn answer button swipe thingy, answer. This was not so hard five years ago. Shit.

Even for the one riverview street in a town hobbling through stage-six gentrification, the squat old bungalow has got unhampered eccentricity fluttering out all over the neighbors' compulsive hedge desecration. Certainly merits the title, not really any route from driveway to back alley without serious bungling. Brimming past overgrown, might rate woodsier than your average hermitable forest cabins. Creepiness nicely staved off by the one well-worn footpath and rabbit-manicured patch around the ivy temple maybe intermittently still acting as a bird bath.

Almost wish he'd Airbnb it just to read the euphemistic respinning of initial disappointment into staunch admiration of the undeniably aphrodisiac guest futon in the laundry room. I guess it suits Harry, but it'd probably suit anyone with a thousand cubic feet of sound gear and indifference to direct sunlight. Possibly not an insubstantial demographic. Maybe an old couple could hack it here. Throw a few eyesores on the porch and a tackier coat of paint on the mailbox. Not-so-small family might be a stretch. Christ, where am I going with this? Either burgeoning realty aspirations or waxing domestic. Well screw it. It's probably not about settling if I'm this worked up over him every time. Right?

^(L) Halloo! I'm here! Put your naked hat on!

^(H) Hey! Come in, just finishing up a really sexy dump.

^(L) Attaboy! Hey you got any of that musty old chai left?

^(H) Think so. Check the drawer under the toaster. Should be milk and honey around too.

Uh-oh, gear's tidy, the ornamental Sweetwater catalogs have been dusted and re-angled for effect. Kitchen floor's much less yellow than I remember. Dishes cleared of stagnant water. He's in full-on dateable mode. I can just about hear the hair on every ovulating woman's neck in a three-block radius pricking up at the scent of eligible cool guy scrubbing grout. Ok, ok. Breathe, boil, steep, stir, contemplate domestic eternity, suppress panic.

^(H) Hey.

^(L) Hey. Glad you called.

Wait, why so needy? Sounds awful. What have I done? Well, that windbreaker I left here's still in plain sight by the door. Good, keep it blunt and cordial. It was a nice run, but I know when I've sat on the souffle, coach. No need to pull me out and talk strategy, still plenty of time to train for state.

Ohp, and he's so horny I could have said "Glad you pooped".

(L) Halloo.

(H) Couldn't find my naked hat.

(L) It's ok. I think I might have seen it on my coat rack.

(H) Well crud. Guess I'll have to just sleep in a sweater and long johns till it comes back.

Mm, hey, jerk. Why are the swoony kissers no fair, to, saying things, back. Shit.

(L) Whatever you say Dr. Fuhnke. You want tea too?

(H) Not just this moment, no.

You can pull me away from a boiling kettle, bub, but I'm not all that into piercing whistle serenades. Heh, taking my bumbling surreptitious snapping off of the gas as a "let's do it here" signal? Your lead, Astaire. I'm all for showing that three-block radius who's eating off this grout.
Alright, sure. Grope, slip, tug, kick, scrape, shimmy, with eyes off doing their own shrill war dance. Closer, good, blurred tight and half panting. Why's the circuit breaker painted blue? Fuck it. Short it. Shunt it? Christ. Shut up shut up shut up.

Pretty striking over there with the vaguely preoccupied look, guy. Could always be a little softer and cramped like this when he's alone. Really mostly bolstering the androgynous cream of wheat vibe, though with makeouts that hungry and going all simian with the rest I have to say he's netting some valued schtupper points.

(L) So are you really that into cooking or do you just have a lonely aunt on call every time you need to make a date feel validated about modern gender norms?

(H) Hm? Not sure. Roommate withdrawal maybe.

(L) Oh yeah?

(H) Fine, you caught me. Ol' Auntie Rubblebutter. Actually my mom's Prussian wetnurse, but she raised us both as her own, after the great rhubarb strike of '88.

(L) So she raised your mom to be inattentive enough to get to raise you too?

(H) Yes, very observant. It was a different time, you know. Tricycles still had luggage racks and sobriety was frowned upon. Had to make do with what God coughed up all over us. Not his fault, of course. Divine Congestions pop up all throughout recorded history. There's some evidence it's linked with trends in folk music, but the Holy Supreme Inoculation of Pious the Twelfth focused mainly on damning geometers— leading to the Era of Ample Fluids and Bed Rest so revered by theological epidemiologists.

(L) Fascinating. Never thought I'd drift off next to someone spitballing essay theses for Absurdists' Philology Review.

Especially not for the third time this week in a birch-shade dappled laundry room love nest.

(H) I've been told I make people drift off in ways they never would have dreamed.

(L) Oh but I bet they did. You know you might still have time to enroll in hypnotists' school for the fall.

(H) Couldn't possibly, that roommate of yours got his buddies at *Manum Nova* all worked up about my robot story and saying they want a novella to serialize through till March.

(L) Jeez. Drew did that? I'm surprised he even still talks to those guys, last I'd heard they'd snubbed him on everything but his condiment essays.

(H) Well, he did, despite it. Had good notes too, maybe he's a fledgling editor in a writer's body.

(L) Always thought he had more of a particularly leggy Smurf's body.

^(H) Can't argue with that. Though I guess there's got to be room for a tortured Smurf auteur somewhere.

^(L) Fingers crossed. So that's what, at least eight months? Paid?

^(H) Yeah, barely a stipend, but it's nice. Probably gonna have to cut down my hours at McGellan's shop.

^(L) Darn, I'll miss those trowely callouses.

^(H) Not me. It's risky though. If March rolls around and nothing new comes up and McGellan can't take me back full time I might have to go work for the city.

^(L) Pouring concrete over ancient burial grounds?

^(H) Or roads and parks if I have to. Station's closer and the Turfblaster probably wouldn't handle the commute to town for more than a few months.

^(L) What a sunny take on your big-shot writing gig. So are they running the robot story too?

^(H) Uh-huh.

^(L) The one you were stuck on when the vampire script arose from the dregs of your soused brain pan?

^(H) The very same.

^(L) So like, death rays and jet boots and a swarthy late-model genetic-algorithm server soothsayer?

^(H) Mm, not quite. It's set in a mind-wrenching future where robots have become meek and affordable and not especially problematic. Augmenting the workforce with dexterity and a terrifying penchant for repetitive ordeals.

^(L) Until a plucky young cracker-jack rucksack hacker discovers a fatal glitch certain to terminate every vestige of life on earth down to the nanobots monitoring the core?

^(H) Oo, good, but no. More like a kindly old piano tuner who's glad to have the extra pair of hands for abundantly obvious reasons.

(L) So, no until?

(H) Huh. Always needs an until, right? Ok, until he gets a little concerned that he's treating the droid too much like an apprentice but thinks better of it since it's on loan from the library and stands as good chance of carrying on the craft or passing it down as anybody else in town.

(L) Neat. So it's up to the whip-smart droid buddy to stumble upon the fatal flaw in the old man's constitution?

(H) Hm, sure, ok fine.

(L) Which is?

(H) Uh, mild solipsism and overpowering sentimentality?

(L) Egads! Sounds suspiciously autobiographical.

(H) Me, solipsistic? Well, maybe when I thought Dubya's re-election was cosmic retribution for calling my stepdad a tool and fracturing the arch of my foot against his fender. But I've since become confident in my lack of effect on anything I please.

(L) Fascinating. I'm still working on convincing the dog I'm a hallucination he's better off blocking out. So our hero, Mister–?

(H) Stu.

(L) So Mister Stu channels his indefatigable symphonic prowess into?

(H) Into a wholesome smile that has kept his client list full, well into his seventies.

(L) The sheer audacity! How does he cope?

(H) Pastrami sandwiches and a stout with dinner when he's up for it.

(L) Remarkable. The essence of human perpetuity in the face of modern sappings. But come on, off the record, what's it really about?

⟨H⟩ Uh, well, let me think where I was going before you so pleasantly interjected.

Possibly not the first time he's flopped out that candy-crusted euphemism, but in this context I'll call it a milestone and be ever so slightly flattered.

⟨H⟩ So it's basically Stu sitting having coffee with a client while the droid does a coarse pass. He's holding out his gnarled fingers, spitting out a bunch of hopefully refreshing and not-so-conventional wisdom on retirement being a general trademark of obsolete professions. Of course the client is dubious and goes off to be miserable at the firm. Then Stu just jams with the droid, calling out for intervals and waveform projections and hundredth-cent increments and things like "Fluff up the felt around A5 a bit" to which his stalwart companion replies "It's fairly compacted and brittle. It appears we have stock on hand for me to cut a new form." Then they play a duet and pack up, having done a better job than Stu ever would have had time for, even with the hands of a twenty-year-old, and with none really the wiser.

⟨L⟩ So you're shilling for some auditory robot overlord ambassador?

⟨H⟩ Yeah, kinda how I felt when it was done, but it's a little more metered than my usual overblown dreck.

⟨L⟩ Sounds like a treat, Hare. Ray guns only get you so far. So when do I get to read it in print?

⟨H⟩ Soon, I think. I'll leave a copy in your mailbox if the chimney's full.

⟨L⟩ Oh, did I tell you about all that Paul stuff? Jesus, that was a ridiculously huge joint you rolled, wasn't it?

⟨H⟩ It was.

⟨L⟩ Well I'll keep 'em both clear in any case. And assuming by chimney you mean the extractor fan vent that occasionally decides to distressingly smolder.

⟨H⟩ A chimney by another name, really. Just remember if you smell burning, that's my first professional vindication on 110-pound acid-free charring your drywall.

(L) Mamma always said only go for the ones who burn your kitchen down with the best intentions.

(H) Wise words. I grew up with "A house aflame in tenderness keeps the shine on the fireman's pole".

(L) How sweet. Aunt Fussyrudder?

(H) I believe so. She crocheted most of our beloved mantle-worthy taglines.

(L) Naturally. She sounds just so real special to ya.

(H) I'm glad you say so. Because I was a bit nervous saying but, aw stuff it, she wants to meet my new potential old ball and chain to be!

(L) Hoh?

(H) You, dummy!

(L) Yeah?

(H) Tomorrow.

(L) Ah-huh.

(H) Where she works.

(L) Yes.

(H) In the cemetery.

(L) Ahhh.

(H) Stealing granite.

(L) Eeeewhh.

(H) I know, recession's not been kind on the crocheted sappy innuendo market. But she's a winsome old gal, you'll see!

(L) Gosh! I'll be needing a pair of good hoisting boots, I suppose.

(H) And how! I'll get you sized up at my guy's in the morning. He's a grabby old lech, but I wouldn't trust my

best good gal's dainties with no fast-talking toe bender while
he's among the living.

⟨L⟩ Your best good gal? Heavens to pew, Heeree, you
keep sneaking in blushers like that and I'm liable to march
right down to the druggist's for a pound of rubbers and a
toothbrush.

⟨H⟩ Now hush. Everybody in town knows old Tom Gru-
boorg's got 'em going eight'll netchya nine on size eighty over,
and he just throws that toothbrush on top like you'd been
eyeing it from out the window all week.

⟨L⟩ No!

⟨H⟩ Oh indeed yes. And you can slide over an extra nickel
so's fer he'll let you rub his goiter.

⟨L⟩ Swell! Well I'm near-a-tizzy furrit. May'ps you'll be
a right beau and have my arm at it? Comes a chance a lass
oughtn't be seen alone with a sack of old Tom's these days,
if you can reach an itch that high up the back.

⟨H⟩ Much as I hear "these days" this and "those days" that,
can't say it's all so much a matter whose sack it is, s'long as
you've got pearly dew drops like that under a set of lips to
set them dowdy old chatter-munks stompin in off the porch
for their old man's strop and a squirt of old Doc Squebb's.

⟨L⟩ Ok, wow, fuck, gross. You win the old-timey off. "Doc
Squebb's"?

⟨H⟩ Actually may be a real thing I think, I had some
clipping with it for a marketing project in an art class.

⟨L⟩ If you say so, pearly-D.

Huh. Odd moment for a ping of shallow horror. The
room's soft, cool, nurturing even. Certainly it's no mood
for bracing self-awareness, more like the opposite. Maybe
that's the pang: a tipped-over pair of self-this and that. Self-
opinionated-ness draining a bit if I'm lucky. Good riddance,
ought to vet my opinions on occasion at least.

⟨H⟩ You as hungry as I am?

(L) Read my mind, Hayrble.

(H) Sunflower-seed cheesy cakes?

(L) If that's a nickname, I wholeheartedly but gleefully abstain. Otherwise, would you care to elaborate? Or should I speak with the saucier?

(H) Somewhere between a pancake and a crumpet. I did it with that crumbly Austrian white cheese last time but the leftover chèvre will have to do. With a side of butter, maple syrup, not-quite-sure-why-it's-green aioli, and chocolate-covered corn nuts.

Good holy gods of dairy, I might as well stop asking.

(L) Hmph. Sounds passable. But I keep on hearing about Mr. Paisley's butter-rum-covered corn-nuts down at the club, and it'd really brew up something sewerly in the cribbage circle if you keep ushering me out without our own batch to brag about.

(H) Well the old bags are free to my almond bark supply as you see fit.

(L) And here I thought I'd finally wrung that lip of yours for its last smarts.

(H) Oh cork it, shug, we both know how lost you'd be without that extra pinch of salt on your kiwi.

(L) Now don't start presuming all– wait, time out, really?

(H) What?

(L) The kiwi thing.

(H) Hm, maybe. Might mellow it some. I was raised in a fruit-salting home.

(L) One please.

And he winks, stumbles to his feet, snags some shorts and elbows through the door in the space of a yawn. All with a sort of cloddy Marceau or under-wound Chaplin traipse with a double slathering of slovenly glee. Must be a honeymoon type. Must secretly swoon at the sight of tabbed binders. Must be weirdly permissive leaving kids unsupervised with fireworks. Clearly doesn't mind doing laundry at any rate. Fair enough. Can't say I wish I'd do better. No undertones of that dry passive haughty clinginess or whatever you call it that burrows in like somewhere between forgetting to wring out the dishcloth and wiping your ass with it. Beats par there for sure.

9

There's a nagging edge to those early fall nights where you're getting used to being up and about through so much dark again. Something churchy to it almost, or just a Sunday dread permeating the whole week. Old Gor-dog's been bolting in and out from his little fort-hole, asserting his elated stupefaction at oddly punctuating moments.

Rob's got a macho casserole half in the oven, I'm dazing over the mandatory informal half-assed praise cover sheet for a string of unintelligible stanzas on Van der Walls interactions on its way to a fourth-rate rag.

New Jen is helping Anne with lyrics at the piano. Not too clear who Old Jen was, I think one in the line of Rob's pot-customer crushes with enough classic chill seshes on her punch card to have sidled up unannounced for a back porch socioastrology colloquium or two. Flappy Tom's been gone an hour and Jen's looking a little off-kilter. Not just kindly obliging Anne's sense of muse. Was it Rob speculating on some history there? No, Drew wasn't it? But we'd been baked enough he'd have bet the neighbors were swapping wives as a tax dodge. Still, this has the stink of that old roommate-as-sexual-tension-sublimation-prop feeling I've come to know and itch at. The lyrics are basically steamy, classy though. If the subtext doesn't boil over soon they'll start getting those little cartoony glintzy clumps just a bit down and to the left of their pupils.

Shit, maybe I'm going full yenta over some sappy rapport they've had for years. Or I'm mischanneling an unrequited longing for unbridled platonic yuks into some "everybody's out to get laid to the point of seriously overlooking other facets of existence" conspiracy. So obvious it's insidious. But Rob's barely tamping down a spatula-accented gape I'm fairly sure is not for my benefit. Let's call it two-to-ten odds he's just marveling over the essence of rarefied creative poise. Something tells me my catalog of significant looks can't do this justice. Plus, the fact that Rob's assembling something edible with the three-footer still wispy on the counter leads me to suspect his perceptron's mostly cached.

(L) Rob?

(R) Hhh?

(L) I think you might need to preheat that thing again.

(R) Whoa, yeah. How long I been venting it?

(L) Like, two and a half bong rips.

(R) Shit.

(L) And I'm not completely sure from here, but I think your ass has been slowly lowering the dial.

(R) Heh, so it has. Thanks Leige. You seen the paprika?

(L) One of the ones clanking in the apron?

(R) Thinking with your ears. I like it, buut, nope. Thyme and, Jesus, cardamom? What am I getting myself into?

(L) Not sure I've seen you complete an entree without a large majority of the spice rack, Rubbles.

(R) Pwaahh. If I were the glum type, I might consider taking offense at that.

(L) Oh come off it. You know I'll eat anything you cook without complaining.

(R) Color your criticism any way you want, buster. Nobody's eating tonight until I find that paprika.

(L) Ok, let's keep it civil in front of the guests, Wubbie. Weren't we dusting our fries with it the other night by the fire pit?

(R) Fuck, yes, yes we were.

(L) Better hope we left the cap on. Rained pretty hard last night.

(R) Dammit. Watch the rice? It keeps looking about ready to boil over.

(L) On it, chef. Don't trip over Gene-o on your way out, he must've dug up a dead weasel or something.

(R) Who?

(L) The dog? Our dog now apparently?

(R) Geordie?

(L) Really?

(R) Yes, I finally have it on good authority. And yes, ours now. Or mine technically. Jen One's in Peace Corps boot camp as of last Wednesday.

(L) Oy. Or, good for her and also us? Sorry. Was she the one with the bug-eyed map of Maine juggling Delaware and Rhode Island on her hip?

(R) No, that's Rhea. We had eel bowls with Jen in town right when you got back?

(L) Right.

And he's back hovering over the soon-to-be-called either bisque or gravy.

(L) Rob.

(R) Huh?

(L) Paprika.

^(R) Ah fuck, shit, God, fuck.

^(L) Best of luck out there, skipper.

Well, he does pull off a frustrated stoney tromp with just enough lighthearted sniveling to keep things breezy. Meanwhile I'm staring at a finished letter, too numb from the last unpaid pity proofread pass to remember if I checked my own margin-note fluff in these damn unscannable three-word-wide comment boxes in the template. Screw it, spell check's a go. Save it, dump it, take the first free breath for the next glorious three to four hours off. Take that, massive untenable debt.

I wonder how long I've been tuning out the biweekly trashy squabble across the alley. Almost at a fever pitch before dinner, too. The last two had such a decisiveness to them that this one's got more of a rematch tone than any sense of holding plausible hope. Subconscious angling for epic breakup sex? And the chronic barker three doors down is almost sounding miffed at the competition this time. The sound really carries on a night like this, but the poor thing's rhythm is all cramped.

Our duo seems to be channeling it, or the Goodwill shag tapestry's proving its mettle. Ok, Jen's eyes are more watery than I should be able to tell from this far off. Better squish the clamshell down and curl up off to the side if they're to stand any chance getting through the third verse without me breaking out the oil paints and a cheap jug of port. I am Quanta Obscura, importunely refracting mystically uncollapsed wave functions in a single bound. Rob, yes, thumbs up on the paprika recovery, but get your ass back on olfactory duty without jarring our virtuosos or I'll spool that casserole through your keyhole while you sleep.

Aw, damn, an unscheduled Drew entrance. En route to settling in with tired waves and a few courteous artisanal head bobs to the bench, but an ambulance rears through and shuts up the alley fight and barker for one of the itchier stillnesses any one of us can have encountered. And cue Geordie scratching his neck so hard it sounds like a rubbery automated washboard.

^(J) Shoot, I forgot I gotta drive Tom to his early shift

tomorrow. You mind doing the last few lines without me?

⁽ᴬ⁾ Sure, no problem. I can run 'em by you next time you're at the club.

⁽ᴶ⁾ Yeah, cool. Night you guys. See you Saturday, right?

⁽ᴿ⁾ Yup. Drive careful, looks like it's really starting to come down.

⁽ᴰ⁾ Yeah, it's getting pretty mucky through old town. You probably wanna hop on the highway instead unless you've got tires with those beefy sci-fi treads.

⁽ᴶ⁾ Cool, good idea, thanks. See ya guys.

⁽ᴸ⁾ Later Jen.

And Drew stays posted butler-like at the coatrack. You live here guy, act like it.

⁽ᴬ⁾ You sure Trina's in her room still?

⁽ᴸ⁾ Pretty sure. You need something?

⁽ᴬ⁾ Well I had showed up on the pretense of us Skyping the folks at a reasonable hour.

⁽ᴸ⁾ She looked pretty beat when she got in. Probably dozing until Scrubs comes on, or Doctor Who or Phil or whichever. You can use my laptop if you wanna cover for her.

⁽ᴬ⁾ Yeah, I owe her one anyway. Where can I–

⁽ᴸ⁾ Rob's room's got the best wi-fi, but it smells like dog farts pretty bad lately.

⁽ᴿ⁾ That is unfortunately quite accurate.

⁽ᴸ⁾ Mine should be fine. Just lilac farts and illicit projectile mace paraphernalia. Password is "feefiefourfive" all spelled out, no caps.

⁽ᴬ⁾ Fie?

⁽ᴸ⁾ Eff, aye, ee.

(A) Cool, thanks. Can you let Trina know if she gets up?

(L) Yeah, you got it.

And Drew has graduated to a metered fidgeting. Never seen him this flummoxed on home turf.

(L) Drew?

(D) Huh?

(L) You look like you forgot to tip the doorman or something. And we're probably at least 600 miles from any doormen.

(D) Ah, no, actually I've been stringing together a song in my head all day and I'm sort of rewinding to make sure I still got it all.

(L) Really? Not like an R. R. Martin, capital-S song?

(D) No, like a song, song. I was in like, twelve bands, remember?

Ah yes. The checkered past as a stalwart metal bassist with too many brittle egos to swat away and eighth-grade lyric consultations to navigate for him to keep his heart in it.

(L) Right, right. 'Tis this season I guess.

(D) You can play a little, right?

(L) Ahgh. Yeah, no, sort of. I can probably help you get some chords down, if that's all you need. Just let's take a seat before you work a divot into the doormat.

(D) Huh? Oh, yeah, sorry it's been a weird day too. I'm surprised I made it home without consulting a psychic.

(L) That begs several questions, without really making sense. I'm impressed. Scoot in, maestro, I'm just the medium.

Can't say he's seeming really that miffed or like he's shouldering any mild trauma. Wouldn't really gel with a pestering tonal buildup, I suppose. Not that it usually takes that much to get him into orbit, but this is a pretty patchy

long-wave band, even for his begrudgingly functional end of
the hipster spectrum.

(L) You're welcome to elaborate, or just start humming
what you've got, but I left my cattle prod in my other pants,
so...

(D) No, no. Just need a sec.

(L) Is this some elaborate Halloween prank or something?
You realize it's still like six weeks away, right?

(D) No, I'm fine.

(L) Ok, then the weirdness. Spill it, or you can go whistle
into a tape recorder.

(D) It's really not much, just odd shit. A hobo on the
trolley started interviewing people like it was a talk show, then
a crackhead snapped at him and it turned into this slapping
match where the hobo kept apologizing with a completely
sincere tone, but they both kept tugging and flicking and the
crackhead finally rattled his pointer finger at the other guy's
face with all the gravitas of some old-world curse.
Then at lunch my boss got a little drunk and started
venting on everybody in the department who doesn't meet
his anti-bro standards, which wasn't particularly awful.

(L) No?

(D) Not particularly. But anyway, he gave me the afternoon off, which he probably shouldn't have, and I went over
to the *Manum Nova* hovel to bum around and see if they
needed a hand with anything, and they're all excited about
"me and Harry's stuff".

(L) Didn't you just pass his story along? I thought yours
was yours and Harry's was his.

(D) Yeah, so did me and Harry. But I mean, they're
running it as if we're part of a new scene with some deep
underpinnings with a glorified Letter from the Editor and
everything.

(L) So? I mean you do pretty much run in the same circles
and drink from the same dilapidated water tower.

^(D) Yeah, I know. And you guys are, eh–

^(L) Sleeping together?

^(D) Yes, that.

^(L) So should I step out? Rob, you got this?

^(R) Hm? Yeah, crackhead fight or something? You'll get through it, bud.

^(D) No, I mean it was just all their over-the-top, what you call it? Not enthusiasm.

^(L) Mildly overzealous good intentions?

^(R) Gusto!

^(D) Sure. Maybe it felt more transparent to me than it was, so I guess I should have been flattered, but I just got all, I don't know.

^(L) Overcome with wrenching dread for lack of faith in your ambitious cohorts?

^(D) Yeah, maybe. Anyway, it wasn't so bad and I went over some notes with them and helped pick out illustrators and stuff and it turned out feeling like a worthwhile afternoon. But then at the Park-n-Ride there were like twenty birds on my car.

^(R) No shit?

^(D) Yeah. And kinda weirdly, no actual shit. And they were really half-assed about flying off when I came up and blipped the lights. Like I was the last guy they would have expected to break up their little confab.

^(L) You know I do count your non-authoritative air as one of your better qualities.

^(D) Gee, when you put it that way.

^(L) Ok, fair enough. That is a lot of curveballs for one day and I'm now grateful for having spent the better part of it safe and indoors slouching against the radiator with Gerdle gnawing at my socks.

⁽ᴰ⁾ That's all I wanted to hear.

⁽ᴸ⁾ You're welcome. So what's the song about?

The awkwardly retracted pointed look toward my room means either Anne or mounting frustration over my dabbling in mildly noxious foaming agents and other nominally non-lethal deterrent concoctions.

⁽ᴸ⁾ Oh?

⁽ᴰ⁾ Yeah.

⁽ᴿ⁾ Guys, I gotta go put a load in the washer and air out the dog stink. Shout if everything catches fire.

Rob, either you know all about it and that's a hell of a poker face or you've got a subconscious sixth sense for ditching when the mood dips from odd to baffling without any overt cues.

⁽ᴸ⁾ You know she's not so, uh, phallophilic lately?

⁽ᴰ⁾ Yeah. But there was a thing, I don't know. It was a while ago.

⁽ᴸ⁾ And now it all finally foamed up on your creative shores and you walk in the door ready to chart it all out and she's right there and now the thing's weighing weirder and thicker than before?

⁽ᴰ⁾ Perfect opening line.

⁽ᴸ⁾ Mm, at least it's raw. You got a melody or what?

Not half bad, and with about 32 bars down pat and fairly clear ideas on a bridge and some weird inter-chorus percussive rally. Probably beyond my pay grade. Better mash around some susses and oddball ninths so he doesn't get his hopes up. Oops, backfire.

Oh well, a lot more fun catering to "no, more grimy" or "yes, but like, flat but not tranquil" than decrypting wincing head bobs from latter-day glom punk gurus with deep super-stitions against treading beyond the two-and-a-half sacrosanct liege-chords. Hear us, oh open-mic God, with our offering of wholesome meager grit. Bestow us your mercy, for we know not what pentameters we breach. Whoa, when did he start singing? Words and everything.

⁽ᴸ⁾ You just coming up with those?

⁽ᴰ⁾ Yeah, sort of. Had some bits and pieces in mind.

⁽ᴸ⁾ Keep it going. I'll try and jot 'em down.

Good stuff, abstract but not flighty. Mumbleable but keeps you attentive. Poor sod could have been an offbeat heartthrob if he'd had the right impetus for a thorough soul-bleaching.

⁽ᴰ⁾ You get all that?

⁽ᴸ⁾ Pretty much.

Two more run-throughs and a drummer and we could have all the low-hanging groupies in the county instagramming themselves eating out of our hands.

⁽ᴸ⁾ We should probably do that tricky part in the middle a few more times, I think I'm clobbering out something different from what I wrote, but it might be better anyway.

⁽ᴰ⁾ It's alright. Or, you can. I should really get some air or something.

⁽ᴸ⁾ Hm, yeah might be a good idea. Got an umbrella?

⁽ᴰ⁾ I think like three of the eight by the door are mine. Thanks Li.

Can't say he's any less spaced. Maybe he's better at savoring catharsis. At least he got his coat on without breaking anything.

⁽ᴸ⁾ How long you been standing there, Rob?

⁽ᴿ⁾ Little bit. Thought I'd scoop up Geordie to keep him out of the way, then we started grooving in with the woodwork a bit.

⁽ᴸ⁾ That's not how the saying goes, you know.

(R) Oh stuff it, Mincealot. I'm stoned and that was– what the hell was it?

(L) Uhm, sublime unbundling of neurotic flux?

(R) Shit, I must be high, you almost sounded succinct.

(L) Smelling good in there, chef. Biscuits and bisque?

(R) Well I can pop in a tube of Pillsbury's if you want, but the casserole's probably about ready.

(L) That's fine. I'm gonna pick at a few of these ear-biters in the breakdown.

The whole prickly early fall thing's got its traction and we're into whatever passes for cheeky domestic tranquility in a house this slobby. It's a shame just the more blunt moments stick out. Plenty of the stranger nights keep on slipping by, knocking apart whatever resolve I had going in.

(A) Hey.

(L) All done? How's the homestead? Cheesy, teary, and odd?

(A) No, we're more of the bland and tiring sort. They liked your song.

(L) Oh, shit, sorry. It was Drew's actually. You staying for dinner?

(A) No, I ate already. Don't let Trina nap too late, ok?

(L) Sure.

Her customary goodbye peck goes a bit softer and more central than I remember. Maybe it's the angle. Tracing a few fingers across the shoulder on the upswing. Then a perfectly guileless wave and inconceivably well-polished brobye to Rob.

(R) She seem alright to you?

(L) Yeah. I don't know. Why?

(R) I think we need that party. Bad.

^(L) You may be on to something. Hey sleepy butt! You just missed Anne.

^(T) Myyahh. Smells good. I was sort of dreaming all this weird music. Were you guys, like auditioning each other or soundtracking Rob's kitchen hijinks or something?

^(R) From what I could tell, yes.

^(L) I imagine your version was a bit more colorful though.

^(T) No. It had more to do with chasing the dog around trying to get him to wear a bib. Thanks for cooking again tonight, Rob. Probably wouldn't have gotten back up for pizza rolls.

^(R) No sweat, Tee. I'm too baked to stay out of the kitchen anyway. You guys wanna rip?

^(T) Sure.

^(L) Nah, go ahead, I got an early deadline.

Plus I might as well see how long I can remember tonight. Something better stick. Geordie's damn name finally, for one. A smattering of new tonal synapses is bound to get burned in there too somewhere. Or I'll get swamped tomorrow and slide into another eleven, eleven-hour day streak till I come to my senses seven drinks deep on somebody's lazyboy.

^(L) I have a suggestion though. We have any of that gummy bear fudgey goo left?

^(R) Ooo, yes, we do. Looks like we got another ten minutes or so for the cheese to brown, too.

^(T) Ugh, no I prefer my fillings intact, thanks. How long's it been, Li? You sure you don't wanna go all Nostredittimal then conk out?

^(L) 'Bout a month. And don't I do that regardless?

^(T) Just wondering if I need to hide my sidewalk chalks.

^(L) Jeez, I'm not twenty-two anymore. I reiterate my abstention, your honor. C'mon now. Cradle bowlrabbus betwixt thine humble palms and embidden the butanic glow.

132

⁽ᵀ⁾ Uh-oh, she's even worse vicariously. Better feed her something soon or we may need the tempera paints.

⁽ᴸ⁾ Silence, wretch! The sugared petals of Nabbacanna-banezra await their measured singe.

⁽ᵀ⁾ So the last time you smoked was when you called me from seven states away ranting about fireworks and wondering if I had any graham crackers?

⁽ᴸ⁾ And you did! And I ate some the following week, I'll have you know. Anyway, a rip this exhausted and I'd probably have to visit the hallway rug and ask you to turn down the lights if I start writhing.

⁽ᴿ⁾ Aw, but that's the Liya we all know and love. And I bet Geordie'd be extra damp and snuggly for ya. Taffy's up by the popcorn I think.

Still vacuum squished to an inverse casting of Rob's fist in its ziploc and way too geological looking for something edible.

⁽ᴸ⁾ Trina, you sure you're not gettin' down on this?

⁽ᵀ⁾ Alright, fine, fuck it. Just let me cough my head off another second.

⁽ᴸ⁾ Did you try it yet?

⁽ᵀ⁾ Hm? No.

⁽ᴸ⁾ Here. Prepare for all confectionery rules to be cracked and reformed around a locus of semi-opaque and not-too-chewy fructal indoctrination. Ah, that's it. Ensnare your palette in swirly discord.

⁽ᵀ⁾ Wow. Good. Did you just melt a bunch of gummy bears?

⁽ᴿ⁾ Yeah, basically. There's a protracted debate over which or how much of the assorted starches and flours on the counter at the time may have found their way into the mixer. We may never know. I am in the miniscule-to-none camp.

⁽ᴸ⁾ Did we rule out agar?

(R) Good question. The starburst-brittle definitely didn't turn out as well. Though in any case, some twelve-year-old on YouTube had beaten us to it.

(L) A hex on mEgganthyme02 and her plucky showmanship.

(T) Hear hear! So you cribbed her recipe inadvertently?

(R) Yup. Our combined, thoroughly concentrated efforts match that of a bored pre-teen.

(T) Aww, it's ok. You'll grow into your big-kid pants soon, I promise. Just remember to wish for it next time you're blowing bubbles off the roof at the neighbors' dog.

God, Rob, please not so gingerly with the contagious chortle. But yes, we should have definitely gotten that on tape.

(L) Robe-robe, if we don't eat soon I'm liable to wander through the neighborhood until I step on a hedgehog or find a Whataburger or something.

(T) Do we have hedgehogs here?

(R) Not on this continent, as far as I know. Are there Whataburgers?

(T) Porcupines maybe.

(L) No ganging up, please. It's getting hot-boxy enough to turn my drowsy brain into a fragile snowflake white-knuckling it not to shit its wingsuit.

(T) Snowshit?

(L) I don't know, slate, slurry maybe.

(R) Wait, why's a snowflake worried in this situation really?

(T) Being melted alive in a mobile neoprene coffin while its friends are all doing naked loop-de-loop high fives?

(L) Just because I'm laughing doesn't mean you're not being cruel. Ok, no, you're not, but Christ, where'd you get that shit, Cambodia?

^(R) The store.

^(L) Right, your card. Whoa. Well that last spitfire of yours caught my left nostril head-on.

^(R) Oops.

^(L) Yeah, might have to stop drop and loll for a minute. Anyway I still got that at-work ick a little. DNR, brauwhs, at least for twelve minutes. But I'll keep my feet sticking out from under the piano in case you really need me.

^(R) Go for it, rug master.

^(T) That's what, you said.

Oh God. She didn't.

^(R) You want me to blend up some of the crusty bits of the casserole and leave you a turkey-baster full next to your bed pan?

^(L) Awww? Would you?

^(T) Sweet dreams, snow pants.

^(L) Good night, sweet jerks. Just pretend I'm not in earshot and keep saying funny stoney stuff. Or go for a passive Jane Goodall feel if anything.

^(R) Stonerus Habitulus, normally skittish to the point of abject paranoia amongst unimbibing onlookers, would certainly gore her in a frenzied munching but for the patchouli-stuffed pockets and a hard-earned status as itinerant witch-doctor.

^(L) Mm-hm, yep, more just like that.

Howdy floor. And hello to you to ripe probably more of a pug after all than I initially thought, whose Halloween test-run muumuu is now a preferred garment. Hello surprisingly intricate detail work on the keyboard undercarriage. Let's all bow our heads and attempt a neat conking without all the doughy reflection. The throw pillow in leg's reach ought to be just fluffy enough to help steel the gut for a four-alarm casserole and whip the bleariness into an appetite for two to five glasses of whatever red's left. Mazle tov.

10

If the whole judge a joint by its bathroom rule applies to potential employers, I'm basically sold already. Playful mod sink that's still deep enough to be practical, and a convex-rim mirror that's got a hazy flattering spread without being preoccupying. Nothing cheap or gaudy in the brick and tile work. An honest-to-God oil still life, just so irreverent to not mind classing up the place, irises and poppies maybe. I suppose it all screams literary magazine with a dose of "let's buck the trend of being flare-assed off putting". Beyond a shadow of a doubt please start tomorrow interview as it may have been haphazardly pitched, I am lingering more like an in-law than an applicant. Well, they're probably used to it.

Uhp, yep, after you. Can't fault you the knowing, unimpressed, but clearly a bit delighted smirk of a fellow toileteer.

[L] Sorry to linger on you Debbie, but jeez, I mean you guys could be selling post cards in there.

[D] Not a problem. Kinda easier to manage that sort of thing with just the six of us.

⁽ᴸ⁾ Wow, really? On a quarterly? I was thinking at least double that.

⁽ᴰ⁾ Has been, but we're paying contributors more this way, mostly by printing longer form and less fluff and me spending twice as much time hounding offbeat newsstand merchants at book fairs instead of cooking up viral marketing schemes.

⁽ᴸ⁾ Imagine that.

⁽ᴰ⁾ We are trying to hire back a couple of the real workhorses that are still in the area, so we can get back to showcasing more print media like we used to. Plus our guy in Prague basically works for expenses and half the time gets in so good with the artists they send us the drafts you see now crowding out into the hall. Uh here, I'm back this way.

⁽ᴸ⁾ So I take it that leaves me in the running for something a little less glamorous?

⁽ᴰ⁾ Yeah, a lot less, sorry. But it's a solid twenty hours if you need it. Guys, Lianne. This is Rhea, Sean, Jerome, and Ebba.

Nice dutiful crew. Mostly post-hipster or pupating one way or another. Not so much of the angsty entitlement but still well clear of any corporate do-gooder tinge. Eerily picturesque in this cramped arrangement.

⁽ᴰ⁾ Sean and Ebba are doing the bulk of the compositing these days. Which I'm sure they're falling dangerously behind on.

⁽ᴱ⁾ Not my fault. Percolator's on the fritz and the shelf life on that instant's debatable.

⁽ᴰ⁾ Ok, last eight clobbered deadlines are also forgiven on that note. I'll get us a Mr. Coffee from Goodwill after lunch. Whoever can solder Old Spateful back together again gets out of the bean pool for two months.

⁽ᴶ⁾ On it.

⁽ᴰ⁾ That's me over by Sean and the pop-art-deco nipple parade. But let's go over in to the, uh, what are we calling that sweatbox again?

(S) I think we finally ruled out fainting room, refectory, and pinacotheque. Nobody closed the poll, but it's been a dead heat between tepidarium and adyta.

(D) Christ, just pick one please. Li? Or... sorry.

(L) No, Li's better.

(D) Ah, okay. Go on ahead.

(L) Office nomenclature politics?

(D) Yeah. To their credit it has gotten pretty tedious trying to refer to the sole meeting room that everyone prefers to have lunch in despite the fully furnished kitchen at the far end of the building.

(L) Maybe it's the invigorating two square-inches of natural light filtering in over that AC unit.

(D) Or the ironic grimy brick wall view it offers while your ass slowly melts into the pleather. I think most of the candidates had to do with that, one of them is some old archo-linguistic mystery most likely meaning "no admittance".

(L) Riveting.

(D) Yeah, I gotta stop getting caught up in all their cavalier garbage. My husband's a guidance counselor at the fine arts school and can barely hold his shit together hearing about my day half the time.

(L) I guess every whackadoodle outfit needs a sheepdog. No offense.

(D) Hah! No, glad to wear it on my sleeve. Whatever I manage to do here keeps us afloat longer than the six-issue pseudo-activist rags we unfortunately resemble, while the hundred-year-old brunch-table heavy hitters are floundering toward esteemed large-print Reader's Digests.

(L) Amen.

(D) Sorry, I got into this business just long enough before everyone lost their shit about the internet screwing us all over to have a sliver of sentimentality left.

^(L) Nah, it's really fine. I'm a bit starved for self-deprecation lately.

Not to mention someone with the chin to complain about the cushiest dumpy chairs I've encountered, and all hemmed in by dotingly careless heaps of old photography journals and unsolicited art samples.

^(D) Anyway, we've got this sideline thing. There's a Mr. Owen, an eccentric subscriber who happens to run a thriving hardware catalogue. He's been siphoning off most of the copyediting and a fair share of the compositing to us. It keeps his staff down to a warehouse crew and a couple assistants for chartering buses through sub-tropical weeks-long sojourns to find the most decently made bolt cutters. Not that he's some eco-warrior, just has this otherworldly sense of frugal workmanship. And more often than not he'll turn a thing over twice in his hands and ditch some extensively brokered deal if he senses something neglectable or "wanting misuse" to it.

^(L) Sounds like you read his manifesto.

^(D) Yeah, nailing down the contract with him did entail "aw-hawwing" to more than a few surprisingly cogent machining-tolerance-related email essays. Anyway, he's pretty shrewd about it all, has a lot of supervisors on high-profile job sites with his catalogue in their glove box. So I guess he sees himself as some renegade die-hard capitalist keeping his domestic suppliers on their toes. The rub, for him, is that he ends up fronting products that often only faintly resemble their conventional counterparts, or are tangentially related to what you'd expect. In other words, if he sees a doodad he gets a gut feeling will come in handy and last a few lifetimes, he buys it.

^(L) So not wanting misuse but wanting explanation for what the hell they're for?

^(D) Right. So he mails us a stupendously exhaustive prospectus on each galvanized wingnut holster and we give him fifty to a hundred words of cheeky shop talk on it.

139

⁽ᴸ⁾ Like a sagely old neighborhood voice-from-beneath the jalopy sort of deal?

⁽ᴰ⁾ Sure, yeah. No hard selling. Just plain-spoken home-spun know-how with a hint of smug self-awareness at hawking potential bells and whistles to the tried-and-true crowd. It's no glamour, as promised. Something tells me you might enjoy it, though.

⁽ᴸ⁾ It does sound fun, actually. Like I said in the email I would probably have to beef up on my handyman lingo.

⁽ᴰ⁾ Good. As I imagine you've noticed, I'm on maternity leave soon and it's either you or sorting through a stack of bubblegum cover letters that would all mean more time for spoon-feeding than anybody has around here. And honestly I wouldn't mind unloading it altogether, copy-wise, if we can convince Mr. Owen I hand-picked and mentored you with the utmost care.

⁽ᴸ⁾ I do have a knack for being treated exceptionally.

⁽ᴰ⁾ Ha, ok. You really know somebody who can walk you a few times around the hardware store for a crash course?

⁽ᴸ⁾ Yeah, and I've got more backups on that front than I need, cross my heart. It's the robot story guy, in fact.

⁽ᴰ⁾ Really? And you're roommates with Drew Mallerin too, right?

⁽ᴸ⁾ Yep.

⁽ᴰ⁾ Wow, cool, don't let their egos get wind of it, but we're banking on a new market or two with their next few serials leading. Good stuff.

⁽ᴸ⁾ My lips are sealed.

⁽ᴰ⁾ Alright, well Sean's got most of the compositing on this thing. The templates are a breeze compared to our froofier stuff, so it's mostly a Friday thing for him. I know the commute's a bitch for you, but in my experience spitballing with petulant poetry majors makes the day go a lot faster. So one or two days a week here at least is probably best.

^(L) That's fine. The home office loses some charm once you've worn through enough work pajamas.

^(D) Personally I don't think I could ever see minding that.

^(L) Yeah, you have to cherry-pick complaints about it. But a slightly overzealous fix-it guru is a hell of a lot more interesting client than my usual fare. Plus that bathroom has biweekly pilgrimage written all over it. Sorry, I just can't get over it.

^(D) No, no, I get it. I'm given to the suspicion that it's related to our eerily high punctuality rate. Ok, do your crash course and I'll email you the HR stuff. Good?

^(L) Uh-huh. Next week was light anyway, so easing off the extra hours should go pretty smoothly.

^(D) Great. Now I'm sorry to rush you out, but I've got to go either regret the double-lax and everything I got when Einsteins' unbolted their doors this morning or dry heave until my eyes water.

^(L) Oh, ok, you got it. Need a hand with anything?

^(D) I'll pretend to show you out if you keep yourself in human-crutch range. Deal?

^(L) Deal.

Some small talk would probably quench the expectant hush of the bullpen, but it looks like we've blundered into an air of no-nonsense nod speak that will probably sprinkle some business-acumen mystique over both our reputations for hours to come.

Something maybe a little too deeply rooted about the wave of relief coming on. Tempted to call it empathy for a vagrant nauseatic finding an oasis of tastefully lit porcelain. Probably more to do with the prospect of six fewer deadlines a week. Should have known I'd be too restless or competitive or whatever it is that's got me gulping down twice the burnout-safe workload.

Modest celebration's due at any rate. Maybe Vegahroo's still serving those compacted agar butter and roe sorbet

hambones with the oily beet-jelly marrow Harry's been biting
his lip about. But can you really gnaw at it? Probably a
glorified twenty-dollar popsicle, but then it's got to leave you
so primped with meloney succulence that you don't care.

11

I'll call it promising that the first to show up besides the regulars are a van full of roadies and a tagalong auxiliary percussionist or two all clearly too stoned to be gravitating toward any distinct light source, yet undeterred by our standard roof's worth of icicle lights warping the front window into a throbbing wash of substantiated migraine.

Next, the better part of the band, even the elusive Lewis, whose busking days he's rumored to have admitted were essentially a call-center sick leave stint. And, tactically spaced, comes the minor star they opened for, hopping from her modest tour bus, seeming pleased enough to have outmaneuvered her entourage to show no outward resentment at being grievously upstaged by Anne and the county's finest half-conscious stool leaners. Then two-thirds or so of the chorus from the touring cast of some swing-heavy musical on its eightieth sesquiannual revival who, coincidentally or not, roll up blaring the same starlet's one recognizable single, as if they've been using it as warm-up fodder for months. And topping it off for the moment, a rented bubble buggy of touring-cast stragglers, maybe a few principles and a woodwind or too from the pit, far and away the most non-temperamentally groomed arts or craftspeople to grace the property.

[L] Rob, how long have we been sitting out here?

⁽ᴿ⁾ Not that long. It's this wax, man. Some old-timer in Boulder told me he was pretty sure he'd been 58 and pissing bullets when he'd first sat down for a puff the night before.

⁽ᴸ⁾ It does have a strong porch appeal, I'll give him that. You realize that at least three of the guys who just walked in can do backflips and you left Drew in charge of the music?

⁽ᴿ⁾ Well, I'm wagering there's not nearly enough shitheads in the mix to stir up any real sinkhole of a lull. And I don't think that much gear would've gotten brought in just for safe keeping.

⁽ᴸ⁾ Don't get my impromptu acoustic nerve all in a tizzy now.

⁽ᴿ⁾ Tizz not, afliverrable one. Everybody's still all sweaty from the last set or grand finale or whatnot. Puts us at least three rounds shy of any true afterparty encoring. Should give us time to get beer-bolstered enough to stand frigidly by the piano and stare the bassist into submission.

⁽ᴸ⁾ He knows what he did.

⁽ᴿ⁾ Eugh. How far am I supposed to read into that?

⁽ᴸ⁾ Let's just say he won't be apt to do or say certain things he'd been wont to before.

⁽ᴿ⁾ Oh my God, you couldn't shoot the moon any worse. Might has well have actually done a wink-wink nudge-nudge.

⁽ᴸ⁾ You're welcome.

And here come the neighborhood it-supremes to round it out, heralding an autumn of puffy cowls with all conferrable nonchalance. I guess half of them walking their bikes paints a chic austerity, but the actually riding and actually audible trailing crew of roommates and hammock surfers are snapping enough wayward hedge tops with their handlebars and swerving with that 0.12 vestigially destructive frosty glee to give the whole procession a sort of medieval charm.

⁽ᴸ⁾ This turnout's getting so chummy and eclectic I'm afraid I'll start blurting out overbearing truisms from some deep-seated waspy mediocrity instinct.

⟨R⟩ Now, now, you'll get all swept up and you know it. Anyway, the hardcore banality slingers don't know any better, and are even more desperate to get their drink-in-hand sashay going than you would ever know how.

⟨L⟩ Ok, I believe you. I'll claim eager, but rarely desperate. So they're safe when outnumbered, but in force they run their tactical picks on the dance floor and groom their cubicle banter with rigid proximity to the uncannily most obstructive, unfurnished area of floor they happened to collide at?

⟨R⟩ Yeah, yeah, those damn Vanillinati. Can't we all go a little tame here and there? Maybe we're all a little too aspirational and sarcastic anyway, right?

⟨L⟩ If you say so, then so's good for me. Can't beat an old dog with today's newspaper and all that, eh?

⟨R⟩ If that's your version of inane, I'm curious to hear your insufferable chatterbox.

⟨L⟩ Not in my repertoire, sorry.

⟨R⟩ You sure about that?

That's got to call for a dead arm by any metric. But a clunky ribbing with the heel has a more affectionate ring to it.

⟨L⟩ Chortle out your vape with that in mind, butt-stir.

⟨R⟩ Jesus. Uncle. Shit, that feels like a meat tenderizer.

⟨L⟩ I stiffened up my corns just for you.

⟨R⟩ Wow, what's your secret? Spray shellac?

⟨L⟩ Nah, plain old crazy glue with a smidge of Vermont maple.

⟨R⟩ Extra dark?

⟨L⟩ Only if you're into alfresco floor hockey, man. Okay, clinical as your grip is, we're still pushing past platonic corn inspection to undeniably plausible offhand affection.

⟨R⟩ Wha?

^(L) The bane of small-town roommate gossip. Release.

^(R) Oh, with pleasure, my corned companion.

Actually, uncharacteristically clinical, come to think of it. Really is lacking his just barely tolerable slime trail of general libidinousness, even in the more unerotic personal-bubble brushings like hefting unwieldy furniture together.
One of Robeo's purported irons in the fire must have cracked. Would explain the lack of grinny bitching over logistics he's partial to for his dozen-DJ's balls. Better hope whoever he's showering with winkey face emoticons won't be put off by backflips.

^(L) You know. Remarkable as this turnout's shaping up to be, I'm starting to worry this many performers and peanut gallerians such as ourselves might end up flirting with those bohemian lulls our cocktail sipping counterparts of decades past bantered so hard to rescue us from.

^(R) Nahh.

^(L) You invited your punk friends, right?

^(R) On tour. Half of them haven't shaken off their prep school nerves anyway, wallflowers in punk-appreciation regalia.

^(L) Oh, that's right. They still add something though.

^(R) Chain-smoking and well-rolled blunts?

^(L) Mm, yeah. Hey Tee, how's it going in there?

^(T) Fine, drinks starting to materialize on every flat surface. Couple rotos going with a spliff and bubbler or two in each and nobody being dicks about butt-ins.

^(L) Well we're lacking a measure of garrulousness at any rate. What about the guys from up the street?

^(R) Flyered their mailbox.

^(T) We had flyers?

146

(R) No, but hard to call it an invitation. Just a map and a time signed by "that guy you always toss a beer to on his way home from work".

(L) Haven't we spent like, six hours at least standing out in that yard?

(R) At least.

(L) And not one name exchanged?

(R) No, they're too fun. There's always a point where small talk would ruin it all. With them it's just basically as soon as you catch the beer.

(L) Paradox of instant social lubrication.

(R) Why? There's just never the nagging thought to present my digital baboon butt cause I'm always wandering off on a high note hearing that dinky little beach box chirping out 1480 AM most of the way home. Honestly I count those fence-leans as one of scant few moments of provincial what-do-you-call-it...

(T) Chubless abandon?

(R) Watch it sister, that's our word.

(T) I beg to differ.

(R) Euggh, don't you get a more obtuse name for it?

(T) What, tidal swell?

(L) Not bad.

(R) Boh, no, worse.

(L) So you pine for the days when everybody knew their neighbors well enough to never ask their name? I can't pin that down as anything but prehistoric.

(R) Call me Ook, then. You'll have to pin me down and loogie their names in before I yoke the frail dazzling blossom of our chillness with a double-Windsor noose.

(L) Trina, you remember when Rob let us squirm over "rhymes with geezer"?

(T) In fact I do. Teaser. Asshole.

(L) Ok pinkbelly, payback's due, might as well just start hitting yourself cause I got a nasty orange one hanging down the back of my soft palette I've been saving for just such an occasion.

(R) Just try it. You're as spineless with how d'ya do's as me and you know it. You'd forget the mayor's name after pulling his... kids from a burning wheelbarrow.

(L) Yeah, yeah. Refuse to speak of your bestie devils. 1480 fanfare and all. Rescind?

(R) Never!

(L) CURTIS! YOU MADE IT!

(C) FUCK YEAH!

(L) S'THAT MIKEY AND TEEMO TOO?

(S) YEAH MAN! HEY LI! YOU GOT SOME MAIL STICKING OUT, WANT ME TO BRING IT UP?

(L) YEAH THANKS. It's ok, you don't have to swallow it all at once. Leave a little to savor.

(R) No fair. You've been there like twice.

(L) Yeah and the first time was when we all met. You were baked out of your head. Like, better clean the oven baked. We were wandering the streets calling your name because you could have easily humped the wrong fire hydrant. –Hey guys! Tons of beer inside, party needs ya. Ah, thanks. Mailwoman'd probably leave a nasty note if there were any room for it.

(R) Hey.

(C) Hey Rob. Oh hey Trina.

(T) Come on in, I'll show you where the good liquor's hiding. You two gonna keep playing hooky?

(L) Yeah, I think Rob needs a minute.

(R) Phhh. How?

(L) How what? How does it taste? A little sweet.

(R) Insanity. You were calling Drew Darrel for a week.

(L) So what? He mumbles and is exceptionally non-confrontational. If you must know, we all practically played the name game with their light-up frisbee while you rolled around in the grass with Lucy.

(R) The fuck is Lucy?

(L) Their basset-oodle. It actually almost got a little weird. Lucy really wasn't having it after awhile.

(R) Wow. I thought I'd never blacked out. I guess frolicking while your friends play frisbee doesn't leave you with too many unnerving gaps the next morning.

(L) Guess not.

(R) Huh. Edibles, man. Any good mail?

The grocery store two counties away is still certain their tangelos in their Sunday best are worth the extra gas. Trina's dabbling in latter-day goth couture has ushered in a cornucopia of unlikely-bedfellow catalogues. And my first issue of *Manum Nova*. A volcanic but only scantly euphemized labial landscape with a freshly erupted copyright-safe Blanka inaccurately caterwauling mid-splitter.

(L) I think this is Drew and Hare's big debut. Back-to-back right after "Zombies Ate My Babysitter" if memory serves.

(R) Nice cover. I'd almost call it inspiring, but I'm not sure what that'd say about me.

(L) Meh, anything that irreverent makes me want to go all LaBeouf up in whatever respective piece.

(R) Well, on that note. Should we host this party or just valet it?

(L) After you.

Already hard to say it needs much hosting. Somebody authoritatively curtained in metal bangs planted on the piano stool, a guy using a kick pedal backwards on that group housewarming impulse-buy box drum and some transductive monster of an electric set de-backpacked lustily, comprised of various non-stripped dry-goods cans with open ends angled obliquely. From single-serving Jolly Green corn to a vintage Folger's family-size tom. The progenitor's too proud to cave to the pianist's chin bob and come-on-already warmups and cut short his rousing, painstakingly understated thesis on the requisite phase-mod scheme he probably got lucky on with some optimizer button. But can't really blame him with a toy that kooky. His pet design gimmick is bent lids hot-glued into scooped dishes jutting from all but the Folger's in order to "bounce in a few extra wavefronts". And with each piece topped by belt tensioners on the stringy polyester mesh covers so a lone tap on the corn only "back echoes through" when he really wants to open her up.

Longhair Junior's meanwhile onto a riff too drippy not to drain the gall back down into our stalwart curator's gut, and tight enough that if he doesn't interrupt himself with a dutiful smile and jump in within four bars, he'll be teetering dangerously toward the rusted chops for love of tinkering camp. Ok, takes it up in two, and with a somehow conclusive finger and a half to the lip gesture to the captive snoots, Harry among them.

⁽ᴸ⁾ You have anything to do with that?

⁽ᴴ⁾ The can kit or the vagina comet you're pointing with?

⁽ᴸ⁾ This? No, the can thingy. I know they don't let you in the conference hutch, Hare.

⁽ᴴ⁾ Ah, well no, not really. I did actually meet him over at the makers' shop before, but we just argued about atypical waveform generators.

⁽ᴸ⁾ Do those exist? Should they?

⁽ᴴ⁾ Well, oboes exist.

⁽ᴸ⁾ Uh-huh.

(H) He was being very pedantic, I don't recall much else. But I'll give him way more slack talking up his chariot like that seeing you actually have to play it so bizarrely.

(L) And seeing our limber ringers beelining for the dance nook. I never would have imagined saying this in my living room, or this century for that matter, but if we don't start dancing soon, people may stare.

(H) Oh gee, you know, I should have mentioned this sooner, but I'm a tremendous dancer. My partners have been known to suffer protracted ululaic convulsions.

(L) You do have that certain vasovagal charm. Must be one of those hyperactive putrescine glands I've been hearing about.

(H) I'd pin it on my bedtime steak rub routine, but you never know.

(L) I'd advise against putting any pins anywhere near it just in case. Shall we?

More sparse in the backyard than usual, despite Drew's heroics with the soggy fire pit and the music carrying out at the neighborly tolerance limit through a cracked kitchen window.

Whatever tricked everybody into a newfound appreciation for "American Girl" and melded latter-day Fiona Apple with Nylons instrumentals is finally petering out, on to straddling "Baby's on Fire" with a martial angst over symphonic Marsalis and The Monks.

(L) I'm verging on awestruck at the music situation here, Drew.

(D) It does beat Rob slapping hands off his playlist.

(L) Yeah of course, but I mean it's all over the place, yet nobody's had a chance to slink back to twirling their dicks and whatnot.

(D) Meaning?

^(L) Not a dull moment?

^(D) Yes, it's almost as if they've tapped into the hottest mix of the 60s, 70s, 80s, 90s and even today.

^(L) Har har, you know what I mean. Just in a twirly mood, huh?

^(D) Born twirling.

^(L) And unswayed by the professional dancers tipsying up the kitchen who've been cooped up in a tour bus for eight months with ne'er a leery straight guy in sight?

^(D) They're bound to have run across a truck driver or two.

^(L) Be that as it may, your abject lack of game may be just the ticket. C'mon, there's like three people in there with their shirts on who are less drunk than me.

^(D) Yeah, yeah, fine. You need a drink or something?

^(L) No, just the satisfaction of seeing you pioneering new cross-arm postures through the window. Okay, go, shoo, hot pants, hot pants on the prowl, watch your garter belts ladies, he's a collector.

A little something atypically damning in that eyeroll. Shit. I'm drunk enough to be oblivious to all but his most staunch aspieisms. Alright, situational awareness audit. Trina is hovering and I didn't notice, despite what must be my drink in her off hand. Jen is looking her lackadaisical ten-plus self on a log opposite us, though maybe conspicuously sober and unaccompanied. Ewha is here, lord, how? Small town customs I suppose. Not as big yet as I'd have guessed, and flirting? Yes, with Flappy, keeping it at a kosher proximity to a clump of neighbors and Rob's basement-horticulture disciples. And Anne's aloof off by the back gate. Ah. Well dammit Drew, she's about as enigmatic as they come.

^(T) Well that's one down.

^(L) Really hadn't the slightest. Is there some love quadrangle I'm not picking up on?

⁽ᵀ⁾ Or pentagram or tetrahedron or something. You'd have to ask Anne.

⁽ᴸ⁾ I'm afraid I'd interrupt the seminal moment of her next creative milestone.

⁽ᵀ⁾ Tell me about it.

⁽ᴸ⁾ And Tom is clearly ignoring Jen on account of?

⁽ᵀ⁾ Can't say for sure. I think I caught the tail end of him getting a bit hissy over something trivial. Either he's rubbing it in or has a taste for crazy I wouldn't have expected. Wait, holy shit.

Ewha's pawing him out through the back gate with commendable nonchalance. Now there's an odd match. Their engagement photo would probably have to be them wearing zoot suits in the palm of a water nymph.

⁽ᴸ⁾ Shit. Do we console now? That's what we do, right?

⁽ᴸ⁾ I guess. Not sure if Jen was looking. I'm thinking the dumping might have already gone down. God, they'd make a strange couple.

I'll concentrate all my empathic mojo into the weighty stare we're sharing, Trina, but we both know I'm a few drinks past putting anything resembling a considerate sheen on it. The clump's dispersing at least, leaving the more aimless bits drifting our way, one of which is teasing loudly enough into his phone to mask the awkwardness of eight strangers noticing each other clearly for the first time around a fire. Meanwhile Anne's making her way straight to Jen's shoulder without a word.

⁽⁾ Nah, man. All's you need is like thirty cigs and a patch of floor. Come fucking on! No? You no. Shit. Alright, thanks, yeah, happy trails to your mom too. Yeah I'll be fine. Later. Fuck. Fuck that guy. 'ssup.

⁽ᵀ⁾ Sup.

⁽⁾ Ahnngh man. Probs aweigh m'yarties. 'Bout to be shroomin balls here. Like, anybody else here really need a cold rag and a bathrobe?

⟨L⟩ I'm good with the fire.

⟨⟩ Yeahh. Good. It is good. But I mean, how's it so all full around but I could just walk without touching?

⟨L⟩ I'd bet against it, but your chromatic mane does have a pretty full berth.

⟨T⟩ Now don't fuck with the poor guy, Leem.

⟨L⟩ I'm not, ditz' honor. Just happen to be fluent in Shrumulen.

⟨⟩ Noooooo. How the fuck?

⟨L⟩ Luck? Spite? G-rated disregard for social reciprocation?

⟨⟩ I wish I met you about forty-eight minutes ago, man.

⟨L⟩ Nah, we'd probably be getting tired of hearing ourselves attempt to talk politics by now.

⟨T⟩ Not too loud Li, the gentry in the dining room was getting into some heated preening last I checked.

⟨⟩ Yeah, politics is a big fucking sopping dickhole of not worth my time.

⟨L⟩ You said it, man.

⟨⟩ You guys want? I was saving the rest for my fuckadoodle ass friend, fucker. I think if it's for two it'd be a nice little bitta shrur, shrup, shruppy.

⟨T⟩ I'm alright, thanks.

⟨L⟩ No need, I did a headstand earlier and I stopped making sense about six years ago.

⟨T⟩ I can vouch for that. Excuse us.

I am not completely ambivalent about being dragged away from this encounter. But as he's capable of getting back on

the phone to give his uncle stock tips in the time it's taken
to settle in around Jen's stump, it's probably for the best.

⁽ᵀ⁾ Not sure if you noticed, hon, but Tom's being a complete shitheel.

⁽ᴶ⁾ No, I did. I'm not all that shaken up, to be honest.
It's just dawning on me I've been sticking it out because he
always had such cool friends around.

⁽ᴬ⁾ Like he was showing you off?

⁽ᴶ⁾ No, not like that. Maybe like showing me the local
highlights and expecting sex.

⁽ᵀ⁾ Gross. So who did the honors?

⁽ᴶ⁾ I don't know, him technically. He was scooping up
guacamole and just looked up and we kinda had a moment
that was like we were mirroring each other's distaste and
he just said, "So it's like that, huh?" and walked off. I was
honestly just wishing he'd have gotten me a plate too.

⁽ᵀ⁾ And they say blunt, dispassionate pricks are harder to
come by nowadays.

Coopey as we're getting, there's a dissonance registering
under the synth, with a vague familiarity, and which is too
off-pitch to be intentional.

⁽ᴸ⁾ Is that our doorbell?

⁽ᵀ⁾ Fuck if I know.

Some would be discouraged by the undivertable throng
of dance-floor bystanders you'd have to beggar through to
answer the door. I'm just short of flat-out drunk enough
to see it as a rare opportunity for a reverse tap-you-on-
the-wrong-shoulder trick presenting itself. The side gate of
unassailable shrieking agony is already cracked, robbed of her
first opportunity to be of service to my unsuspecting prey.
Let's see, five-nine, male most likely by the shoes and
unwitting slovenliness in the pants, but can't be sure with
the porchlight cutting a deep shadow from torso up thanks to
a box just a hair too big to be casually walking into a party

with. Kudos for actually having rung the bell for a reason, though it's draining my deviousness. Better switch gears from cheap startle to gravelly salute from creepy neighbor in a tattered nightie.

(L) The real party's on my back porch, handsome.

( ) Oh, Jesus. Hey Li.

(L) Shit, Paul? How in hell did you get here?

(P) What? You invited me on Facebook.

(L) From eight states away, yes. Some would call that a gesture.

(P) Some would call that padding your guest list.

(L) Two flightless digital birds. But really, man, I mean what the fuck?

(P) Swindled the division chair into sending me to a Jordan Rift Valley Antiquities and Speleology summit at Tulane without so much as an abstract. Realized the other night that this would be on the way if I left three days early and put in a new radiator.

(L) You came in The Boat? I didn't know that thing could still break forty. How's she holding up?

(P) Pretty well. Knocked the rear-view mirror loose when I stopped to change out my coffee-soaked shorts on the shoulder.

(L) And you never looked back?

(P) Oh God. That was just hanging too low.

(L) Yeah, like bulging with wasp larvae but somehow still on the branch.

(P) Yum. So much for the apple brandy I brought.

(L) What is that, thirty bottles?

(P) Nope, just one. And some gifts.

⁽ᴸ⁾ I'm suddenly grateful we don't have a chimney.

⁽ᴾ⁾ Huh, that'd be sort of fitting, actually.

⁽ᴸ⁾ How so?

⁽ᴾ⁾ You'll see. First one's in the cigar box on top though.

⁽ᴸ⁾ Boy oh boy, is it another flight risk kit?

⁽ᴾ⁾ Not really. Well, if you put your mind to it I guess.

⁽ᴸ⁾ Ok, I'll open it in a minute. Let's go in and set this down.

⁽ᴾ⁾ Gladly. Is somebody actually playing an eerily faithful rendition of "Spoonful" in there? It's hard to see through your window blob.

⁽ᴸ⁾ Most likely. As far as I know the guy who showed up with a turntable hasn't squeezed in much more than a few James Brown samples.

⁽ᴾ⁾ Wow, so this is what not giving up on your late twenties looks like.

⁽ᴸ⁾ Nah, we're good and crotchety day-to-day. There just tends to be a decent standing cavalry around town for this kind of night. And overabundant well-paying venues in both neighboring cities without many good afterparty dives.

⁽ᴾ⁾ Well in any case, I'm starting to see why you've stuck around. Though your mom's condo did have those really nice chairs in the lobby.

⁽ᴸ⁾ Oh man, I dream about those. Here, please, I got that. I don't think anybody's claimed the air mattress in the studio so we might as well mark it now. HARE! That's Harry, he brought the vegemole or tomacamole pesto brioche cups, I forget which.

⁽ᴾ⁾ Isn't the first one a little redundant?

⁽ᴸ⁾ Oh, no, the "vege-" is for Vegemite, believe it or not.

⁽ᴾ⁾ Rad. And nice going. I don't think I would have ever pictured you with someone drinking a Schlitz in well-coordinated beige dress socks.

^(L) Must be losing my edge. Ok, let's let him see me slip away with a debatably handsome stranger then, yeah?

^(P) Debate my hairy toe knuckles. But yeah, your party.

Uh-oh, two and a half groping couples in the hallway may not bode well for the empty bed situation. False alarm, just a rattled pug. Must be the age-old aphrodisiac of nearest dimly lit point of egress.

^(L) This is Geordie. He's not a compulsive leg humper yet, but we've got him on a waiting list with a miracle worker.

^(P) Wow. I can only imagine what kind of pants they must wear. He does look about ready for a little practice.

^(L) Yeah, maybe better to start him slow, out back by the fire I think.

^(P) Perfect, we might as well bring the box too.

^(L) Buh. Ok. What the hell are we doing in here then?

^(P) Letting the dog out? I'll go and bring my bag in later.

^(L) Ok fine. But I won't hear any whining about backaches if you end up sleeping under the kitchen table.

^(P) Deal.

Down to one pair of gropers and some weighty fumbling from Rob's room.

^(L) I think the room at the end of the hall's free if you guys need a sit-down break.

Remarkable. Advice followed with eyes closed and lips locked. I'll call that my good host deed for the night.

^(P) Whose room is that?

^(L) Drew's, I'll introduce you. And ten bucks if you get him to walk in there shirtless in the next fifteen minutes. Twenty if the door closes behind him.

^(P) Seemed like they might be into it.

(L) Easy money then. Alright, I'm gonna scoop up the runt and we'll make a break for it. Stuff your ears to the deepening funk of the sirens at the piano.

(P) Is that Canned Heat?

(L) No, Chilliwak.

(P) Damn. There really are heroes combing the bins.

(L) Gah! Resist the beat! Go through! Oh, hey, hello, sorry, Drew, Harebert, this is old friend Paul.

(D) Hey.

(H) Hello Old Friend.

(L) What are you two up to in our lovely mud room?

(D) Is that what it's called?

(L) I dunno, not sure where I picked that up. Not really a patio and not really room for a washer.

(D) Huh. Well, I had been explaining to Harry how I farted a perfectly arpeggiated octave this morning, which led us to one-upping each other on un-googleable phrases, as in, "bespoke dog fur socks" or "images of ridiculously large books used in movies".

(H) I still think "limp dick porn addiction" won.

(L) Does sound like a winner.

(D) Which somehow led us to a debate on near-term game changer tech viable for long-form fiction.

(H) Which poetically circled back to butts.

(P) Oh?

(H) Synthetic toilet paper made of algae or lawn clippings or whatever.

(L) Like your robo-mower drops off its load and, voila?

(H) Yup.

^(P) You realize that presents the possibility of the dog getting to wipe first?

^(H) I did not.

^(L) So, back to leaves, basically?

^(D) Yeah, but it's got some handy enzymes genetically tailored to consume the bits your granddad's roll never would've dreamed of.

^(L) Dirty little fecal eaters. Hm, wouldn't it leave some weird powdery residue or something.

Well, maybe that's a plus, come to think of it.

^(H) No, your butt bugs eat what's left.

^(P) What if your butt bugs become dependent on the residue?

^(L) Uhp, there's the rub.

Two out of three sickened guffawing eye rolls in unison. Gotta work on my delivery.

^(L) Ok, somewhat sorry for that. I'll switch back to beer again. In the meantime, Paul's mystery box is apparently an outdoor mystery box. Or a fire-pit based one? I may be mistaken.

^(P) Half of it's definitely outdoor. Fire pit strongly recommended for thematic emphasis.

^(L) Well anyway I'm getting terse blandishing licks at my heels here from our dear Gwurdle. So head out or make way please.

^(H) I'm in.

^(D) I've never been known to turn down a mystery box. Lemme go get a jacket.

^(L) Alright, no–

Thank you Paul. Gotta let the lion think he penned the gazelles himself.

(L) We'll go on out Dreweley!

(H) So you're the one behind the aquarina thing, right? Li showed me the video. It's nuts, man. So churchy and, what, elegiac? But nimble. I've been trying to work one up with old brass fittings, but I can barely get a warble out of it.

(P) It's, ah, you need ceramic for the right timbre, salt glazed if possible. Maybe the metal's too, uh...

(H) Reverberant.

(P) Yeah, 'scuse me, sorry.

(H) What? What are you two owling at?

(L) I'm about to lose a ten spot on dumb luck.

(H) Oh.

(P) Door's cracked.

(L) Five then. Leave it to Drew to be polite with somebody screwing on his bed.

(H) I would have put money on him offering them fresh linens.

(L) Well let's get scarce anyway, just in case.

Shroomey guy is tending the fire without eliciting any white knuckles, while two effectively sober men at my side inspect the dog's anus for grass stains. Makes it tempting to believe for the moment in whatever Rob was spewing yesterday about psycho-symplectic vortices.

(L) Screw it, I'm opening the little one.

(T) Paul?

(P) Tee ra-ra!

(L) Oh yeah, Trina, Paul's here.

(T) Wow, same old Paul, only slightly less hair. I'm impressed.

(P) You have a lot less hair.

(T) I do. Thank you. I was about to come in and suggest we see if our trippy acquaintance wanted to go shoot some of your zap darts at the old couch in the alley, but it looks like you've got your hands full. What the hell is that thing?

(L) A cigar box with a crappily mâchéd screwdriver-sized box inside. Do I get a hint or is it a mini piñata for grownups with Werther's and floss picks? Geordie's kinda got me in a punting mood, or should I get the badminton racquets?

(P) No, no blunt force please. That's from Kate and delicate and probably would be extremely expensive if there were a metric for unsanctioned grad student labor. The mâché's just left over from God knows what.

Ok, slide as directed. And lo, a box indeed. A bright, yet rosy-dark wood, flowy grained with a nice heft. Ironwood maybe. Inset techno-floral reliefs and wispy scrollwork borders with deviant triangular divots taunting the eye not to rest easy. A frosted glass plug, flat and round, flush on one end. Cascading steps to nowhere on the opposite end.

(L) An unfinished cataracted spyglass! Kate really knows me.

(P) Not quite. It's a more of a, hm, how much do you know about optics?

(L) Not half as much as I will in three minutes, I'm guessing.

(P) Anybody?

(D) I know it's strange as shit the first time you get fitted for astigmatism lenses.

(H) I audited a glasswork and lens-grinding course when I was getting into stage lighting, but it was pretty bong-oriented.

(P) Ok, we'll put the group at intermediate to advanced then. Uhm, ok first let's see if me and The Boat didn't jostle it to death on the way here. Try holding the glassy end up to the fire. Shouldn't need to get it all that close, really.

^(H) Ooo, neat. Really glows.

^(P) Yeah, good. Just a dinky LED sandwiched in between two panes and an old SLR mirror feeding a little solar cell set into the bottom panel. Nothing particularly fancy so far, right?

^(T) I'm thinking our friend whispering sweet nothings to the poker over there may beg to differ.

^(P) Well, I assure you, that's not really the fun part, which might have you all equally transfixed. Any rough guesses so far?

^(H) A sheep-grade laser razor?

^(D) A really shitty ophthalmoscope?

^(P) Excellent guesses, but pretty far off the mark. This, flitties and toddlermen, is a somewhat analog cryptomathing.

^(T) Bullshit.

^(P) Well, semantically, sure, but no, my IT-savvy compadre. S'f'real.

^(L) What, do you flash Morse code into a webcam with it?

^(P) Nope nope. Hand it back or you'll never find out.

The man clearly has no appreciation for the sensual gravity of a glowy totem.

^(P) Thank you. Alright, in my handy sunglasses case I– shit. Oh right, cargo shorts. You see here I've got a bunch of old slides. Actually, mostly new slides just printed at high DPI on transparency and stamped into standard slide mounts for posterity's sake. Now Li, if you'll be so kind as to retrieve the slides of the old man in the leaky Speedo and you laughing at me puking into a drinking fountain at Six Flags.

^(L) Aww, that poor windbreaker. Really brought out the green in your neck fat.

^(P) Did you start that sentence assuming it was going to end up a compliment?

^(L) Wasn't it? Your jowls were so regal. What would your mother say if she knew you had them removed?

^(P) You leave my turtleneck phase out of this.

^(T) Alright goobers, focus or I'm gonna need a few more drinks to keep up.

^(P) Sorry. So, Li, if you'll go ahead and insert the Speedo slide into the slot up near the glowing end. Good. Now that first click is the mirror getting pushed down, just like how it'd work in a camera. So the cell's no longer getting light, but the big capacitor should be about charged for what we need. Now just press it in all the way and hold it for a second or two...

Must be the part where it ejects India ink and confetti when I happen to be looking right down the barrel.

^(P) Good. Heard that little second click?

^(H) No.

^(T) Yes.

^(D) I thought I did.

^(P) Well, that was it. The slide locked in front of a randomly checkered mask. Then the masked image hit a condenser lens and on the back focal plane met a little bead-curtain-looking screen of optic fibers stripped and scuffed on the side facing the light. With me so far?

^(L) Of course not.

^(T) Sort of. Is the back plane where it's upside down?

^(H) Shit, I should know this.

^(P) Not quite, Trina, it's actually the point where all the rays squeeze up cozy and it *starts* to flip.

^(H) Yeah, and you see the funky little dots.

^(P) Right. It turns out there's a hefty branch of microscopy dealing with those funky dots. For our needs it keeps things compact and ensures there's always something to work with in

the middle of the frame. Now here I guess they could've used more camera guts to just pipe out amplitudes from the fibers, but some sentimentalist had a multi-channel thermocouple sensor lying around with small enough leads on it to get a reading or two from each fiber, and I guess keeping the whole thing relatively low-tech in terms of chippery.

(L) So all that flibbertigibbet to make it click open a peephole to stare at a slide we already have in our hand?

(P) Nope, the peephole was always there, just to check the alignment. The click was this far panel unlocking just far enough to slip in a few folded sheets of paper.

(T) Deposit mode.

(P) Right. Now if we insert the slide of me barfing in the drinking fountain instead– Li? Thank you. We'll now hear two clicks, and the panel opens entirely to reveal your prize.

(L) A box of quick-drying fountain pen ink cartridges? Oh golly, I'd been squirreling away for months.

(P) Ah, no, that's part of the failsafe, anything else?

(L) Oop, yeh.

A used gum wrapper wadded around a grimy old bolt with a crusty rubber band. Kate's signature bouquet.

(D) What's it say?

(L) "Lick my throat sweat." And there's a little drawing of a butt with a welcome mat tramp stamp.

(T) I'd say frame it, but I'm almost done with this Trident.

(H) So what if you spill coffee on the slides or something?

As the only one familiar with the coffee stains upstaging the better part of any original varnish work in his kitchen, I can't tell if there's a tinge of klutzy self-deprecation under that discerning front.

(P) Well, that's kinda the fun part. As you might have guessed, you can load one of the ink cartridges into that cylinder doohickey down in the corner. It's a one-shot spring-loaded atomizer, so if you do need to reset the keys, you want to make sure to pull that out first.

(L) Which also explains why you've lined a piece of wood that would probably hold its nose at your mom's jewelry with gnarly yellow shellac?

(P) Yep. Well let's say your slides got a bit moldy and can't pass muster against the fairly forgiving blurriness threshold of the stored signature, or I guess more importantly if your secret barf memory has been compromised. All you need to do then is get a paperclip and punch in a PIN sequence on those four little gorgon nipple eye things just under the slide slot on the opposite face. Like...so. There goes the atomizer spring, and you'll note a little brass cover slid back.

(L) So everybody knows my PIN now?

(D) Not me, that was way too fast and blurred by gorgon boobs.

(P) No, it resets each time you use it. Type in a new PIN and the cover shuts. Now all you have to do to reset the electronic-tamper-proof EPROM holding the image keys is to leave it under the sun for a few weeks.

(L) Swell!

(P) Or a germicidal UV lamp for a few minutes. Or! You can get it done in seconds with this handy-dandy, particularly blinding and skin-cancer inducing quartz xenon strobe gun, which I had the honor of outfitting with a light-proof muzzle so you don't have to wear arc-welder's goggles to use it.

(L) Now Paul, I oughtn't be showered with hot-glued ionizing radiation guns in front of my beau like this. You need an extension cord?

(P) Not if my calculations are correct, but maybe just in case.

(L) That's what I like to hear.

(H) I'll grab you one.

^(T) So it's EMP-proof?

^(P) Maybe. I think the idea was having it be time-capsulable.

^(D) Can I be the first to say I do get it, but not really completely?

^(P) Me neither.

^(D) I mean is something supposed to be self-evident about what it's for besides magic shows for six-year-olds?

^(L) A paddle-sized monument to misused student labor?

^(T) It's two-key encryption, with probably more solder points than lines of code.

^(D) Which is?

^(T) Big part of how the secure internet works. Uh, almost like a hotel room safe but with a deposit slot like this. The management and whoever you feel like can get a key to the room, but you're the only one who sets the combination to the safe. Which, in this case, has a little mail slot in it. And, in this case the management can zap the door open with a ray gun if the guest lost their keys. Or whoever you may or may not like can do so for whatever nefarious pretext, but it sets off, what, the fire sprinklers I guess? No wait, well, ok, sure, but also a fire sprinkler inside the safe filled with ink, and presuming your valuables in there consist of messages written lightly on low-weight paper.

^(P) Couldn't have said it myself.

^(D) But those safes are always digital, and people must forget their PINs all the time and you have to trust the management could crack it.

^(T) Yeah, hopefully not without resetting the PIN while you're out at the gerontology museum. There, you gotta trust the hotel to a degree. But to a lot of people it's more assuring than leaving your jewels with the concierge.

^(P) But a little seedy.

167

^(T) Yeah, true. Your lock gets picked instead of the back office's. But the old days of goons in ski masks going after caches of passports and foreign currency are gone.

^(L) Traded for new days where nobody's really too excited to leave their shit behind a keyless door they never met before.

^(T) Sure. Or in our case not without jury-rigging some anti-shoplifting pop tags all over the place to blow if anybody opens the door without the guest key. And having derailed the analogy about as horrendously as possible, this box, inside a safe, inside a reputable hotel, would probably be the most discrete means of sending a message any of us would ever have access to, or the most tamper-proof at least.

^(P) Ok, that I couldn't have said better.

^(T) I know. You copied my notes in Comp Sci 121.

^(L) Yeah, don't be fooled Harry, Paul's a VCR-repair qualified pioneer of nascent interdisciplinary-department exploitation.

^(H) Huh?

^(T) A humanities adjunct in geek's clothing.

^(L) Like Indiana Jones. But with a less tedious day job as his secret persona?

^(P) Did he have a secret persona, technically? Or is he just an icon of the romanticized fieldwork era.

^(L) Yeah, yeah. I'm sure the Balkan Antiquities community will be forever indebted to your findings.

As usual, he diverts his favorite smile—narrow but almost cagey deep around the eyes—to whatever's on hand. In this case the Tic-Tac sized aperture on the flat outer face of the strobe gun's muzzle. Maybe registering some concern operating the thing in a huddle of firelight-dilated pupils, but satisfied with his handiwork. Drew does his best impressed-but-dismissive nodding retreat back to the last open stump near Anne, but just to watch us hold our breath for the sacral joining of plugs and final whirring clicks.

(P) There you go, Li. All primed. You can set five public keys for deposit mode and one private for retrieval. Kate's got her own prototype and one of the slides in there marked as her public key, so you can send the boxes back and forth if you want.

(H) Damn, it's like crypto vinyl. So cool that no one ever heard of it till after it was retro. And I've been saying hipsterism's dead since Dubya started selling his artwork.

(T) Looks like we're at the epicenter.

(H) So what can you call it? Cyphergraph-o-gram?

(L) Cryptocchio!

(P) Oh Jesus. Should I just leave it in a basket outside the next DEF CON?

(L) No way. He's already earned a cozy corner of my most prized shoebox. Ooh! Maybe Rob can train Gerdly to go pick up weed from the neighbors with it.

(P) Sure, why not? It might even hold together underwater so you can keep yourself entertained while doing the dishes. Or, if you get the whim up your britches, use it correctly. Let's not forget we're being lured into a totalitarian state.

(L) Well you're being toted into a lurid state.

(P) I... ok fine, two points.

(L) Damn straight. So what's all the rest in your field kit there?

(P) Oh, that's from me. Just a mylar mini hot air balloon kit with a few tweaks, it'll take a little while to set up.

Harry's fighting back drool from a quick peek, but he's in the right mood to concede this one's more spectacle and play my proxy offering fresh drinks to the fire gazers.

(L) Ah-hah. Balloon in the chimney, that was the apropos?

(P) Yup. Wouldn't have really been the same as that first sooty dildo creeping into view behind grandma during Scrabble. You know I don't think I ever found out if you two knew my folks were there for dinner that night.

(L) Bah! You double-booked on us and forgot. We drove by assuming you'd be half-asleep on a pile of Chaucer critiques and saw a Paul we'd never met. Braising a roast or something.

(P) Duck confit. My first and only attempt.

(L) Yeah, apron and everything, with the whole Paul clan probably wondering why he doesn't have any cordial upstanding chums who'd appreciate a break from Los Betos once in awhile and would certainly spice up the old family drollery.

(P) You never have met my family, have you? Huh.

(L) I have not.

(P) And that prompted the whole thing.

(L) You bet your sooty dongs it did. Turns out it's a lot tougher to find personalized helium balloons at nine on a Sunday than sex toys.

(P) "Missing you" wasn't it?

(L) Yeah. "Hang in there" was sold out.

Rob is sheepish coming through the door with the current of live jams ebbed to a solitary but peppy upper octave rambling on one of the less frequented blues scales.

(R) Hi. Rob.

(P) Paul.

(L) Paul's the one in the picture on the fridge where I have green hair and we're holding blocks of glacial ice.

(R) Oh. Nice to finally see the bottom half of your face.

(P) I wish I could say the same, but I don't want to hurt your beard's feelings.

(R) Thank you. His name is Ace.

^(L) You said it was Russert!

^(R) That's his middle name, obviously. Ace Russert Ah-fah-chuh.

^(P) Spelled A-F-A-C-E?

^(R) I don't know, it's never been spelled before. You guys seen Anne? I've got some pretty wailey Danish klezmer queued up, but it's feeling like an acoustic no-hitter in there and a couple of Cherraine's roadies say they've been crying to Anne's SoundCloud all week.

^(L) Over by the fire.

^(R) Thanks. Nice to meet you Paul.

^(P) You too.

Stewing with bat-cave decorum, but I can't say I mind with these two. Better hide the Irish sea chanty book for good measure.

^(P) Nice guy.

^(L) Yeah, actually a great roommate. Even cooks for us.

^(P) Someone always cooks for you.

^(L) I'm a suggestive shopper.

^(P) You know, it occurs to me that your other roommate, Dale?

^(L) Drew.

^(P) Drew. He must've ambled back up to us pretty quietly, and without his jacket.

^(L) Holy shit. Imagine what he may have seen and done before coughing awkwardly and retreating to the bathroom only to contemplate going back for it.

^(P) His shirt's inside out.

^(L) Fuhhhhk.

^(P) So they were into it?

171

^(L) I don't. No. There has to be a pitifully platonic explanation.

^(P) Yeah, the dork is strong with that one. Must've decided on a sweater and didn't notice them panting till the perfectly ill-timed moment. But we can dream, right? A young jay finds his nest aflutter and knocks beaks a bit for hospitality's sake before he remembers us outside and swoops off.

^(L) I don't know anyone who'd do that. Maybe you, but you'd have to be so drunk it'd be a borderline creepy buzzkill situation, and you'd pass out or somebody would start crying.

^(P) The art of flattery disclaims you, love.

^(L) You too, probably, jerk. I missed you, you know.

^(P) It's been like six weeks.

^(L) Twelve. And that's when I do my best missing.

^(P) All right you two-drink tearjerker, can you help me lug the rest of this out to the middle of the yard? Setting up there should at least help playing dumb with the neighbors if we need to.

^(L) Of course.

And of course it's not nearly as basic a contraption as he'd been playing it off. Satisfied at my tipsy, hearthy slow grin, he takes the unspoken go-ahead to do the assembly work without all the oratory, just muttering about 3D printed copper braiding on a translucent fiber-weave something or other skeleton which unfolds more or less like a Hoberman sphere wearing a preposterously droopy silver dress. Plus I think purposely unintelligible tidbits about some shady nano-division postdocs and an overfunded grant for "fanless lightning-rod heat-exchanger home AC sort of shit."

^(L) A what now?

^(P) Eh, so it's like a gasogene-shaped heat reclaimer thingy to convert waste heat off AC units to some white-hot molten mineral suspension then shine it into some intricately etched

3D printed funhouse of bizarrely compressed surface-area latticework with inlaid polished silicon.

⁽ᴸ⁾ A photovoltaic black box?

⁽ᴾ⁾ Well you could look inside, but it might boil your eye jelly before your retinas fogged over.

⁽ᴸ⁾ For household use?

⁽ᴾ⁾ Of course! Nine-inch ironclad insulation.

⁽ᴸ⁾ Of course.

⁽ᴾ⁾ Anyway, this thing's just a materials demo. Supposedly a proof-of-concept for the heat capacity of some such. I happened to be hosting the park-bench soiree where the whole thing originated and was the only one sober enough to take notes, so, reverse party-favor sort of thing I guess.

Fully extended it's like a five-foot chocolate truffle still in its foil, but with disproportionate dainty ties on the ends. On the top he affixes a thumb-sized PVC valve and on the bottom he slides in the only hardware: four slim but sizeable battery packs with zany 90s labels that would only look at home in the chassis of an RC off-roader, which are set in an X and already alligator clipped. He hits the one obvious switch and the thing goes blinding red, dwarfing the firelight with what seems like enough juice behind it to light a little-league diamond if not for the now purplish space-blanket lampshade. It starts crinkling out, sectors of the foil going rigid with a suddenness more like drawing a bow than any inflatable I've seen.

⁽ᴸ⁾ Jesus.

⁽ᴾ⁾ Seven-hundred fifty watts. Got the LED drivers on a cheap CPU heatsink grafted to the frame so it distributes as evenly as possible away from the batteries, which are the only real ballast. Once it's hot I'll disconnect the bottom two packs and it should fly.

⁽ᴸ⁾ Should?

⁽ᴾ⁾ Will fly. But the last one melted through a little bit about twenty feet up and did a really pitiful slo-mo version of the untied party-balloon death dance. I've been assured this new weave should do much better.

The crinkling's already done, and the thing's just barely oblong, bobbing with the wind in an anxious swivel. Last flourish from the box is a cartoonishly antique remote. The throttle's too caked over with its own rotted rubbery bushings and dust covers to function, leaving a big orange button, and a ludicrously long antenna.

(P) Here. I've got another one that can dim the LEDs, but I don't think we'll need it. The one-way valve triggers when the pressure hits two atmospheres or so, somehow maintaining an optimal density band for lift. Push the button and the valve stays open and the thing should sink. Ready?

The campfire crowd's stopped to gawk in the middle of migrating back inside on the promise of one of Anne's rousing hypnotic hymns. Rob peeks out, appraises the situation, and emerges, guitar in hand, leaving the door open and letting the first-of-the-night silence draw the rest of the nearby able-brained out with him. Anne cradles the guitar and plucks out a bow-legged carnival waltz in one of those moments of slipshod grace reserved for the cult of the rhythmic adepts, and with a Chvrches-caliber convulsive brain-bobbing to it.

(L) Ready.

Two last alligator clips and a pair of wire cutters to the ceremonial salmon zip tie and we have bobbling hot-car-interior-scented liftoff.

(L) Looks like MacGyver ought to be handing you the paperclip to the city.

(P) I really should've used the guidance valves. I've got the wiring diagrams and everything.

(L) Why?

(P) It's windier than I realized, and the high-heat-tolerance lining might not be so fun to catch without hot pads.

(L) Shoulda sprung for the double-ply.

(P) It's probably already hexadeca-ply or something.

(L) Ah, it'll be fine. Bask in the brisk evening golf claps, that's gotta be at least thirty feet.

(P) And counting. Be generous with the blow button once it's clear of the power lines.

(L) You got it. Care for a neck-aching stroll down the alley?

(P) You been reading my Christian Mingle profile?

(L) Really? I thought you knew it was me posting all those best-of begat lists.

(P) 4Jezebzy? Aww.

(L) Oh, make sure to latch it. Geordie's fond of the neighbor's snapdragons.

(P) Oh shit, me too, tactile-ly speaking. I probably haven't popped one since I was four.

(L) Me neither, maybe even never. Guess it doesn't matter how many times they tell you not to forget to stop and ruin the flowers.

(P) You've got a weirdly charming alley back here.

(L) I know, patently weird, right? I thought it was all the vines at first, but I think it's just that it's so windy but you can still see all the way through.

(P) Hm. Cool, yeah you're right.

It is a treat walking with something to periodically stop and watch that isn't a dog squatting. But something does reek of unwitting defensiveness here.

(L) You're still completely lost over Kate, aren't you?

(P) Sure, yeah.

(L) Which means you drove something like two-thousand miles for a pep talk from your favorite schadenfreude-riddled wine mate without admitting it to yourself?

⁽ᴾ⁾ Whatever you say, doc.

⁽ᴸ⁾ Did you ask her to come?

⁽ᴾ⁾ No, don't be ridiculous. Or, ok, I might have, but in a really obviously stupid joking way that would have made it more awkward for her to accept.

⁽ᴸ⁾ Great.

⁽ᴾ⁾ Li, we're pushing two-hundred feet at least.

⁽ᴸ⁾ Oh. Ok, I'll start with the button if you promise to soften a little to all that "life's too short" and "love's always been right between the couch cushions" crap. Trite's not necessarily wrong, right? Emotional junk food, but let's just assume we both've been too knee-jerk about it, ok?

⁽ᴾ⁾ I blame bad parroting. You really think I'm the one that needs to soften up?

⁽ᴸ⁾ Yes. Or, yeah, her too, but shut yourself up about her, this is Paul time.

⁽ᴾ⁾ Uh-huh.

⁽ᴸ⁾ Isn't there some counter-intuitive stone-cold bullshit mixed in with the nice guy bit?

⁽ᴾ⁾ Huh. Maybe. I know at least that waking up half-stoned and shivering on the back patio gets me pretty blustery.

⁽ᴸ⁾ Hey, you want your admittedly fantastic toy back or not?

⁽ᴾ⁾ Yes, yes, I do. Sorry. And yes, I'm aware I'm getting grumpier with what I'd thought was a measure of elegance.

⁽ᴸ⁾ Good. So drop that exasperated smirk and hear me out.

⁽ᴾ⁾ Are you levelling with me? This feels like uncharted and mildly clinical territory.

⁽ᴸ⁾ God, has anybody lately? And don't mistake my giddiness at the novelty of it for a blithe misfire. You two are half in love and in denial for I don't know who or what's sake.

Clearly you both have enough time on your hands for stupendously considerate acts, and I can't say I've ever felt more spoiled than tonight getting the whole Mr. Wizard in a Santa suit act without any bitching about dastardly academian shenanigans or any of the other customary agonizing.

(P) My pleasure.

(L) Look, I don't know. Maybe it's relief from some ball-busting streak at work or maybe you're road-weary or whatever. But if whatever it is is just amounting to some decades-dormant pubescent aftershock, it's gonna dry up quick. So whenever you catch up with yourself, make sure it wasn't just for some even-keel spring-cleaning vibe, nice as those can be. You're due for more than that, maybe not just love stuff, or with Kate, I don't know. Just don't mistake comfort for contentment. I don't want you getting that musty wistful aloof avuncular whatever the fuck it is. Either of you.

(P) Thank you Li. I'll withhold any smarmy shit on the matter.

(L) That you fucking better, tinklebutt.

Probably unrealistic of me angling for an all-out flummoxing. Dippy resignation will have to do. No minor feat in his case.

(P) So I've got a question.

(L) Shoot.

(P) Did you just mash the button once?

(L) That I did. Oh. More of a tap and check deal? Where'd it go?

(P) It was somewhere out by those power lines.

(L) Hm. I'm not sober enough to be sure, but I think that means we're clear of any major highways or water towers or haylofts at least.

(P) Good. Battery ought to be getting cheesed too.

Finally setting foot in the stubby little half-park off the

concrete drainage ditch. Always had a beckoning, who gives a hoot if it's a hellscape charm. But really hits its grimness potential with a deformed glowing sack of copper-threaded ABS hinges singeing the orange safety rubber off the baby swing's chain. I guess the huddled figure looking on is more or less a given. With one last wheeze the bag unshlups and manages an airborne ankle-scraping motion to its final perch on the hand bar over the slide.

(L) Oh shit. Uninvited guest.

(P) What, that's your corner or something? Or am I not up on curfew-spooked teenager lingo?

(L) No, crashed the party. History with Anne.

(P) Anne?

(L) Trina's sister. She played us the send-off just now.

(P) Ok.

(L) But uh, this one. Well I haven't really met her come to think of it. Just monumental gossip and I farted at her once.

(P) I always wondered how often that actually happens. Ok, I'll assume that leaves you unphased with her being catatonic, alone, and very pregnant.

(L) Yup.

(P) —on probably the last lump of urban gout in this little emotopia village? So I'll go and try not to burn my thumbs on the doodad. I'll assume you're somehow better equipped for an emotional parlay.

(L) Coward. If she's frothing, I'm telling her you're holding peanut butter and pickle juice.

(P) Two very difficult commodities to pack discreetly in saleable volume, I might add.

(L) Uh-huh.

We've been spotted. Can't be too chilling us meekly putzing to a fork in the conversation, with the flaming placid hot cheeto of good fortune as serene a calling card as you could hope for in a place like this. Still, that's a pretty jarred snap upright for someone lost in pleasant reflection. Especially if it's over Flappy Tom bidding a butt-honking yet chivalrous adieu, with an aftertaste of one of the grenadine-rich mixogasms Rob dared to set out as a technicolor liquid smorgasbord this far from Halloween. Better fly in low, probably not my brand of flak.

^(L) Hey. Ewha, right?

^(E) Yeah. Yours?

^(L) The gasbag or the thing melting to the swing set? Yes to both anyway, I guess. Or, well, he is single.

And with a foot up two rungs, angling the ass into a perfect pre-middle-age testament against whatever cut of dungarees were on clearance at Ross eight years ago, it's really no surprise.

^(E) Oo la-la.

^(L) So we haven't really been introduced, Li.

^(E) Pleasure.

Well. Warmer than I might have expected. Guess I deserve the squirmy seat here. The hell kind of hand have I got to play anyhow? "I feel like a shithead saying it, but I've heard quite a bit about you, in the gushy standoffish 90-proof gossip sense, that is."

^(L) I like your name.

^(E) Thanks. Sorry I crashed your party.

^(L) Did you?

^(E) Mm-hm. I live down the street and saw the lights. Sorta been getting cabin fever to be honest. Boss's been adamant about reducing my hours. Wasn't counting on skirting an ex, but you guys do have a hell of a house band.

^(L) Yeah, we pay in vintage grooming supplies and mummified sundries.

Ok, not technically a non-starter. But still, Jesus.

(L) I should probably tell you something, doubt it's gonna brighten your day any though.

(E) Shoot.

(L) That bassist you swerved out of the back alley with had just pulled a pretty icy and dickish breakup with a girl who's as far as I can tell a saint-in-waiting.

(E) Fuck. Like nasty icy or white rapper icy?

(L) Maybe more the second one. Too dry and reptilian to even earn the moisture points. Let's say a chilled tin of horny-toad flavored enema powder.

(E) Is that a reptile?

(L) Ehh, yeah I think. It has a neck, so let's say yeah.

(E) Well you're welcome to pass it on that Mr. Toad promised me leftover s'mores cupcakes then ran off puking through his fingers after a Pappa John's guy drove by.

(L) You'd think he'd have a sense of propriety about something like that.

(E) Nah, could have just as easily been me if it were Domino's. To his credit, he was probably way more plastered than I realized. Not much warning with a quiet drunk like that.

(L) Yeah, you know I can't remember seeing him do much tonight besides gulping and pouring, and somehow fully akimbo throughout. I wonder if he was working up the nerve or just boiled over.

(E) Who knows. I must've been taking his garbled come-ons as eccentric disaffection or something.

(L) Maybe it's a sort of autopilot charm. May be all he's got, who knows. I've known so many happy-go-lucky drummers and bassists. I'll assume he's just at odds with the typecast and there's some punk chick out there just waiting to smack some angst into him.

(E) I'm sure you mean well, but that still kind of pisses me off.

(L) Yeah, sorry. I'm probably too quick to assume a silver lining or noble underdog or whatever. I'll just wish he gets a good smacking one way or another.

(E) Works for me.

With madcap blundering of this scale at any point in the past, Paul would've been injured or kicking something by now. But here he is, contraption all reclaimed except a blown-out patch twenty degrees up from the basket and half-folded into its no-nonsense bagpipe valise form. Man boy becomes man eagle scout.

(L) Will she fly again?

(P) Think so. Frame's probably intact. Got most of the gunk off the slide. It just left a little funky bluing.

(L) Well aren't you the urban achiever. Oh, eh, Paul, Ewha.

(P) Hi.

(E) Your bag freaked me the fuck out. Couldn't you put a propeller on it or something?

(P) Yeah, it's in the works. I left the throttle in the hands of an inexperienced button masher.

(L) Oh? I seem to recall a certain Firehouse Frenzy pinball leaderboard that speaks otherwise, not to mention the ratio of quarters invested per increased top-ten average high.

(P) God. Nobody should ever bring graph paper to a bar. But, yeah, I am sorry we spooked you.

(E) Hard to even start getting mad at this one, eh?

(L) Nah, don't fall for it. He goes for that slow-burn conniption.

^(E) Hm. Whatever dragon needs feeding I guess.

^(P) I'll take that as a near-miss compliment.

^(E) By all means, slow-Burning Man.

Nothing really shifting in the thin splay of moonlight or piddly breeze clawing a few upper boughs. The barometer might be doing some triple-time samba though.

Or parlaying a toughie on the outs has some leavening factor. Whatever it is easing the gloom gets full marks for fluidity and a difficult terrain bonus.

^(L) You mind if we raid your kitchen for ice water and saltines before we head back? Remy usually doesn't slump off the piano stool before three.

^(E) Yeah, that'd be nice, actually. But you may have to settle for aquavit and Twizzlers.

^(P) Darn.

Not either of the tidy or bohemian extremes I'd pictured. Neat on average, a few sparse but homey landscapes sprinkled in, and understated with a squint-for-immersiveness quality at that. Gonna go with early works of a fresh grad from a European academy only second tier for being accredited after the advent of the metal paint tube, having a handful of alumnis' works elbowing up past whatever slop-drop glut half the world's seasoned curators are wishing they hadn't amassed in the swirly lude-a-lope through their early career. Nice drapes too.

Pauls' looking antsy. I'll go for broke and say it's that traveler's dilemma when you're too dog-tired to change course and realizing you're stuck somewhere that doesn't involve sleeping in a real bed anytime soon.

^(L) You know, Paw-Paw. We're actually not too far from Harry's and he's got two-thirds of a five-piece sectional in his laundry room. And I know where his spare key's at.

^(P) Huh. Actually sounds nice. He won't mind?

182

^(L) Fuck no. Company just gives him an excuse to tear up the kitchen. I'll text him. I LIKE YOUR PLACE EWHA!

^(E) THANKS! GIMME JUST A SEC.

^(P) Man, how can she afford this?

^(L) Two bedrooms and a raspberry bush? Paul, this town's two rib joints and a busload of commuters away from being zoned as a commune. As much as we joke about it, you can't really fully gentrify on willow density and laissez-faire leash laws.

^(P) Guess not. Be vigilant though. Life's too cuddly and precocious here not to start popping up on top-ten hep-gawk getaway clickbaits.

^(L) God forbid they have to start baking fresh scones at the cafe. But yeah, waiting for a table at the catfish place would be a travesty. Shit, you've tripped my inner inordinate nativism routine. Thought I'd tapped some real Magister Ludi wayfarer's zen too.

^(P) Bah. Proto-neo-liberal archetype dripping with impotent mysticism Hesse probably couldn't have foreseen turning so piggish, which Stephenson had the sense to slap lipstick on and take to the state fair.

^(L) What, that recent one?

^(P) No, before that.

^(L) Ohhh, right. Monks. Well, despite it being one his finer romps, quantum mysticism's not so bonery to me either. Hey! Thank you.

Scandalously mismatched art-deco saucers and the platter and everything. I guess you pick up a few tricks with globetrotting parents.

^(L) Why's this so much more enticing than Rob buttering up the night's bong-onauts into monosyllabic profundities?

^(E) Come again?

⁽ᴸ⁾ Sorry, went a little heavy on the wax myself. I meant to say this looks lovely and your sense of easygoing hospitality is staggering.

⁽ᴱ⁾ Comes naturally with a pinch of stir-crazy.

⁽ᴾ⁾ No lucky someone hovering nervously and catching plates? Sorry if I'm not pirouetting around your unmentionables.

⁽ᴱ⁾ Nah, fine by me. Cale's off to preach the undead video game fan-fiction gospel in sunnier 95-plus climes.

⁽ᴾ⁾ Woof. How'd you possibly resist joining on the path of herbaceous scarcity?

⁽ᴱ⁾ Well, my patient disinterest in almost everything he had to say sort of festered into a kind of knee-jerk authoritativeness.

⁽ᴸ⁾ And that was that?

⁽ᴱ⁾ No, it backfired. He'd always been sweet, and this got him fawning or trying to spar like he thought I had an itch for some emotional S&M or something. I mean, maybe I do, maybe we all do, but I was just pissed usually, and I'd liked something about his blunt conventional front to begin with.

⁽ᴾ⁾ I'm picturing an Episcopal church with weak knees wearing a Hawaiian shirt.

⁽ᴱ⁾ Yeah, or more like a big red barn full of Dr. Thunder barrels and aisles of shrink-wrapped media arts textbooks. I don't know. He was always crazy about me. I mean, even after he had every right to get bored or complacent. It's not easy passing that up.

⁽ᴸ⁾ So, in the end it was his literary fetishes, or?

⁽ᴱ⁾ No, he left. I didn't kick him out or anything. Just finally scared him off not keeping my disgust quite in check. Took a minute. Sheer relief the first week.

⁽ᴾ⁾ Now more of a morbid acceptance of what awaits?

⁽ᴱ⁾ Shit, you should charge by the hour.

^(P) Yeah, sadly I lent myself to a higher calling.

^(E) Flying neon canker sores over peoples' houses?

^(P) In more ways than one. Close enough to how it feels steering Hittite epistemology dissertations from blegh to meh.

^(E) I'd ask you to enlighten me, but I might need a C-section and a few stiff drinks first.

^(P) Shoot, I left the ether in my other pants.

Nice of them keeping it so cute for civility's sake. We're into a drowsy hunky dory at least. They're both too exhausted to show any tooth, and there's no way not to be obtrusive if I keep bringing up Bropop.

^(L) I'm sorry, I'm sort of monumentally curious if you feel ready or, how ready, or, shit, never mind.

^(E) To move on without a couch sore to feed?

^(L) No, but he did leave a hell of a divot now that you mention it. But I mean, you seem like the type to take it all in stride and just be the cool mom, but, something's gotta freak you out, right?

^(P) Excuse my friend. Sense of tact's got a low crit roll.

^(E) No, it's fine, too much tact and you end up with a bunch of rogues doing backstab do-see-dos.

I can't tell if she's accepting the deflection or reflecting on whatever it was I asked. So this is what sudden admiration feels like.

^(E) I do get miffed with all the griping in the childbirth class. Of course it's living hell with let's call it a continuous hangover on top, but it gets to me how surprised some of them seem. A weird one-upmanship I guess, or just show-and-tell venting. But it's got such a cliquey feel sometimes. Plenty of perks in the cult of self-perpetuation, and I've never really given two shits about partying all night, but you see the alienation. Not really minding all their old friends still out there stirring shit up without them.

185

(L) And not realizing they'll regret it in forty years when they can't find a bridge partner worth a damn?

(E) Something like that. But, uh, shit, what were you asking?

(L) Anything really keeping you up at night? Besides grotesque tech demos on rundown moonlit playgrounds?

(E) And besides general overwhelming discomfort and borderline incontinence? And sensing my personality fracturing under the pressure of immense hormonal tides?

(L) Sorry, my empathy gland has severe limits.

(E) Nah, more fun to vent on the innocent. But ok, yeah, more than once I've gotten more than reasonably concerned I'll do a passable job on the day-to-day stuff, then totally fall flat in those sappy touchstone moments. Like all the pithy sage advice is supposed to start bubbling up spontaneously.

(P) Maybe having a three-foot self-inflicted misery machine underfoot just has that effect?

(E) Yeah, or I watched just enough Global Guts reruns growing up to flush out any of the family standbys.

(L) I'm sure there's at least few cases of parents making it all up and doing just fine. Half the gems I inherited are all crabby 80's TV narc-sounding innuendos.

(P) That's... no, no, example please or I call bullshit.

(L) Oh, you wish. Probably twice a week, more through puberty, my dad sees a haughty, sex-charged beer ad or something and turns to me with "That's a table nobody's gonna want to remember sleeping on," or "That's how you end up with your gramma signing your paychecks," or just "and that's what a room full of screw-ups looks like".

(P) Ok, that does sound like your dad.

(E) That sounds like *my* dad, with a slightly more lubed stick up his ass.

^(P) You know the only good advice I ever remember getting was to lightly gnaw the tip of my tongue to get to sleep, or it could've been to sleep without drooling. Maybe both. Shit, I don't remember.

^(E) The fuck?

^(P) No, serious, it sorta works. But I remember waking up with a bloody dribbling hamburgerized loll once and swore it off. Might've come from my great aunt.

^(E) Is that advice for me, or for me to give?

^(L) Cautionary anti-advice?

^(P) Beats me.

^(L) You can't keep beating yourself forever, friend.

^(P) Har har.

^(E) So only chew your own tongue until you're half asleep?

^(P) It is senseless enough to ring poignant.

Which puts us at conspiratorial new-buds smiles. Probably something to savor if it ever happens not drunk or distracted to the right state of abandon. I'd worry quitting on a high note might send a half-assed intimacy phobia signal, but Paul's barely holding his eyes in sync despite his tongue. A bit of veiled eyebrow theatrics should get him up and moving bedward without his trademark sweet-and-sour sarcasm tightrope.

Christ, how did my camaraderie get so intricate over the years? Good thing it's so tittering her doing the preseason forty-tire two-step through it, or I'd be getting the drunk knocked out of me realizing the lion's share of my jocular digs are coming across way more conniving than intended lately.

^(P) What are– oh? Nah, Iduwanneh, my tea's still warm.

^(L) No buts, mister, and Ewha's mugs have immaculate insulation.

^(E) My God, you're right.

187

^(L) Plus I'm drunker than you and you started nodding off first, which is a Class B party foul.

^(P) Bah! When I'm tenured such constructs shall be stricken from the vernacular.

^(L) That's right big guy, just as soon as you go night-night.

^(P) Flagrant bourgeoisie child-revering hobnobbery. Thanks for the tea Ewha, you have a lovely home in dire need of a prime coat of spittle and diaper leakage. Please excuse my companion's crooking me off the threshold without my ballooning gear, she has a proprietary implacability, or implacable propriety, I'm not fully certain but will make sure you're the first to ascertain when I am.

^(L) Ok, Jolly Twit, we get it. Glad we ran into you Ewha.

^(E) You know my friends usually call me Evie.

^(L) Really?

^(E) Yeah, anything else they tried ends up sounding like toddler babble.

^(P) Then Evie, we beg your leave on account of waning civility—solely of our purview—and bid you the warmest of beddy-byes.

^(E) Night guys. Li, stop by if you ever feel like wallowing in pumpkin rolls and emotionally undaunting Netflix filler.

^(L) Ooo, I'm not one to take such an offer lightly, y'know.

^(E) Good. Really, come over any time. The doorbell never wakes me up so don't worry about my delicate state or whatever.

^(L) You got it, I'll bring extra canned pumpkin guts.

^(E) Deal.

12

Dear Kate,

Please bear with the whole outmoded pen and paper approach here, Roommate Rob nearly electrocuted himself turning a ceiling fan into a multi-faceted disco apparatus and managed to smelt enough copper to render an impressive block of the circuit breaker inert in a feat our renter's insurance flunky dubbed "disturbingly reckless". As such, laptop juice is at a premium for the moment, and anyway I'd been missing my 50th Anniversary Disneyland Pen with the floaty biplanes, etc.

To it: if Paul's acting funny lately I deny any involvement. Unless he's generally manned up and made himself more emotionally available and started wearing age-appropriate underwear or stopped wearing underwear altogether. In which case, you're welcome and don't think I don't remember you confessing him getting you all hot and bothered just riding shotgun in his cat-puke wagon way back when.

If, however, he's same-old, then you have my explicit scrunch-nosed triple nod to unprompted dead-armings or shoe smooshings on my behalf (preferably followed by life-congealing ultimata and inevitable teary embraces regardless of the outcome).

SRSLY THO 4RLZ: sorry for stirring up all possible shit.
I know you've both been pretty mum on mushy stuff in general
lately and I don't know what's got into me thinking I know
best, blah, blah, blah. This here's in the spirit of full disclosure
I guess, but if you two have been cozying up on the reg for
months now and are just keeping me out of it as snooty
punishment for not visiting enough, then fine and I hate you
both forever and wish you the best with all my heart and expect
to give the most party-chilling/lugubrious toast at the faith-
ambivalent partnership commitment ceremony of your reckoning.

However it goes, fitting Paul's dodges and rebuffs together is not exactly a precise science. As you're well worn of,
I'm sure. So good luck on whatever nebulous bumper boatery
you end up facing.

In other news, the party he ditched you for was admittedly bitchin, with highlights including couples slow dancing to
Lithium (with jarring piss-faced head bangs miraculously fused
into swing throws and appropriately grungy tango fights on the
yelly parts; short video clip on miniSD enclosed in the event of
professional curiosity).

Roommate couple that shall not be addressed as such
has since absconded on an inaugural legal recreational weed
pilgrimage while our home-team band that shall settle on
a name pending the outcome of a highly doctored poll is
mini-touring the middle-most flaccid jazz circuit under the
alias "Grimbline y los Chiflados", leaving the block/town/my
perception thereof oddly becalmed.

Roomy Drew may be going gradually unhinged despite
a favorable reception to his and boyfriend Hargibold's literary
concoctions and perhaps too steady work-as-needed optimizing
acoustics for corporate pep-rally luncheons in the city. Having
put that down intending to spare you the details, I realize I
must digress full back-flop, in hopes you'll burn this letter
sentence-by-sentence as your read. I say "unhinged" as in
there's been a few manic non-sequiturs sidling by that I count

myself as at least functionally empariffic enough to have missed anything like it earlier on. I'll give an example. It is par, but maybe the most distinct: In the snack line at the movies, to the let's say morbidly nondescript woman in front of us, apropos of not a goddamn thing, he says "Better pick something sweet!".

Harge was in attendance, dazing off at a cardboard triptych of bulbous anthropomorphic shrimp bandits or quark farmers or whichever they're on to. I can say with certainty they were cuddly enough to keep it PG while getting their teeth kicked in. So Hayree doesn't really register the oddity and does a sidelong retort thing, thinking Drew'd been talking to him, which would have been the least bizarre reconstruction for a half-alert brain, given who was standing where. This throws the woman further, as if the guy offering unsolicited enthusiastic obvious grandpa-isms was also a gifted ventrilo-schizo.

We got between there and the seats without incident, or with Drew's uncharacteristic bombast just too low key for any more red-flagging. Then, when the house lights came up at the end, he just popped up and traipsed off down the aisle and out into the night without looking back, while the inevitable peppy second credits song hadn't kicked in yet to rouse Hayre. Since then it's just an infrequent Tourette's-ish spurt, almost passable as glib except that it's about 180 degrees out of character. Not every day, but enough to be unnerving, especially sharing a four-inch chicken wire and meringue wall.

Update: felt like a shit unloading on finely aged stationary about a friend sitting out on the porch hammering out an Innocents Abroad retread concerning Jupiter's post-colonial era, as if he was beholden to delicate psychosocial mores. He was, in a sense, but didn't make it feel like prying either. Long overdue blubbery tell-all for both of us, it turns out. In hindsight, I may not have owned up to any more than a vague sense of mortality and chafing down my wits in various digital voyeurship roles. He unloaded about having been on an old-school anti-psychotic for the better part of his post-pubescent life and went off it cold turkey recently against his shrink's better judgement on account of some nagging tremors and a carnal penchant for inordinately salted everything it apparently piques. For my part I was steadfast, stoic, staunch, stalwart, staid, etc. in offering bloated reassurance and stark reminders of my daunting ignorance on the subject. Needless to say, we are both paragons of humane tenderness after the exchange, and mutual corners are avowed occupied indefinitely—OUJELLY?

You know, for all the corners I've sworn to inhabit or facsimile thereof, I can't help but feeling they outnumber the uncredentialed coaches I've collected in mine. But let's face it, and strap your feelers in tight now, you're the only one I really need holding up my spit bucket anyhow.

But ok, keeping this all about me, I did feel thrust into the deep wearing naught but, let's say, a metaphorical pair of novelty jumbo New Year's glasses. It's surely all for the best getting it all out in the open, but did I blunder into an unspoken obligation to decommission future meltdowns or artfully defuse them with that metered, pander-resistant hostage negotiator rapport? God forbid. He did mention he's calling the trial a bust and going for another in a long series of wean attempts, so I should probably come off it and let the guy be, dammit.

I hope you'll excuse all the homefrontery. I really did have every intent of just laying it on distastefully thick about Paul and leaving you nonplussed enough to put our friendship in jeopardy. But, you know, life brawh.

On a lighter note, do you recall Paul confiding in us how in tatters he was when he realized his dad had mis-taught him to count to 10 through 90 before 11? If you don't, forget I mentioned it and burn the letter again.

Signing off for now, you lose light faster than you'd think up in these here hills, and the sub-lumen LED shard in my 80-cent curlicue desk lamp is inching me past the bounds of frugal sensibility.

Word to your mother if she still puts out.

Tshya,
Li

13

Guess I wouldn't have noticed until she hit stride on it, but Jen's dishing out with a clomping, sedate weariness that can only be further described as that campy, outmoded sisterly balm I've been starving for and never would have let on about since admitting to myself I've moved here for good.

And on the best rooftop table with the best plate of whiskered silt beast still steaming while the normally starchy waiter jaunts off, humming his dippy repertoire of cult Broadway clunkers reserved for the between-services crowd. Maybe something to be said for taste begets intimacy.

She draws rapturously on a stub even a veteran smoker would have taken a close look at first—would be well past Joe's ankles if it weren't an off-brand's distant cousin. No perceptible shame in violating probably a Marvin-the-Martian sized stretch of the de facto public smoking propriety scrolls, letting it hover over a virgin fillet, with the ash about ready to dangle, and a row of biddies nearby but assuredly upwind—dreary, duly disaffected, and bedazzled—none of which would ever say anything. At least two of them must have their reasons, or who having lived this long may have always found it noxious to begin with, to not think twice on glaring nakedly in unison. Or it's just the horrifying kernel of truth to "it'll stick that way" in motion, apparently a rare mom-ism with more sense to it than eight-year-olds think they've gotten wise to. Does make me wonder if it's worth venturing a pervasive resting bitch face overdiagnosis theory to Jen, but it would probably lay plain my spacing out. As a topical pivot-upon-entre it may go gracefully, but probably too rocky a landing zone to get any footing. Not that I haven't known a few sour-at-easers, but they sure as shit weren't clamoring for unflagging solidarity from the occasionally pouty crowd.

⁽ᴸ⁾ Sorry, I'm gonna be totally honest, I just completely glazed over once the food landed. Must've been hungrier than I thought.

⁽ᴶ⁾ Can't blame you. I think I was starting to ramble a little anyway.

⁽ᴸ⁾ No, I was actually reveling in getting down to some uninhibited shit-talking after a pretty hefty dry spell. Please, pile that dirt. I want to stand on top and smirk at everybody from it. You said Anne knew, right?

⁽ᴶ⁾ I don't see how she couldn't have. Ok, well in the food-service vein, you know how you said you felt when Harry laid out that soup souffle thing all apologetically like it was pauper's porridge.

And like the Sheriff of Nottingham was about to peek in from the kitchen window with an accusatory sniff at the remnants of cubed ham on the cutting board.

⁽ᴸ⁾ Oh you mean the meager potato-meets-skin on double pork, mushroom, and orange roe with eggy unsweet rice pudding, buttermilk, and feta fluff he had the audacity to drizzle over chopped mixed greens and call a meal?

⁽ᴶ⁾ Besides the marble rye melt.

⁽ᴸ⁾ A fawning afterthought. But do go on, Jeanette.

⁽ᴶ⁾ Oh God, you peeked? That's why I pretend I don't have a driver's license half the time.

⁽ᴸ⁾ Ah, own it. Plenty of just-Jen's and -iffers putzing around already.

⁽ᴶ⁾ Yeah, sure. Thanks Grandma.

⁽ᴸ⁾ Any time, pumpkin.

⁽ᴾ⁾ But, anyway, that's about how I felt hearing it come from her. I mean, she gets up there pouring her heart out, but still just as cool and polished as the band. It's transcendent as hell, damn near flawless, and as shoed-in for some big contract as a biased friend can think, or at least for scrounging up a living at it and all that.

⁽ᴸ⁾ But not really the same old egos in space story, is it?

⁽ᴶ⁾ No, not really, but it seems like part of it's eating at her still. Maybe there's less glitz than you'd expect, but that in some way makes it easier to worry about her losing touch a little.

⁽ᴸ⁾ Can't just call it an undistilled moment in the sun for now?

⁽ᴶ⁾ Nah, I don't know. She's probably still a bit miffed over a kinda brush-off I'd rather not go into.

⁽ᴸ⁾ Not asking you to... directly. But was I there for that?

⁽ᴶ⁾ Yeeah, yes.

⁽ᴸ⁾ Ok. Just if it's the moment I'm thinking of, it was damn weird in general. Which I'm sure must be a huge relief.

⁽ᴶ⁾ Wow, yeah, like a weight on my chest has been inched a little off-center.

⁽ᴸ⁾ But ok, sorry, not-prying over. But good, alright, something totally unrelated: I was meaning to ask if you or Anne maybe had any idea where the hell Rob's been going lately?

⁽ᴶ⁾ Oh, shit, yeah I might. Why, is Trina pissed?

⁽ᴸ⁾ That's a tough one. I guess. I'm only getting barfy eye-rolls bringing it up. They're still hiding their sappiness worse each morning, but then he's rushing off probably four hours before I've ever seen him use an exterior door and gone half the night, most nights. It's almost as if he's started working split shifts at a real job, but aside from the fact that he's probably never heard of a split shift, his soul doesn't seem even remotely mangled.

(J) It's the opposite? All pepped up and a little more swagger than usual?

(L) Hoh, yes. Crystal ball's spinning out freebies today or what? More please? I'd offer my first born's first-choice preschool seat.

(J) Hah, ok, but I'm giving it to a dried newt and nobody better ask any questions.

(L) Fine, sure, sure. C'mon, c'mon, spill 'em.

(J) No, it's not like that. Or, I came by it honestly anyway. There was some super-lame macho nerd pow-wowing going on at the party after you went off chasing that blimp with your friend from out of town.

(L) Uh-huh.

(J) At some point, Drew started getting into a book he'd been reading on old-school radio tradecraft snafus, sounded like the electronics espionage version of all the weird pre-Wright Brothers planes from the old newsreel clips. Big goofy waffle antennas mounted on roving horse teams, that sort of thing. I don't remember which one it was, but at some point Rob said something along the lines of "I'm gonna do that. I'm doing that. I have to. I'm totally doing that." Which, of course, no one took seriously.

(L) Oh shit. And why would they. That's basically stoner for "I might fervently watch a short YouTube video of someone else doing that, and maybe even leave a smug, but encouraging comment."

(J) Right, but, sounds like–

(L) He's doing that. Jesus. He's probably up there right now. Tallest hills just across the water. Roads are kinda shit, so hardly any hiker traffic.

(J) Yup.

⁽ᴸ⁾ And he's always bitching about the shitty reception on the highway.

⁽ᴶ⁾ Uh-huh.

⁽ᴸ⁾ Well at least he's got his CPR card.

⁽ᴶ⁾ What good's that gonna do him up there alone?

⁽ᴸ⁾ Tragically timed recognition of his juvenile sense of misplaced confidence?

⁽ᴶ⁾ From anyone else that'd be pretty off-putting.

⁽ᴸ⁾ It's a gift.

⁽ᴶ⁾ If you say so.

⁽ᴸ⁾ Somebody's gotta sheepdog all the deadpan ironists. Lately I catch them veering off so vapid they just start saying pathetic things about themselves with no inflection whatsoever.

⁽ᴶ⁾ Isn't that what deadpan is?

⁽ᴸ⁾ Well sort of, but it's not like you need to wear a veil in a convent, or, let see, throw a masquerade in a monastery?

⁽ᴶ⁾ What? Are they all wearing their hoods normally, or? Can you English that please?

⁽ᴸ⁾ Let's say the deadpan alignment chart has one very vacuous extreme. Or, ok, taking an axe to most of the limbs of my analogy, there's a point where it's like winking through a threadbare veil.

⁽ᴶ⁾ What is?

⁽ᴸ⁾ When, say, sarcasm evaporates to some chalky residue of disjointed meme speak and sloppy pith impressions.

⁽ᴶ⁾ Who's Pith?

⁽ᴸ⁾ Anyone's.

⁽ᴶ⁾ What? Oh, like pithy. Ok, then I want Sheepdog 101. Do I need to start watching more Dragnet reruns or something?

⟨L⟩ Can you even call them that anymore?

⟨J⟩ On Channel Nine they do.

⟨L⟩ They're still playing Dragnet?

⟨J⟩ They do a whole grab bag of vintage nap-hour delights. My lunch breaks are usually a lot less scenic than this.

⟨L⟩ But no less pithy, I'd think.

⟨J⟩ Well, after soaking up more of a cross-section than I ever would have hoped for, I do think that all the wholesome greatest-gen banter probably had as much aimless fluff as anyone else's.

⟨L⟩ Huh, yeah, guess it'd be hard to tell for sure. Ok junior sheepdog, name that bird.

⟨J⟩ What bird? I only see doves.

⟨L⟩ No, don't you hear that? The one that sounds like its honking a beak full of rancid dicks in a pachinko hall.

⟨J⟩ Oh yeah. Euyygh. Has to be a heron, right?

⟨L⟩ No idea.

⟨J⟩ But how exactly does a bird come by that many old dicks to begin with?

⟨L⟩ Well obviously she was once a fair young street hooker who crossed the wrong fishmonger and fell under his curse.

⟨J⟩ What, stole his wallet?

⟨L⟩ No, nono, no. Stole a cod– his prize cod.

⟨J⟩ And, then he gave her dicks? Multiple dicks? Fish dicks?

⟨L⟩ Nah, he just turned her into a heron. Couldn't shake her knack for getting dick, I suppose.

⟨J⟩ But didn't know what to do with them once she got 'em?

(L) Yeah, a pity really. Could there really be a simpler explanation for a creature ending up sounding that excruciating?

(J) I don't know. Little bit of a Queen of the Estuary vibe in there. Maybe it just translates a little flakey coming from bird-ese.

(L) I'm not sure if that's patent cheerfulness or a remarkably high tolerance for miserable noises.

(J) I'm the eldest of five. Plus three parakeets, two cockatoos, a small feral cat dynasty and whatever dogs would have us, as my mom put it.

(L) As someone who once lived next to a guy with a territorial roof-dwelling peacock, I can say with confidence I know exactly what your childhood was like.

(J) Oo, still, must have been tough.

(L) We called him Duck, which got a rise out of his owner in that clenched, ear-steamy way which I think you only see any more in adults who spent more time watching cartoons where that happens than actually seeing people interact.

(J) I see. Very neighborly of you.

(L) Nah, we all lightened up. He turned out to be a formidable 40K ally.

(J) No shit? I wouldn't have guessed you'd go any deeper than digging out the old Magic deck once in awhile.

(L) Yeah, me neither. I'd say it's more a chronic Stockholm Syndrome for the de rigueur tabletop preference of a given gang's alpha dork.

(J) By junior high, we'd amassed about three closets' full of warped overlays and mismatched figures and handmade tokens and transcriptions of chewed up manuals with official cul-de-sac ruling committee council minutes in the margins.

(L) Damn, I'm jealous of your clearly storied and character-building upbringing. And I'm sorry but I grossly misjudged you when we met.

^(J) Ugh, yeah, I think I milked the whole lemonade lip gloss routine more than I'd meant to.

^(L) Well I didn't want to say anything, but you might've been pushing appletini footbath for a minute there.

^(J) Yum.

^(L) Anyway, I did always end up getting tired with all the tape-measure diplomacy, but there's something to be said for going full war room with chipboard on sawhorses.

^(J) True. No mistaking it for lackadaisical rainy-day family time.

^(L) Well, here's to not too boldly proclaiming your tastes, lest they be diluted, dissembled or worse.

^(J) Hear hear! Rhubarbinis on me! And may we get too tanked to remember me ordering them.

^(L) That's almost the spirit. And may the name-draggers forget their galoshes and workday jeans.

^(J) Sure, yeah, may they!

^(L) It's drag or bedraggled, man.

^(J) Rabble rabble!

^(L) And down with the underlying conceit in anything resembling a testimonial, even the knee-squeezing misty eyed ones.

^(J) Yeah! Presumably! I have no idea what the hell you could possibly mean by that.

^(L) I mean we must thwart the relentless dissertators before they swallow themselves whole!

^(J) Hyargh!

^(L) To the understowed discontentionalist anti-social media-tors!

^(J) Yeah! Like that angry letter to the city about bird carcass clean up that I ended up not sending because I was so embarrassed of sounding old, or just incurably crass.

(L) Yes, that's exactly what I meant while distractedly slobbering those words into a slogan.

(J) Good! I'm going to stop falsetto shouting now because I've never felt so dizzy and hoarse all at the same time!

(L) Fine with me!

(J) So, distracted, huh? Crabs or something?

(L) You know, maybe. I was thinking it had been a slice of mid-relishing ennui over the bitchiness of such moments probably getting rarer as you learn to appreciate them. But yeah, crabs squares with the facts a little better. I'm gonna have to start calling you Doctor knows what's wrong with me, MD.

(J) That's so pleasantly dumb. Hats off to ya.

(L) Cheers. Sorry, I forgot how quick Sigge is with those refills.

(J) No, don't let me slow you down. I could do pretend toasts to vague convictions all night.

(L) Flattered, but I think I'm tapped. And I believe our fellow patrons have swiveled against our ruckus to the brink of decency.

(J) My God, like a little patch of stiff wool sunflowers in revolt.

(L) I think the one in the oyster print scarf's got our backs.

(J) Here's hoping. By the way, whatever happened to Harry showing up? I feel like he'd naturally counteract their humbuggery without realizing it.

(L) Yeah, he could out-sidelong glance those tramps any day. But, oh shit, apparently I'm still a child of the AIM era, who assumes it's normal for text conversations to awkwardly piddle out at some point.

Sure enough, a queue of causally interwoven prompts, disgustingly GIF laden and emoji drunk and wholly lacking any arguable decisiveness, planning, or resolute terms whatsoever for the past several days. Probably half of my rolodex is now stuck with looming evenings of binge watching an epic trilogy's worth of seven-year-old, not quite prime time, lesser cable-network dreck on some pretense of scholarly intrigue in its apoplectic tropes for an occasional smug half squint at some festering glossy hyucks. And this domino-ing to all the fuzziest personalities within 88.7 MHz's alleyooping range if not for my hasty intervention.

(L) Yeah, no. Shit. He's on the way I think. "All...right...Haribeaux...bring sloppy joes in a ziplock...if you don't want...the best freshwater fish in probably 1000 solar systems." Ok.

(J) On the way you think?

(L) No, he'll come. Sorry, is it weirder that I dictated that? Never really got a handle on thumb-typing a quick "yes in fact I am still hoping you'll still show up" before the actual company has time to roll their eyes.

(J) Well, only weird given the contents, but endearing. And props for doing it geriatrically and not giving the early birds any tooth-clucking fodder.

(L) True, but I would be interested to see how they'd take us just going dead quiet then tapping at our phones in unison and slowly panning around taking pictures of the empty tables and winking a lot.

(J) Like with some really creepy nostril flares like a game show host out of an old MAD magazine?

(L) Well, here and there, but can't oversell it. Do we dare?

(J) Sure, why not?

Catatonic, spirited, and revolting without all the histrionics. Even a little ear spasm to boot. Must have been refined with each successive sibling to be prompting that type of swallowed low-frequency groan from at least nine feet.

(L) Astounding. Shame I left my oils at the coat check.

^(J) Thank you. I always felt left out when everybody would start showing off their innate gross-out talents.

^(L) So you made your own?

^(J) No, I just made that face to make them stop.

^(L) Clever. I'd gotten down wrapping my arms behind my back and twiddling my ring fingers over my belly button, but puberty is a cruel mistress.

^(J) You sure? C'mon, I promise I'll never make that face again.

^(L) What? No, the opposite of that, please.

^(J) Well, I'd been hoping to avoid chronic lockjaw till at least forty.

^(L) Ok, if I get at least three twiddles in, you make that face every time I say "This is my friend Jiffnit from Pattahyugich" to anyone you haven't met.

^(J) You're on. Uegh, so close. Ooh, almost. Yeah, tuck in your chin some more, it's helping.

^(L) Lies! Muhh, that was not pleasant. How close? Four inches?

^(J) Maybe three. But look at it this way, you probably had really disproportionate forearms before puberty or something.

^(L) Well that explains why nobody invited me over to play with their Stretch Armstrong.

^(J) I've still got mine, you're welcome any time.

^(L) Whoa. And I bet he's all patchy and brittle too.

^(H) Am I interrupting?

^(L) Always. But sit, sun's in my eyes. So, ducks in traffic?

^(H) Basically. I thought you got my text.

He ought to know by now that's grounds for a toothy, stiletto-eyed lean-in of interminable scrutiny.

^(L) I read plenty, bucko. There's room under the table if you need a minute.

Yes I'm kidding, but keep playing along with that squishy galoot on the wire bit. I promise your text was bubbling direly somewhere in the periphery of the vague mess I aimlessly glanced at at least twice.

^(H) No, I was just thinking of going to ask the maître d' to turn the nose down a bit. Hi Jen, sorry but I just have to say when I walked up you looked like Li'd just laid a rubber egg and started putting on football pads.

^(J) Well you look like somebody tried to put you back in the egg, but then decided it wasn't worth the trouble and now you're all slimy and shelley and unsure about your place in the world. So there.

^(H) So much for that new conditioner. Can I be off the hook now please?

^(L) Nope. You just wandered in to body mod night at the old meat packing plant.

^(H) Oh?

^(L) Hook. Lots of hooks. And cutting slack is heavily frowned upon.

^(H) Dang. Not even a hint on how to chip away at redemption?

^(L) Well, I can't speak for the mobile beauty parlor squad at table eight fumbling to keep us in healthy subtext range, but regaling us of your last forty-eight minutes' foibles may please the consort.

If I'm not mistaken, this marks his first reluctant-to-share out of genuine apprehension moment. Bit of haughtiness to it, but that could have rubbed off.

^(H) Well it's definitely not going to sound like an excuse.

^(L) That's fine, I didn't bring my stabbing goggles. Unless Jen has spares.

(J) You know, they're usually with my phallectomy kit, but I had to drop some shit off at Tommy's this morning and must have accidentally chewed them into a paste while I was waiting for his dog to wake him up.

(H) I'd make a crack about two tipsy stunners in punked-out power suits picking at each other's fish skins, but I didn't bring my crack-making kit.

(L) This here's off the rack 'Roldy.

(H) That makes nothing clear to me, but I will not complain about the divine hand who sheared the stirring rendition of Breugel's proverbs as breathing room for your thigh.

(L) Thank you. You may remain seated. Excuses aside, where the hell were you anyway?

(H) Groaning over a legal pad and occasionally glancing at half a tuna sandwich from earlier, feeling like it should remind me of something. Which it eventually did, hence the text.

(J) Big deadline?

(H) Sort of. I imagine the offbeat genre-traipsing middle-Southeast literary scene could find its way without me, but I have it on good authority that my benefactors have been mentioning my name with a fainter disdain, which somehow completely snuffs my pride.

(L) So postpartum groans over a work leaching truths too incisive for even their creator to mull unabjectly?

(H) Not really, or maybe a little of that, tough to say. Twenty pages of something anyway.

(J) What? Cool, cheers.

(H) Nah, it's all outline.

(L) Oh, muffinbutt, you want me to put an ad out for a ghost writer?

^(H) Would you? I do feel like I've really accomplished something by jizzing anthropomorphic feline geopolitical speculation for an afternoon. But anybody can sit on that egg, right?

^(J) Yes, that's a perfectly lucid and conventional turn of phrase that I can relate to.

^(L) Cat people. Almost a bold choice.

^(H) Ugh, yeah. It was all from that cat story at my old apartments. When I saw them do that big circle committee at four a.m. taking diffident passes at the stray I'd been feeding?

^(L) Oh right, Jesus. That gave me weird dreams for a week.

^(H) Sorry. Anyway, I kept thinking it was too engraved in my psyche to subject to high-concept whoring. And then imagined fleshing out an era-spanning epic just to be sure.

^(J) How many eras, exactly? Are there cave cats?

^(H) That probably would have worked better. No, it's all an ascetic agrarian backdrop. Tribal, but sensible. Under the assumption that cats wouldn't really go for millennia of fanaticism between rudimentary trade and advanced metallurgy.

^(L) So, establishing shots on idyllic cat-topia, hulking mouse-beasts under the plow, young Toms leaving lizard-skin bracelets on a sweetheart's window sill?

^(H) I was thinking long-since veganized after generations of overhunting in whatever sacred valley led to a manna in the form of a particularly succulent root vegetable. But mouse-cows would be pathetic and adorable.

^(L) Or rat-cows and mouse-pigs and sheepsters, but just regular goats on the grounds of inherent peculiarity.

^(J) Not stoat goats?

^(H) So then squonkeys and ottopottami?

^(L) Precisely. Which leaves us with cowlephants and, eh, trunkosaurus?

^(H) Sure, get that into a four-thousand-word prologue and have it on my desk by the end of the frankfurter. Anyway, some brazen young calico has one too many sojourns into the catnip forest and ends up tyrant, which is a first as far as anyone can remember.

He's possibly so dispirited at this point he'd drop it and sulk at the slightest interjection. Should I read that as quite so immature? I can relate, but it is a bit heavy on the adolescent dough-fisted angst. Better lean breathy and compassionate. But still keep him off-balance and swinging hard so he's too phased to pontificate after the denouement. Oh, Jen, no, the tinder's too damp to poke at yet.

^(J) Lemme guess, Catholemew?

^(H) Not bad, I was thinking Torvald.

^(L) Mmh, all I got's Cathulius, but out loud it's really hurting for oomph.

^(J) Chthulius?

^(L) Ooh, I believe we've just had a bit of what you might call winkandnodico.

^(H) Oh for fuck's sake.

I dishonor you, Exalted Barber, but the Flailing Crayfish strikes fluidly under the cover of tablecloth. That's right, puckaroo, I bet that is the first time in a very long while you've been playfully but firmly thwocked in a soft and sensitive zone a careful few inches off the mark.

^(L) And?

^(H) And the first, let's say, twelve-hundred pages is the escalation of his grasp and ego into that befitting a right C-Rex. To be honest I had just done a dab when I started, and from what I recall, that half of the outline is mainly exclamation marks.

⁽ᴸ⁾ Oh, Tittybear. You told me you were saving those to blowgun out through your busted peephole at Jehovah's witnesses.

⁽ᴴ⁾ I knoww. I just looked down and my bong was full of ice and the nail glowing and my inner crackhead doing his little jig.

⁽ᴶ⁾ Jesus.

⁽ᴸ⁾ Yeah, they're intense. We were eight or so deep and his mom texted she was thinking of dropping by with some banana bread and we hid in the pantry for two hours.

⁽ᴶ⁾ Lord.

⁽ᴴ⁾ Yeah. Which explains the large part of an afternoon lost to catty diplomacy in an age of sectarian hubris succumbing to utilitarian pomp. So, when I come to, Ch-what's his name was at an impasse with the elder chieftains of the more influential clans, most of them expecting to die for their insolence. But one of the more mavericky ones–

⁽ᴸ⁾ With gnarly bands and tattoos and a rook-feather cape?

⁽ᴴ⁾ Naturally. So this heretofore inconsequential elder had once noticed a squirippo or cowadactyl or whatever doing something I guess you could call anathemic to a race more rooted in self-reliance and poise than our crude simian pack mentality: she sits down on her haunches.

⁽ᴶ⁾ So not once in the course of going full agrarian biped did anyone accidentally squat by the water pumps on a hot day?

⁽ᴸ⁾ Well, can't assume they hit the iron age, per se.

⁽ᴶ⁾ Then milking the, what was it, rats?

⁽ᴸ⁾ Really good stools?

⁽ᴶ⁾ Fixing a fence, then, dammit.

⁽ᴴ⁾ No, no, alright. Let's just say it's one of those things like, eh, picking your butt. Or she just bows her head, same idea.

^(L) So, Caesar I effectively pick my butt at thee?

^(H) Exactly.

^(L) Ok, I buy it.

^(H) The point is, it's never been established as a gesture of supplication. It still is, objectively, but with everyone standing around having been expecting a show of force proportional with the tyrant's mood, it comes across as a pretty ballsy affront. Basically saying "I deny you the sport of my slaughter".

^(L) Yuh-huh.

^(H) So that ends however it ends, ages pass.

^(L) What? What becomes of Cthempkin?

^(H) Uh, he... loses.

^(J) Tragic.

^(H) So ages pass, mostly as a regression in fits and starts to an essentially medieval era. Or, well, no church powers really in the mix so feudal's probably more accurate.

^(J) But, so many cat church puns.

^(L) If mouse is to pork as rat is to cow. Then it has to be "quiet as a..."?

^(J) Church roach?

^(L) Beats "quiet as a Sunday ham".

^(H) They're both winners. If you'll excuse me, I'll be curled up in my backseat listening to my Enya mix tape.

^(L) Come on. No half-stories at this table, please. Right Sigge?

^(S) Not on my watch. Can I get you anything?

^(H) Ah, yeah, trout cakes and an Abita.

^(S) You got it.

⁽ᴸ⁾ Ok, ok, please. Low-res thumbnail of the Cliff's Notes at least.

⁽ᴴ⁾ Yeah. That's about what I got down anyway. Thing's go feudal, standard crouch and/or head bow and all. And again it comes to a climactic impasse, this time with an entire town's population having been called before the royal seat or council of plutocratic senate or whichever goon collectors have the most ducats.

⁽ᴶ⁾ Not Ca'rowns?

⁽ᴴ⁾ Ugh. That was, from the bottom of my heart, not intended.

⁽ᴸ⁾ We believe you, Hare.

⁽ᴴ⁾ Thanks. Cheers. So the crowd's haunched and it's got all the stink of the groundwork being laid for some happy medium between a random culling ritual and a kangaroo court for known or would-be dissenters. But a vanguard shows itself along the diagonals and sprints out, leaving the civilians in perfect wedges—and plenty of them perfectly not in on it. The vanguard flanks the royal goons. Maybe there's a scuffle or it's so damn quick to qualify as a bloodless revolution. At any rate, the head honcho—

⁽ᴶ⁾ Haunch who?

⁽ᴴ⁾ No, wow, that was, sorry. As unintentional as it gets, and no, the head baddie cat person or persons ends up just getting stared down off their perch and ushered out of town.

⁽ᴸ⁾ I sense a catch.

⁽ᴴ⁾ Of course. Again a few generations pass. Things veer democratic now, but when shit does in fact go down, it tends to be out on the square with cowering innocents as barricades.

⁽ᴶ⁾ Then some asshole just plows through?

⁽ᴴ⁾ No, maybe once or twice, but I don't think he'd garner much of a following. I mean, everybody loves the baker, he's the pride of the town, assuming in the absence of religion the more prized artisans enjoy a saintly immunity. But that's all the more reason to stage a coup between his cart and the green grocer's. Your opponents are obliged to defend themselves without endangering the livelihood of the revered, which puts them on poor footing if it's crowded enough.

⁽ᴶ⁾ But if they're so dignified, why not just Cat-Fu face-offs up in the hills somewhere?

⁽ᴴ⁾ Sure, but let's say the tacit rules of engagement go this way more often than not. Or, like the only way to stem or spark a coup depends on intricate timing and placement of your allies and precious non-combatants in the market square.

⁽ᴸ⁾ Wait, so it's prancy cat flash mobs as the unspoken rule of law?

⁽ᴴ⁾ Yeah, when you put it that way, I suppose I am drowning in cynicism and grasping at straws thinking any feedback could cheer me up.

⁽ᴸ⁾ Aww, there's that ever so dick-twaddling and slightly pissy smile we've been missing. You should think about letting it out more, looks a little cagey.

⁽ᴶ⁾ In all fairness Li, I grew up around plenty of restless dicks and I'm blanking on the whole twaddling concept.

⁽ᴸ⁾ Mhm, I guess I was picturing one of those delicate moments, say just after a much-needed readjustment on an especially swampy afternoon.

⁽ᴶ⁾ Oh, where it's just private enough to fluff things up with a one-two tug and bobble kinda deal?

⁽ᴴ⁾ That was surprisingly insightful.

⁽ᴶ⁾ A marching band uniform is essentially hormonal camouflage.

⁽ᴸ⁾ That I can attest to. So that's the whole outline? Fade out on Cats wholly unironically doing West Side Story?

⁽ᴴ⁾ No, that's all backstory. Hobos swapping tall tales over a pot of sterno chicory and nettle brew. Subtracting the dab fugue, I had most of it all down halfway through

the first cup of coffee this morning. The hours I spent after-
wards were essentially gauging out a bunch of snaggletooth
reductive caricatures into a soupy Hamburger Helper plot.
Mystique, high intrigue, inevitable lengthy descriptions of
claw-augmentation-based weaponry.

⁽ᴸ⁾ Gawhh, how awful that the side job that you love that
sometimes pays you to sit around on Saturdays fleshing out
PG furry fantasies is sometimes stressful.

⁽ᴴ⁾ No, "sometimes" is a stretch. I'd go with exceedingly
rarely.

⁽ᴸ⁾ Rendered all the more soul-tautening by its scarcity.

⁽ᴶ⁾ I don't know how you cope, man.

⁽ᴴ⁾ Pills. I don't even know what kind. I just tell the guy
on the corner "Fuckin' pills, man" and he hooks it up.

⁽ᴶ⁾ Whuhh, mystery trip.

⁽ᴴ⁾ Hyahh, I know. It's like my palpitations even go numb.

⁽ᴶ⁾ Dank. Got any left?

⁽ᴴ⁾ Well I crushed 'em all up in a laffy taffy then melted
it into a frosting and put it on a cupcake so I could share it
with my gramma, cause she's tight, but you could probably
still lick the beaters and the bowl if the ferret didn't get to it
yet.

⁽ᴶ⁾ That's chill.
⁽ᴴ⁾ Yeah, I know.

The chief offensibility chair of the probably otherwise
smotheringly nice old ladies can't be catching every word, or
coming close to reading the spotty trailer-park thug affect at
face value, but God I've never seen ears so pricked before. Of
all my cross-threaded wingnut Facebook aficionados, I can't
picture any of them turning out nearly so crimped. Probably
begs some eternal question I'm too sated to kick at.

⁽ᴸ⁾ I move to venture this unofficial washing of he-who-
shall-remain blue-balled from Jen's hair to a more culminatory
venue; vis-à-vis Peanut Buster Parfaits.

⟨J⟩ Hear-hear.

⟨H⟩ Good idea. It's getting too chilly to go without fudge sauce. Sigge?! Sorry it's urgent. Li, you get the cakes and I'll cover the DQ? Thanks, man what a pro.

⟨L⟩ I've been struggling not to call him Sigwig.

⟨H⟩ Li, I mean this in the most forgettable way possible, but I'm afraid you'd struggle equally not to hang a bedazzled moniker on a Bill Smith as you would an Engelbert Humperdinck.

⟨L⟩ Well, that nearly cuts to the quick, hon, but you're right it's so forgettable it almost feels affectionate.

⟨J⟩ You guys have an odd sense of sappy.

⟨L⟩ Well please pipe up if it's in any way putting a damper on the express phlegm-chunk hating premise of the evening. The delegate whipping boy can be defenestrated on the merest outward poot of your displeasure. I recommend a sour smile with just a peppering of the upward Jonathan Winters flutter, as so.

⟨H⟩ Dear God, put it away.

⟨J⟩ No, wait, wait, let me capture this moment of genetic regression for future generations. Holy crap, how can you hold it so long?

⟨L⟩ If my bathroom mirror could talk.

⟨J⟩ Yes? Please, we have to know.

⟨L⟩ It would... probably be... exhorting a small parish of Steel Reserve cans in an underpass to repent or suffer the maw of eternal discord?

⟨H⟩ Not spearheading a YouTube community for transliterating traumatic moments into time-lapse hedge-trimming vignettes?

⟨L⟩ C'mon man, I broke its sanity not its dignity.

⟨J⟩ I could say worse for my old Strawberry Shortcake compact, but it got wise and jumped ship in a Waffle House bathroom.

⟨H⟩ Oddly fitting. Ok, should I start jangling the keys and clearing my throat?

⟨L⟩ No, no. Lead on Aychely.

14

Sorry Drew, I'm tapped for banter. Please take the slobbered niceties as they're intended and keep doing whatever intricate handicraft you've suddenly taken up that produces all those soft, comforting shuffling noises. Same goes for you Geordie, and you too bathroom, as much as I know we have catching up to do. Shoes, you smoosh off quick or I'm getting out the glitter pens. Fahh. Trina, why are you sitting on my bed half-dazed and doing the reflective phone-cradle thing?

(T) Little drunk?

(L) No. Verydrunk. Martinis then Dairy Queen then forties.

(T) Fun.

(L) I need to put my head down now. Without shirt. Oooup. What? No. Wheee! Thank you. I'd say jeans too but you look about eight beers shy.

(T) Rob fell out of a tree and broke his foot.

(L) Ohhhy. That's, garbage. So that's why so glum?

(T) I guess.

^(L) Or it made you wonder, and you're not a contented wonderer?

^(T) That's all you got on me? You realize we've lived together for the better part of a decade, right?

^(L) Sorry. I mean you're not the quietly wondering on your loving roommate's bed because everything's just fine type.

^(T) Is that a type?

^(L) I don't know, maybe in boarding school.

Blundered into a case of mistaken intimacy. The mark had just taken my slipshod cave-in of a basement office for a two-bit speakeasy. She wasn't the first. Only the real mistake was mine, the not-quite sullen pout had been all not-quite, and now I was up to my ears in misread emotions with half a gut-full of buck-twenty-seven malt and the other half too drunk to remember.

^(T) Actually I waved at you from the kitchen window, and it looked like you gave me a "c'mere" back.

^(L) I would wager the odds of that exchange having occurred the same way in my mind as not worth putting on the board. Oh wait, paint me utterly mortified. That look was intended for a squirrel standing on Drew's car giving me a tough guy look.

^(T) You wanted him to follow you into your room?

^(L) Beats me. Really, sorry. My horizontal brain's kicking in and it has some strongly opinionated fuzzy notions of disgruntlement with how I've handled the last ninety seconds.

^(T) It's fine. I probably should have something to vent, it's too dreary out not too.

^(L) Undefinable malaise triggered by me thinking you looked pained?

^(T) Well, that's jabbing a finger at it maybe. Does sorta put me in the mood to nitpick about Rob. But really I'm finding that dating a slovenly boisterous dork has a few perks.

⁽ᴸ⁾ And I wish the best of completely inaudible sex to you both.

⁽ᵀ⁾ Ugh, you know that could have almost been sweet.

⁽ᴸ⁾ Oh, oops. Well honestly when I hear you two go in there I just take the dog out on the porch and stare reproachfully at him for ten minutes to balance things out.

⁽ᵀ⁾ You're assuming no reproachful stares factor in to our fetish palette?

⁽ᴸ⁾ I know, how pedestrian of me. You really think it's that dreary out?

⁽ᵀ⁾ Yeah. Cold gray winter days have a fuck-off charm for me. This early fall crap gets everybody all reflective and serene. Gives me the creeps.

⁽ᴸ⁾ Total nightmare. You know it's already November, right?

⁽ᵀ⁾ Mid-fall, whatever, worse. You know what I mean.

⁽ᴸ⁾ Kryptonite to your powers of crass bullshit quenching? Sweet spice and all shades of squash tamping us capsaicin fiends back into our hovels to the distant roar of too many major sports to keep track of all suddenly in season?

⁽ᵀ⁾ Don't you dare call me glum then think you can cheer me up that easy.

⁽ᴸ⁾ You.

Little toe to right cheekbone. Disaffected swat at fifty millisecond delay. Recalibrate.

⁽ᴸ⁾ Are.

Heel to right trapezius. Too-unamused-to-shrug downward open-mouthed eye roll just about on cue. Call the bluff and give at an ooh how comfy sigh.

⁽ᴸ⁾ Behggun fer it.

⁽ᵀ⁾ Are you gonna fart or something?

⟨L⟩ Mm, if only. I fear it would be a prelude for works better suited to porcelain acoustics.

⟨T⟩ Don't let me stop you.

⟨L⟩ Muh, maestro's still pestering the sopranos backstage.

Now there's a groan I could almost mistake for my rumbling colon.

⟨T⟩ For fuck's sake, Li.

⟨L⟩ I know I ought to be put off by that tone, but I'm just so blanketed by these fuzzy autumnal anesthesias that it just makes me feel all hindful and namasthetic of your deeper antigasms.

There's the flop. Strange as this mush is to sleep on, it has a knack for sapping the will for maintaining any kind of posture.

⟨T⟩ You put up glow stars?

⟨L⟩ No, came with the room. Can't say I've ever entertained the notion of painting them over.

⟨T⟩ Still a little weird.

⟨L⟩ Muh, someday somebody will publish a study about how great it is for you.

⟨T⟩ May we live to see the day where nobody reads it.

⟨L⟩ Amen.

The few mostly botched constellations and majority of improvised ones around the corners do balance pretty well the area closer to the fan and its manic disregard for entropy with a sort of almighty brush flick look.
Thanks, presumed eighth grader, who either stayed too sentimental to carefully weigh the chastity-belt factor or discovered pot.

⟨T⟩ You know my sister's got the hots for you.

⟨L⟩ I can't say I blame her. Look at me.

^(T) I see an underwear tag, three pieces of a leaf in your hair, and an actual hanging drop of underboob sweat.

^(L) The sum of my imperfections is unfettered grace.

^(T) Who said that?

^(L) Shit, let me check my quote dictionary.

^(T) So, can I register any minimal show of concern for her emotions? For my sake?

^(L) What, due sisterly diligence? Sure you're not more prone to let her squirm on it?

^(T) Kinda lost its thrill after we were twelve.

^(L) Hm. Tempting as it'd be to probe Harry for a reaction, I'd feel contrived about it, and too good with him to leave him in the dark. But yeah, I'd hit that.

^(T) How thoughtful. I'll definitely not pass that on.

^(L) Not verbatim at least. So, you sure nothing's up? I know it's my ass on the elevator button, but you can't be this bummed I didn't walk in with a toejam-sweet sack and a three-pack of Dutch Masters.

^(T) Can't I? Sounds pretty fucking fantastic.

^(L) Oh man, yeah, I think I'm drooling a little. There might be a roach in the old-fangled candle holder thing over there. Probably like, eight good puffs.

Yes I'm aware I'm narrowly skirting little-shit territory. Please take my flat blinking stab at bare minimum charm as assurance I'd never get off putting you to task, but recognize my taking the initiative beyond a painstaking belly roll runs a credible risk of backfiring in a flourish of klutzing misery laughable only to the less worldly who've never seen a backup roach slip through the porch decking at the height of a regional dry spell.

^(L) Pweeeeze.

^(T) Thin ice, bub.

⟨L⟩ Well aware, marm.

Lighter jumps up from her smoker's trick sleeve, with roach and bobby pin propped and ready for a casual and lengthy pre-roast of debatable necessity. Fine diversion for regarding me with that dinted severity usually reserved for clipboard fanatics or much drunker strangers.

⟨T⟩ You really had me convinced I didn't have anything to unload, Li. But since your half-assed prying is so gawsh dang en, en– shit, what is it?

⟨L⟩ Entubating?

⟨T⟩ Endearing. There was a weird thing, still kinda eating at me, just as a bystander.

⟨L⟩ Entitillating.

⟨T⟩ Mmh. I was doing my luxuriant brown bag in the square routine on Friday and there was a guy with one of those creepy fish balloon things.

⟨L⟩ The clownfish one?

⟨T⟩ No, way more boring. Cod or perch maybe. And it was sort of funny and I was enjoying myself thinking maybe I'd go show the guy some postmortems of Paul's levitating souffle when I finished my sandwich. And the guy has a buddy sort of plodding around in some equally hypnotic but not as noticeable smart-phone trance. So they're kinda zoned out in sync and oblivious to this other guy who comes plowing through on a longboard. I mean, he knows what he's doing but it's not exactly open pavement by the fountain.

⟨L⟩ Right.

⟨T⟩ And the longboarder must be zoned out on his earbuds too, because he nearly collides with the fish. Which must be a pretty startling obstacle, I mean it's just about at eye level. So he just almost bats it away, a reflexive pat if anything, but it gets whipped around in his draft and ends up right over one of the fountain jets so it almost looks like it's catching an updraft.

^(L) That's, awesome.

^(T) I thought so.

^(L) An airborne trout bobbled around by pressurized water bursts. Maybe that's fish hell.

^(T) Maybe. This fish didn't seem to mind, but the RC club attending to it went, like, cartoonishly apoplectic.

^(L) Like Ren and Stimpy?

^(T) Like two Stimpys.

^(L) Ooh, that's too bad.

^(T) Yeah. And the longboarder stopped and was apologetic, but still obviously in a bit of a hurry, and these other two were just, so pathetically inconsolable. And what got to me wasn't their failing to see any of the absurd levity of it, but how totally ill-suited they were to being pissed at all.

^(L) So, like anger so shallow it just splutters around everywhere.

^(T) Pretty much. And I don't know if it was just me, I wasn't really completely in earshot, but it was like they were speaking a branch of English so steeped in meme-logic, and I don't know, some Xbox Live senseless cusspot jargon. I could barely fucking piece it together. I should probably just feel old, but it's more like I wanted to slap them, so much. I mean they were our age.

^(L) Sure it wasn't some elaborate Space Team LARP? It is strange, I grant you that. I guess even the most rudimentary maturity is sort of an opt-in thing these days.

^(T) For the dorks.

^(L) You really sure they were our age?

^(T) Pretty sure. Old enough to be indignant and not just pissed.

^(L) Hm. So no gramma's basement vibe, or?

(T) Could be. Nothing resembling a getting laid in recent memory vibe, for sure. Like dressed to get in a Pokemon brawl with the local Mormon toughs. And all that barely parsable effrontery gibberish on top of it all.

(L) Real-life PERL, then? Let's assume the worst and call it a biennial sojourn into daylight from the deeper recesses of a 4Chan support group.

(T) Here, it's got a run, careful. Whatever the case, they ended up getting pretty nasty about it. And I probably wouldn't have done shit anyway if I could make sense of it, but because of that I fucking couldn't get properly irritated either.

(L) Yeesh.

(T) You asked.

(L) Did I? If it's any consolation, despite it sounding like a barely passable Kidz Bop lyric, I've got this nagging sense of not knowing at all what to say lately. Or, no, maybe it was worse over the summer. Too much in my head, even for me.

(T) Huh. You weren't just practicing your weighty talk radio pauses?

(L) Was I?

(T) Li, weren't you always sort of like that? Or, I mean can be hard to tell with you. You certainly know damn well the best way to say what I wouldn't.

(L) Oh. Neat. I'll redress it as a belated self-awareness spurt then. Or berate it as a distressed one? Either way.

(T) Good for you.

(L) No, but really, I know I'm spacey as poodle farts, but it was like my cozy aloof bubble lost its tether or whichever bullshit, and I was barely keeping abreast of any goddamn thing going on. It wasn't any deep emotional upheaval, or it didn't feel like it. Just more and more casual exchanges started feeling like back when Ashley'd come over and heave a few gravity bong rips and go on yammering about her

unparalleled insights gleaned from AP US History and 4H
Club or whatever it was.

⟨T⟩ No, Unified Lawn Sports Alliance. I was 4H.

⟨L⟩ Holy Christ, yeah. Why did we give her shit for that?
That sounds awesome.

⟨T⟩ Because she was a complete bitch.

⟨L⟩ Right.

⟨T⟩ Li, you realize you're a pothead and what you're describing is kind of par for the course?

⟨L⟩ Yeah, yeah. But feels more like I'm cornily entrenched
in not giving a shit. At least symptoms of debilitating emotional trauma are treatable.

⟨T⟩ That's awful, but sort of makes sense.

⟨L⟩ Oh hey, by the way. What do you call a sun-dried
tomato?

⟨T⟩ What do you call a thing that's called what you just
said?

⟨L⟩ Yes, c'mon!

⟨T⟩ Uh, wrinkly tart flavor pustules? I don't know.

⟨L⟩ Tomazin!

⟨T⟩ Ough, you realize I'd probably have murder–suicided
us if you'd ended up in getting into marketing?

⟨L⟩ Actually, Manua's contracting me part-time for catalogue work.

⟨T⟩ Dear god.

⟨L⟩ What do you call beef jerky?

⟨T⟩ Fuck you.

⟨L⟩ Braizen!

⟨T⟩ That could be anything with a "B". And it's not braised,
is it braised?

^(L) Might be. What do you call a bunch of alligators on the South Pole?

^(T) Dead.

^(L) Ice gators! What are the poacher's vanity plates?

^(T) A pair of old Adidas?

^(L) E-10-D-L-F-N. Credit to Mrs. Rutter's stack of "Jokes for All Ages, Grades 2 to 4" on that one.

^(T) All ages with age guidelines?

^(L) That was her favorite bit, I think. Odd lady. Never laughed in a kid's face, but really knew how to lure us into embarrassing ourselves.

Wouldn't have been my first guess for material to trigger a sharp pensive breath, then eyeing the gauzy blur of reflected desk junk and streetlamp wash making its annual nuisance through the thinning poplar.

^(T) I gain more and more respect for those types.

^(L) Peg-taker-downers?

^(T) Mm-hm.

^(L) Yeah, rare to see someone do it with such a sure hand anyway.

^(T) Guess so. Li, I hate to smoke and slink off, but I have some horribly boring shit to do in the morning and I'm fucking beat.

^(L) Eh, that's what roaches are for. What's so boring in the morning?

^(T) Uh, that Sunday morning Secular Society chess-turbation thing in the square with the work lunch buddy. Flaked too many times now and swore on my grandma's minestrone recipe that I'd go.

^(L) Ahh, silent cleverness church in broad daylight.

223

(T) Yeah. Nice crowd, but in her case, emphasis on the smarmy margarine cleverness that you just wanna pinch on the cheek with white-hot calipers.

(L) What a treat. At least you can maybe hack some pegs off from the base.

(T) Pegs? Oh. That horse has been dead awhile, Li.

(L) I stand by it. Wait, what about the festival thing with the vampire movie? It's at noon right? Or the main program is, I think.

(T) Yeah, I don't know. I still can't get over that documentary they trotted out last year on, fucking, what, "Regionally Cohesive Spontaneous Combustion"?

(L) Oooh yeah. That was a lot of slow zoom-outs on oily rags.

(T) I mean, nobody even walked out.

(L) Oh god, that's right. And like half the crew giving each other such nice ego rubs in the front row all throughout. I guess they couldn't have had any inkling that QnA would have been such a shit show.

(T) Oh, yeah, they were adorable, weren't they? Anyway, I don't know, let's see. And thanks again.

(L) Welcome. I'll look forward to accidentally beckoning us together more often.

(T) Night.

(L) Night.

How nice, no one's ever really put me to bed this drunk. Why is the fan on? Only one glow star above it. Discouragement or pulsar? I'll go with cautious optimism and say both.

Anything else amiss? My hiney sense is tingling, but then I do need to wash the sheets. Quick "thanks for the ride" and emoticon jumble to H-ray to allay the slimy overindulgence shame? No, he's a big boy, and I probably need to learn when to let a good coat of slime keep me pupating.

Why am I still not nude? Oh, sheer reverent mother of clamshells and sea foam, that's better. Gahh, fuck the fan. Subtle hint from Trina on my stank? Couldn't be. Hamper's shut. Can't pick up anything under the lakeside frizzly drink fun. Some faint deep hard-packed clay motif I suppose. Is that the house or me?

No, no, don't get up, sleep fairy, just let me reach the dangling piece-of-shit fan switch chain without completely upending all the delicate spongy glandular miscellany you've so kindly equilibrated. Ugh, no, too far, so much for that. I need to put a ribbon on that thing, might as well have done eight jumping jacks. Ahh, no, what the multicolored blinking bullshit? I thought they stopped doing that on phones five years ago. Must've butt-flipped the silent switch. Butt-flip kinda day, really.

Rob. "Don't tell Trina, but I'm in the ER with a splinted metatarsal." Oh the poor mangy thing. D-minus. He's really been going out there alone? No, he must have roped in that wiry backyard buzz-saw guru from the gas station. The friends you make over blunt wraps.

Let's see. "Dear Robrut. Head 'n butt? The sign for sphincter pliers is a de-pincer movement adjacent a clenched fist. ER staff can most likely accommodate. Trina heard already. Apologize to her if need be, for whatever the hell it is that brought you to asking me to cover for you. And leave the covert signal bending to DARPA."

I have got to find a place to put this thing outside my room. Off the nightstand at least. Well, fuck it, half nauseous now, better preempt the wallow.

Maybe Drew's up for waving the leash around on the porch and pretending we can't see Geordie through the front window. Poor thing. He must kind of get it at this point. Which means we're essentially doing an "I can't hear you" warm-up for a perpetually into-it audience.

(L) Hey, sorry I blurbled past you like that. Passing out seemed imminent.

(D) That's alright. I was pretty engrossed.

(L) Sponge-agami?

(D) Eh, no. Volunteered to do a handful of miniatures for a stop-action dreamscape bog party thing.

(L) Ahh, yeah. Bog stuff. Is that a trellis?

(D) A winding fern trellis, I hope.

(L) Well, I don't want to interrupt, but. C'mon, c'mon, let's do something else.

(D) Like what?

(L) I don't know, debasing YouTube video roulette?

(D) Which ones aren't anymore?

(L) Ohhhh, dig. The webcamogenic population at large won't even be able to leave the house tomorrow.

(D) Or, will they?

(L) Touche. Shall we?

(D) Shall we what?

(L) Euh, stand up and do another thing?

(D) Yes, I get that. Call me crazy, but I typically have at least some vague sense of intent before I get up.

(L) That's what I just gave you!

(D) No, you're off-the-radar vague. No intent registering.

(L) Walk. Walk with me. It's nice out. C'mon. Bughh, yes, you too dog. Where was he?

(D) Warming my feet.

(L) Hm. Think he was enjoying it, or just taking pity?

(D) No, all him. Flung my slippers off like he had an appointment.

(L) So. Ready, or what?

(D) Just a midnight stroll, barefoot, in your bathrobe?

(L) Precisely. Paid good money for that last tetanus shot.

⁽ᴰ⁾ Alright, why not. I'll bring the glow frisbee.

⁽ᴸ⁾ Now you're talkin. I'd offer a jay, but lo, the enchanted pocket only splays forth a chewed-up golf pencil.

⁽ᴰ⁾ Might pass from a distance.

⁽ᴸ⁾ Poser stoners it is, lead the way.

Of all the startlingly many roommates I've had, these ones sure supplant my familial going-on-maternal longings the best. Not ever really tribal in those old lightly squalor-resistant playpens. Sure, plenty of the untempered ecstatic wonder and all that we signed up to be indentured to Sallie Mae for. What was really better back then about any of it? I guess some of the albums I heard for the first time. Barely counts. Well, without Rob I'd probably be doing pensive Sunday nostalgia binges over a crusty jumbo CD wallet, crate filler interspersed with Amoeba-pilgrimage gems, and an unsightly tangle of negligence-corrupted mp3 folders.

⁽ᴸ⁾ Yes Peorgie, come. Why's he so apprehensive all the sudden?

⁽ᴰ⁾ Rob tied the leash between the Roomba and that Star Wars roll bot thing for a few hours for stealing a meatball.

⁽ᴸ⁾ Oh?

⁽ᴰ⁾ Ended up crueler than he meant, I think. Oh, and your floor lamp is completely broken.

⁽ᴸ⁾ Huh, yeah it looked different in here.

⁽ᴰ⁾ I could have probably intervened, but–

⁽ᴸ⁾ Too horribly engrossing?

⁽ᴰ⁾ Yeah, sorry.

⁽ᴸ⁾ Don't worry about it. The hipster bulb was probably worth more. I think Rob bought that, so his loss.

⁽ᴰ⁾ Alright. Shit, it's kinda chilly. You sure?

⁽ᴸ⁾ Yes. Go. It's fine. I got drunk heat pouring off me too slow as it is.

^(D) Drunk heat, ok.

^(L) Don't poke fun at my lexicological shortcomings. It's late.

^(D) Didn't mean to.

^(L) Good. All is forgiven. Past, present, supinum. Intentional and, uh.

^(D) Hale Murray, fallow grease.

^(L) Well fluff my tutu, I just put this mopey fern-twirler in a decent mood.

^(D) Mopey? I've never so much as called you anything but a bright, shining bean of cheeky fun. You realize that?

^(L) Hm, guess not. You've never made a pass either, but in some circles you might have just now.

^(D) Huh? No, just playing offended. Glad you can gauge my sarcasm to know self-effacing criticism from a compliment.

^(L) It does get pretty dense.

^(D) Yeah, I'm on the mumblecore spectrum.

^(L) Oh, I'm sorry. Would you like a lollipop suppository?

^(D) I can't imagine I would.

^(L) Hey don't knock it till you rip out that first clump of sticky butt hair.

^(D) Wow. Who's hitting on who now?

Dog's swerving back. Drew's happy to stop, looking like he thinks he's pulling off snide, but too unguarded to twist me for a real rejoinder. No moon. Stompy old funk on a tinny radio down the block. Mockingbird on duty's spooked for the moment. Fuck it.

Just an unassuming friendly embrace. Alone under a streetlight in the neighbor's grass. Some lower butt cleft probably peeking out. No, definitely. Willing, but no push. Pull back, smile, kiss the cheek, quick gentle graze across the funny temple-drooped cowlick. Yes, you deserve more on that wounded smile alone. No, I'm not that cold. March on, sloppy grin.

⁽ᴸ⁾ I need to say I swear to God I came by this in honest deduction, but I think we're the shorted side of a love triangle, circuit, thing.

⁽ᴰ⁾ Who's shorting?

⁽ᴸ⁾ Well technically me, but, uh, more like a cheezed capacitor or ground than a, what, diode?

⁽ᴰ⁾ Sure? That's a groundbreaking shitty analogy.

⁽ᴸ⁾ Thank you. You met up with her lately, anyway, or what?

⁽ᴰ⁾ Li, I really don't want to get into it.

⁽ᴸ⁾ Mm, probably wise. Soo, how's your... outlook, then?

⁽ᴰ⁾ Full of foliage and wood sprites.

⁽ᴸ⁾ That bad? Musicians, 'murite?

⁽ᴰ⁾ Mmhm. Wait let's stop.

Oh Christ. Well it's a miracle I'm not in the shithouse already on this one. Fine, lay it on me, man.

⁽ᴸ⁾ Why?

⁽ᴰ⁾ This bench is great.

⁽ᴸ⁾ Ohh.

⁽ᴰ⁾ You never sat here?

⁽ᴸ⁾ I have not. Hm, oh, wow yeah. You weren't exaggerating. Why are there so few good benches anymore?

⁽ᴰ⁾ Subtle art.

⁽ᴸ⁾ There's bound to be more design degrees awarded per semester than there are benches this good.

⁽ᴰ⁾ F'only them chiblsn'd lerb'n.

⁽ᴸ⁾ I'm sorry? Are you choking on a four-track recorder?

⟨D⟩ No, my dad used to do some voice like that. From Laugh-In or God knows what.

⟨L⟩ From all these gems you keep sprinkling, I can't imagine your family dinners growing up.

⟨D⟩ There weren't many. Family time was typically by appointment.

⟨L⟩ Oh. Well, if it's any consolation, the word quality doesn't apply to mine in many constrainable senses, or with much sense. Or, ok, no, they weren't that bad, sorry, I'm reaching.

⟨D⟩ Quality take-out menu curation?

⟨L⟩ Ah, yes. You too, huh?

⟨D⟩ Children leading the way.

⟨L⟩ Shit, where's the dog?

⟨D⟩ Halfway up the block, eating somebody's flowers.

⟨L⟩ All that leash talk and look at us.

⟨D⟩ You're the one holding it.

⟨L⟩ So I am. Chortey! Chort-chort-chort!

He turns. Idles, cocks what's cockable, sets to ambling on a plausible return vector.

⟨L⟩ Eh, I claim due diligence.

⟨D⟩ You did probably save some flowers.

⟨L⟩ Nice bench, nice block. Even the crackheads seem nice when they come through.

⟨D⟩ Hadn't noticed.

⟨L⟩ You think we have something to do with it?

⟨D⟩ The niceness of the block?

⟨L⟩ Yeah.

(D) Well we liven things up without pissing everybody off or leaving shitty messes for long. Less trouble than a punk house, more fun than a quiet old lady. Yeah, sure, net positive.

(L) Go team.

(D) What?

(L) Just ever so daintily mocking the deflated tone you took explaining our niceness.

(D) Well fuck me then.

(L) Huh. Wait, are you actually morose instead of the usual mostly pretend morose? Always worried I'd never be able to tell.

(D) Yeah, I suppose. I'm enjoying your little barrage anyway.

(L) What, I'm behaving unusually?

(D) No.

(L) Eh, point taken.

For its underlying perks, the view is no real wonder. Maybe the subtle artisan couldn't bear being upstaged. More of a spot to melt back and file down a day's chipped id than behold with all musterable akimboness.

That last old fashioned may have been the first in a series of bad calls in the making, with consequence number one being hangover-cum head cold I could have easily avoided without the lapse in my dutiful scarfing routine. Well, I'm accepting I can't change it. Which already feels more like aloof dickery than wisdom. Might at least beat that moment waking up assuming I ought to feel fine until the first sore-throat gulp or miniscule head tuck turned bear hug from the disjointed dish-powder-mouthed headache goblin. Another chit in the pile of the joys of getting appreciably older.

(L) What's on your mind?

(D) Huh? Let's see. The fact that I'm no longer comfortable with social interactions lacking digital overtures.

^(L) Well people did used to send each other calling cards all the time.

^(D) Fucking odd people.

^(L) Yeah, it is weird. So did we blindly undergo mass aristocrafication? Or is that putting too slim a prick on it?

^(D) I don't know. We were primed for it, that's for sure.

^(L) Huh. You know if prostitution had been legal, the internet might still suck.

^(D) Remember how often people wished they'd had a camera around? Every fucking day I'd hear that.

^(L) I do. And just a courtesy nose wipe here, but you sound miserably goddamn old.

^(D) Don't care. I mean, did you really see anything back then that would've been, eh, viral caliber?

^(L) Like besides kids falling out of trees and breaking their arm?

^(D) Yeah, guess that's its own artery of distasteful, medium-proving material.

^(L) Actually, you know, I did. I was a junior, there was this get-to-know the upperclassmen arts assembly blow-off day thing. I'd been busy with some jazz ensemble hamming it up, but this guy we knew in the drumline insisted we run across campus between sets to watch them in the gym. Which was fine, nobody wanted to watch the whole damn marching band, they were unnerving enough at the pep rallies.

^(D) Uh-huh.

^(L) So they file out, with a potheads-with-impunity swagger somehow mustered amidst six-week chin stubble and C-plus average GPAs. They stand at perfect nonchalant parade rest till the crowd goes quiet on its own. Normally a miracle for a bleacher-load of freshmen, but the adults had prudently slunk to the corners. Then they get a real, thick, whoopy, martial beat going, y'know like, "whum putta tum putom pa ta-tum-tum whom".

^(D) Ok.

^(L) And they just ride it, good full minute or two. Nobody gets antsy, it's real tension, rare and bloody. One guy's out in front, hands at his sides. Big guy, quite big. Not handsome. Probably never got carded in his life. Half of the drumline could have passed for thirty, come to think of it. I knew most of the other guys out there, but he was, like, a much deeper nerd caste. Could've been a dungeon master trainer. Which, at the time, my proto-hipster peanut brain filed as, fuck I dunno, set dressing.

^(D) Sure, you're describing the majority of my friends growing up.

^(L) Alright. I'm a shitty person, or, was a shitty wannabe nerd in those days, without sound guidance. My sincerest apologies to the brethren.

^(D) Li, I consider your nerd-dom indisputable, and pretty much self-evident.

^(L) Aww.

^(D) So? They vamped the night away and cool guy just swayed through it all?

^(L) Ah, no, he finally walks up to the mike. Takes an eight-count, then blasts out, almost a yell, but with this primal seriousness. Like a sweaty, clenched, gravitas. I mean I guess that was in style, but this was controlled, and he was actually singing the notes still. And, it dawns on me and whoever else had access to cool older siblings' cassette collections, that it's The Safety Dance. And he just stomps through it, like some evangelical Care Bear.

^(D) And everybody went bonkers, and you could hear the bleachers rumbling a mile away?

^(L) Eh, I'm sure they hooted some and forgot all about it, they were still just a pack of freshman hopped up on cafeteria fries and Fruitopia. But I know my seat rumbled in a beguiling new way.

^(D) Ok, I could see that getting some likes.

233

⟨L⟩ We'll never know. One of the more entrancing performances I think I've seen, and I saw the gorilla at ShowBiz Pizza finish a set with his hand twirling out of socket.

⟨D⟩ That dude did know how to hold it down. You're not cold yet?

⟨L⟩ Not really. Practically sober though. Wanna go shoot mace balls at the weed patch?

⟨D⟩ Sure.

Up off the feet and away, tiddleyfarts. Avail us your perambulatory abandon.

⟨D⟩ Corny as it sounds, I keep catching myself wishing I was as carefree as him.

⟨L⟩ I was thinking the same thing. It is striking with him, isn't it?

It ought to be as easy to us anyhow, with the old Sunday night mix of forgotten kitchen lights and living room Novocain network-drama kaleidoscopy. Trina might have had a point about this time of year. But can't really call it stifling either. Catching myself in a hurry. Not for inadequate leaf gazing either. Just some instinct in how the sound carries or being more exposed through the dead branches like those diamond-pattern speakeasy rugs that keep the default to a murmur. I wonder if some old Persian king figured that out. Actually I hope I never find out. We're stamping out too many harmless mysteries in the name of fuck-all knows.

⟨L⟩ Hey, remember at the party you guys were talking about ungoogleables?

⟨D⟩ Yeah.

⟨L⟩ What do you think would be the one worst thing in the world for everybody to be able to look up and have immediately clarified?

⟨D⟩ Excluding deep theological or philosophical insights?

⟨L⟩ I don't know, probably odds are the best answer would at least have its toes over the line into their arena.

⟨D⟩ What the other person is thinking?

⟨L⟩ Nehh, the one worst thing, that's too trick-questioney.

⟨D⟩ So just one idea, clarified, to bring all society to its knees?

⟨L⟩ Yes.

⟨D⟩ Hm, what's left to ruin? Thanks, I'd forgotten how much I usually hate hypotheticals. Or is this an actual old riddle I'm failing at?

⟨L⟩ No, no. Honest weird shitty question.

⟨D⟩ Oh, come now, there's no such thing as an honest question.

⟨L⟩ So we'll never know life's most comforting mystery?

⟨D⟩ Guess not. Or, ok, got one. The average joke vocabulary of dolphins.

⟨L⟩ Come again?

⟨D⟩ Jokes, if there's, you know, 100 pods in a region with the same old dozen jokes circulating and the occasional new ones making the rounds. Or stories I suppose. Something tells me they wouldn't quite have the wherewithal for epic poems.

⟨L⟩ Isn't that just a fifty-fifty ruiner? If they're jokeless, then the "what makes us human" debate gets some closure. If not, it's another point for team "gee, but you know monkeys laugh and crows teach and octopuses can murder you on the toilet given the right plumbing".

⟨D⟩ No, if they're jokeless, or down to one half-remembered knock-knock or something, it's sad because that means they're always so rambunctious and gleeful because they can't help it. If they're not, it's the weightier embarrassment that they're down there enjoying themselves as well as we ever could without really having fucked anything up with the world.

⟨L⟩ I don't know, something tells me they fuck shit up plenty.

(D) You know what I mean.

(L) I do, and I don't fault you for it.

(D) Are you coming in? I think I'll actually take a rain check on the target practice.

(L) No, I'll let the brat keep swatting at the begonias awhile. They're spilling into our yard anyway, right?

(D) You get to field the irate drop-in.

(L) With pleasure. I was raised to wrangle those kinds of things into lemonade affairs.

(D) I believe it. Thanks for getting me out for some air, Li.

(L) Happy to air you out anytime, spud.

(D) Night.

It's getting less tricky cheering him up. Hope I'm doing less fishing for that patronizing accomplishment buzz. Or he's getting better at rolling with it. Must be a sink or swim thing once you're old enough to realize you just got the shit end of being more inclined to having strings of seriously awful days. At least it beats short-cutting to clammy monastic myopia, right Gordo? Spare us, oh sweet lard of deck chair posture, the smugness of half-baked epiphanies, that we may acquire instead oven thermometers of diligence and develop culinary knacks of your good grace that are instead nicely browned and airily crumbed notions.

Christ, I'm glad Harry didn't give me any shit over bailing and stopping for dry heaves on the 68. Who could have reasonably expected any guys our age to even grow out of their unfathomably protracted self-absorbed ninny phase? Shit, has it always been that way? Advances in sheltering must be amplifying wiener traits to new heights.

Nah, that's too petty. There's plenty of stoic shitheels and garrulous saints that don't really factor in. Here's to the cool-headed and selfless anyway, Gordo. And don't think that includes you for being such a discriminating flower eater, I've seen you snuffling at your reflection in the front window at dusk.

This new taste for middle-shelf booze is really messing with my puke and pass out routine. Much more lucidity than I signed on for.

(L) Alright Guggles, you had enough baby's breath?

I'll take that cherubic disinterest as a yes.

(L) Suuu-eee, hep hep. Come on, buttcuddles, I'm probably flirting with strep here. Worth it anyway. Pray hump my obscenely plush slippers, tot.

Gone just long enough to get a tingle of the re-acclimation rush. Order abounds, heater's chuffling, Rob's off eating a tub of peaches in a metal bed somewhere, otherwise no one I know is completely off their shit. Just hope I've appeased the drunken surrender demons enough to let me back into that cradled snug without any more sensory overrides. No matter how ripe with bliss or otherwise gushing. My 78-minute commute already has its curly liver-poking witch nail to the grindstone. And I'm no condition to be in the wrong mood for intermittent thumb drumming and neatly lost trains of thought.